WITHDRAWN

LITTLE APOCALYPSE

LITTLE APOCALYPSE

KATHERINE SPARROW

HARPER
An Imprint of HarperCollins*Publishers*

Typography by Michelle Taormina

19 20 21 22 23   PC/LSCH   10 9 8 7 6 5 4 3 2 1

First Edition

For Elijah, the boy who held fast

BEFORE THE BEGINNING

The sad boy sat on the curb with his head covered in a knit hat, even though it was a hot day. He kept his face turned toward the gutter, staring at the brown trickle of water that ran into the sewage drain. With his arms wrapped around his belly, he took up as little space as possible and looked like he was crying, even though there weren't any tears.

He took some braided shoelaces out of his pocket, closed his eyes, and murmured something as he fed the rope into the drain. He stood up and took a red yo-yo out of his pocket. He pulsed it a couple of times before sitting down and looking at the drain some more.

Celia stood across the street watching him. I should know him, she thought, but didn't know why. She watched him for a full minute before deciding to cross the street and talk to him. She didn't know what she would say to him.

Maybe she would tell him that he looked like the picture of how she'd felt ever since she'd moved to this city, left all her friends behind, and started going to the worst middle school ever. Or maybe she would pull off her own shoelaces and throw them into the drain in solidarity. Or what about just sitting down next to him? He might look at her and smile. She'd say something stupid, and he would think it was funny. Then he would teach her a couple of yo-yo tricks, and she would show him how to make origami cranes out of napkins. They'd spend the day exploring all the places in a city that no one ever notices: crumbly staircases, alleys full of broken furniture, and rooftops where birds roosted.

Celia stepped out into the road, ready for all that to happen, but a horn honked and a bus rushed by. The boy was gone by the time she crossed the street.

She didn't think about the sad boy again—didn't even know she'd made a memory of him—until the night that was the beginning and end of most things, four months later.

1

EVERYTHING FELL DOWN

"I can stay home if you want me to." Celia's mom ran a hand through her frizzy hair.

"I'll be fine. I've been babysitting for two years. I can babysit myself for the weekend," Celia said.

Celia's mom rubbed the crease between her eyebrows as she looked out their bay window at the maze of cars and people on the street below. "Grandma's probably going to get over the flu as soon as I get there. It's just that at her age . . . and she's been sick for two weeks."

"Grandma needs you more than I do." Celia reminded her mom of everything she already knew.

"And your father would cancel his trip; it's just that—"

"That he has a new job and he can't. I know. But one question? If a stranger offers me candy, I should take it, right? Especially if he's in a van without windows?"

"You got it, kid." Her mom winked at her.

"Nothing bad will happen while you're gone. I promise." Celia plopped down on their faded orange couch and surveyed the colorful mess of her living room.

"We'll go on a road trip next weekend to make up for it. We'll stop off at every roadside diner and eat every kind of pie from here to wherever we end up, okay? We'll have fun. Promise."

"Yeah. Fun." Celia looked out the window at the gray day and tried to remember what fun felt like.

Her mom crossed the floral carpet and sat down on the couch. She slung an arm around Celia's shoulders. "You know I love you and that you are an amazing kid. Everything will get better. You'll make great friends soon. All the kids at your school are suckers for not hanging out with you."

"So true." I wish we'd never had to move here, Celia thought. I hate it here and I don't know how to make friends. I'm shorter than everyone else and everything I wear is wrong and every time I talk to anyone they just ignore me or are mean. But she didn't say any of that, because it wasn't her parents' fault. They'd lost their teaching jobs at the University of Portland because of budget cuts, and when they'd been offered jobs at South Youngstown Community College, it was that or flipping burgers. Her parents always said that in academia, you had to go where the jobs were. End of story.

"Bill?" her mom yelled.

"What?" Celia's dad came out of the kitchen wearing a *Kiss the Cook* apron.

"Can you believe our daughter is old enough to stay home alone?"

"Are we still talking about this?" Her dad held a greasy spatula in one hand and a glass of wine in the other.

"I'll worry about her all weekend."

"That's our job. But Celia's thirteen. We'll call her and text her and she'll be fine." He glanced at the living room wall full of framed pictures of their family: Celia grinning with her front teeth missing. Celia riding a bike with her mom. Everyone laughing on a boat last summer. "We'll write up a list of rules that Celia will follow while we're gone, and you'll promise to follow them, right, kid?"

"Of course," Celia said. Her life here was so boring that she probably wouldn't even have a chance to break one rule while they were gone.

"I'll miss you, even for just a couple of days." Her mom hugged her.

Her dad hugged her too, and for a moment Celia's sadness went away.

* * *

Her parents left in the middle of the day on Friday. Celia got out of school and walked behind some kids from her grade. She imagined running up to them and talking. Maybe she could tell them her favorite joke. *What's brown and sticky?* They could think she was going to say something gross, and then laugh when she answered, *A stick.* Or maybe she could agree with them that biology was so dumb. Only, how could anyone not love biology and how weird and amazing the natural world was? And anyway, it wouldn't matter what she said to them. Celia had spent months trying to be nice to kids at her school, and everyone was only mean back.

She hoisted up her backpack and followed the flow of people wearing long wool coats who stomped down the street, barking into their cell phones and glaring at the world. Portland was the same size as Youngstown, but everything felt different here. Everyone moved faster and smiled less. Maybe because it was on the East Coast and an island, so everyone felt cold all the time? Maybe because it was farther north and that meant less sunshine and more grumpiness?

When Celia got home from school, she stepped into her empty apartment and took off her backpack and her coat, and then she shrugged off all the crappy things that had happened at school that day. No one had wanted to pair up with her in PE. She'd eaten lunch alone at the edge of a long table full of kids who ignored her. Then her English teacher had read aloud the essay she'd written on ethics while kids rolled their eyes and texts to everyone but her. People used to like me, she thought. It wasn't like she'd had a best friend, but there had always been kids to hang out with in Portland. She'd gone to the same school, ever since kindergarten, and didn't remember how she'd made friends: she'd just always had them. There had to be some better way to be the new girl, but Celia didn't know how. Someday soon something had to change though, right? She would find a friend. Just one. That would make all the difference. It had been a long four months.

Celia put on her warmest flannel pajamas and went into her parents' room to slip on her mom's fuzzy slippers. She swung the closet door open and glimpsed herself in the full-length mirror. Her straight brown hair ended just below her ears and her bangs covered her forehead in a straight line. No one else at school had stupid bangs like that. Sadness covered her face.

She went into the kitchen to microwave a mac-and-cheese dinner. The typed list of rules her parents had left sat on the kitchen counter, along with two crisp twenty-dollar bills. The list was single-spaced and seven pages long.

1. Celia will not pet stray dogs, or bring home any cats, and if she finds a snake in the toilet like that documentary about Florida, she will flush it.

2. Celia will not open the door to any sales-
   men.
3. Celia will not do any drugs, even if the
   other kids promise they are super fun.

She read through it all and imagined them writing the list late last night with the hope that it would keep her safe, like a magic spell made of paper and ink.

Celia called her mom and told her that everything was fine, that school was great, and that she was going to watch action movies with girl heroes one after another until she got sleepy. She hung up and snuggled on the couch beneath a pile of soft blankets that smelled like cedar as she turned the first movie on. She watched those girls on-screen and wondered what it would be like to wear shiny clothes and always know the right thing to do. It would feel like the opposite of me, she thought, as she stumbled into bed and drifted off to sleep.

Motion shook her. The bedside lamp wobbled back and forth before crashing to the ground. It took a moment for Celia's eyes to adjust to the darkness: a moment before she saw it wasn't just her bed, but all four walls that shook. Books flew off the shelf. What were you supposed to do in an earthquake, again? She'd been through a million earthquake drills at her school in Portland. You were supposed to get under your desk, but there was no desk in her bedroom, or anything else to hide under. And there weren't supposed to be earthquakes on the East Coast, were there?

Celia slid out of bed and crawled over the undulating floor to the window. A full moon lit the city, and the road moved like ripples in a pond. It felt like the world had turned to water, and her apartment was a ship at sea. Down on the street, chunks of building crashed to the ground. Cracks ran up a concrete wall. Windows broke. Celia looked up at her ceiling and watched cracks grow in the plaster. Her room smelled like dust. The world shook and shook.

Then, like magic, the world went still again. A moment later the blunt sounds of chaos—yelling, barking dogs, sirens—came through her window.

Celia sat on the floor amid the fallen books. Her arms and legs felt shivery and numb. That was huge, she thought. A huge earthquake. And I'm all alone. What would Mom and Dad do if they were here?

She righted the bedside lamp with shaking hands and tried to turn it on. Nothing. Same with the light switch. She walked through darkness to the phone in the kitchen. She started dialing her grandma's number before noticing there was no dial tone. She searched for the cell phone next, and found it plugged into the socket near the toaster, surrounded by shards of a broken wine glass. There were no bars, and it beeped strangely when she tried to call out.

Celia moved slowly to her parents' room, stepping over broken, half-seen things in the darkness. She rooted under their bed until she found the two flashlights in the emergency kit. She clicked them on, and two bright beams lit up the darkness. The light felt like a small miracle.

Celia searched every room in the apartment to make sure there weren't any holes in the floor, or any walls about to fall down. Vases, pieces of paper, and broken picture frames lay scattered everywhere.

"Everything is going to be okay," she whispered, and hated the sound of her fluttery voice in the empty room. She said it again and again, until she sounded strong. Through the front door, she heard her neighbors talking in the hallway. Celia pulled jeans on over her pajama bottoms before opening the front door.

Dozens of flashlights danced over the beige walls of the hallway.

"Anyone hurt?" a man called out. "I know CPR and first aid." He stood in his doorway, wrapped up in a thick bathrobe.

Down the hall, another door opened. "We have candles, anyone need candles?"

"Or canned food? We have extra. No telling how long the electricity will be out."

More doors opened, and more people offered help. Across the hall the old Hungarian woman who didn't speak English and hardly ever left her apartment peeked out. Celia walked over to her and handed her one of the flashlights.

The woman's cheeks crinkled into a smile. She patted Celia's hand, murmuring something Celia didn't understand before closing the door again.

"Where are your parents?" someone said behind her.

Celia turned around and looked up. The man in the bathrobe stood near her. "Are you alone?"

7. Don't let strangers know you're home alone.

"My dad is looking for our emergency lanterns: he thinks he left them somewhere near the pepper spray and baseball bat he keeps near his bed," Celia lied. The most dangerous thing in their apartment was the sharp chef's knife her father used when cooking dinner. Celia shone her flashlight in the man's face until he went away.

Celia swept her light up and down the hall, like a lot of people were doing. Nothing looked broken or dangerous. She was just about to go back to her apartment, lock the door, and hide beneath a mountain of blankets when her flashlight skittered across some kids going through the door that led to the roof access. There were six of them, and they all wore worn pants and patched hoodies. One turned toward her light, and just before he lifted his arm to shield his eyes, Celia recognized him. It was the sad boy. The shoelace-and-yo-yo boy. He wore the same knit cap, which made more sense now that it was winter. As he frowned and squinted into the beam of the flashlight, Celia had the feeling all over again that she wanted to know him. He turned and ran up the stairs. The other kids followed.

Who would run up to the roof after an earthquake? Celia thought. Where were their parents? Didn't they care?

Celia went back to her apartment and closed the door behind her. In the quiet, she could hear the stomp of footsteps overhead. What were they doing up there, in the middle of the night? Did the sad boy live in her building? Why hadn't she seen him around?

9. Celia will not go gallivanting into the night.

But . . . there had been an earthquake. Maybe those kids needed help and were all alone, just like she was. Maybe their apartments were ruined and they needed a place to stay or something. Maybe it would be good to go make sure everyone was okay. Besides, she was getting creeped out in her dark apartment, all alone.

Celia slipped out of her apartment to go find the sad boy.

2

THE DREAM GIRL

The padlock lay broken on the top step that led to the roof. A cold breeze blew in through the half-open door, and beyond it, moonlight lit the cold world.

Celia peered out of the doorway and saw the sad boy surrounded by a circle of kids in the middle of the roof. They wore hats or had the hoods of their sweatshirts pulled over their heads. Their clothes were baggy and they wore clunky shoes, like none of them could afford anything that fit right. The kids stood in a circle and held hands. There was something strange about them, something wrong, but the longer Celia stared at them, the more she had no idea what it might be.

Celia opened the door a couple of inches wider. The sad boy

raised his hands and said something Celia couldn't make out. He threw his yo-yo forward and did a complicated trick before it flowed back into his hand. The others swayed from side to side, raised their hands, and said something back to him. Sirens from the earthquake drowned out whatever words they said. Some of them were hunched over and had shaggy hair poking out of their hoods. Others bounced on their toes and had toothy smiles that stretched across their shadowed faces. In the moonlight, Celia couldn't make out more details than that.

The door made an audible squeak as Celia pushed it all the way open and stepped onto the gravelly roof. The kids froze. All eyes turned to her. She pulled her coat around her and shoved her hands into her pockets.

"Hey," Celia called out. The whiteness of her breath curled up into the night air. "Is everyone okay up here?"

The sad boy snapped his yo-yo up into his hand. He stared at her with his hard-angled face as he frowned and pulled his knit cap lower on his head. For a second, his eyes caught the moonlight and glowed. A couple of the other kids took a step toward her. One of them smiled with a mouth full of crooked teeth.

"Go. Now," the sad boy said to his friends and pointed to some large pipes jutting out of the roof.

"There's no law against saying hello," a girl said.

"Go," the sad boy said more forcefully.

The kids turned and ran away from Celia, moving in unison like a flock of birds. One of their hoods blew off and showed wild, spiky hair. They disappeared behind the pipes on the far side of the roof.

The sad boy walked closer to Celia, putting himself between her and the others. He placed his hands on his hips. "This is private property." He spoke with a soft accent. Russian, maybe.

"I know," Celia said. "I live here."

"This is a private meeting." He crossed his arms over his chest.

"But . . . what are you doing up on the roof? Are you in some kind of trouble? Can I help?"

One of the kids peeked out from behind the pipes. Dark curly hair sprang from her hood. She had some kind of birthmark on her face. "That's her! The girl from my dreams." The words echoed across the roof.

Celia shivered and stood up straighter. "You dreamed about me?"

The girl grinned and nodded.

Celia smiled back. It didn't seem possible that someone she didn't know would dream about her, but she liked it anyway.

"Shut up, Daisy." The sad boy stepped between them so Celia couldn't see the other girl. "It's not safe up here," the boy said to Celia. "We're just here because . . . we're kids whose parents aren't home. We're having a meeting about it and it's private."

"Really?" Celia grinned and bounced on the tips of her toes.

"My parents aren't home either," she said, before realizing a second later that she had just broken a rule. "So does one of you live here?"

He nodded and kicked the gravelly ground. "I do."

"You must be new. Apartment 7G, right?" Celia asked.

"Yeah."

"Cool," Celia said, except now she knew he was lying—none of the apartments in the building had letters. She took a step closer and a smell wafted off him, like apple pie and . . . sunlight? That wasn't right, but it was as close as she could get to describing it. "So what are you all doing? I can hold hands and chant with the best of them." There was something about the earthquake and the weirdness of tonight that made Celia feel like she could make friends with them. It had been a long time since she'd even bothered trying.

A panicked look covered the boy's face. He shook his head. "I'm sorry. You can't—"

"She could help us! We could all become friends and do stuff together," a boy's voice called out from behind the pipes.

"I'd like that," Celia said quickly.

"No!" the sad boy said. He stepped away from her. "No. You have to leave right now."

Celia swallowed over a lump in her throat. Why do I even try? She wondered. Why did I even think for one second that anyone could like me?

"It's not you," the boy added. Gentleness filled his voice. "But you do have to go."

"Fine." Celia bit her lip. "I'm gone already." She turned to go, but stopped when she got to the door. "What's your name?" she called back. "In case I see you later?"

"You won't. I'm . . . Demetri." His face had long shadows and dark pits for eyes.

"I'm Celia. I live right below here." She pointed to the part of the roof that was her bedroom's ceiling.

Celia turned and walked away from them. Something strange was going on up here. Something that involved a group of poorly dressed kids, yo-yoing, and a middle-of-the-night rooftop meeting. But whatever it was, she wasn't invited.

Back in her apartment she listened to their footsteps overhead and the rhythm of various sirens going off across the city. It felt like she would never fall asleep.

3

EVERYTHING IS ONLY GOING TO GET WORSE

Celia woke to morning light. The earthquake's wreckage surrounded her, and everything looked worse than she'd imagined. She tried not to stare at the deep cracks in the ceiling's plaster. She tiptoed around the broken things and tried both phones again. Neither worked. Her laptop would turn on, but there was no Wi-Fi. She dug out an old battery-powered radio from the camping gear in the back of the hall closet and found a station where a reporter listed what buildings had collapsed, and the names of the twelve people who had died. Celia switched stations and listened to a scientist explain that an earthquake in Youngstown meant there was some as-yet-undiscovered plate tectonic activity beneath the world's surface.

Celia found a brown paper bag and began picking up pieces of broken glass off the kitchen counter, careful not to cut her fingers.

The mayor came on the radio and said both bridges into the city had been wrecked, and for the moment there was no way to drive on or off the island. Help was coming, the mayor said in her clear, strong voice. Emergency workers would be arriving on trawlers, as soon as the docks were fixed. Aid would get flown in, once the airport runway got repaired. "Stay home and stay safe. Everything will go back to normal in a day or two."

Celia imagined her mom at her grandma's, and her dad in a hotel room, both trying to find a way to reach her. She imagined them worrying and wished, more than anything, that she could hear their voices and tell them she was fine. It felt like if she could tell them that, then she would be fine and the jittery-sick feeling running through her would go away.

Celia poured a bowl of raisin bran, cut up a banana, and opened the fridge. Milk and vegetables tumbled out. The refrigerator had a rotten smell. She rescued the milk carton from the floor and poured some into her bowl. The slightly warm milk tasted gross. Celia leaned against the kitchen counter and ate the cereal until it was all gone.

In the bathroom, she automatically tried to flip on the lights. Nothing. Celia tried to call her parents again. Neither phone worked, same as before.

She was just wondering what she should do next when her apartment started to shake again. Another earthquake? An aftershock? But before she could run to the kitchen table and duck beneath it, it stopped. Then started. Then stopped again. It came from the ceiling. Something massive and heavy was stomping around on the roof.

Were those kids still up there? Celia wondered. She hadn't heard them walking around for a while. Were they okay? Maybe I should go up and check, she thought, not that they would be anything but annoyed by that. Before she could make any decision, someone pounded on her door. Celia ran to it and peered out through the spy hole. Demetri stood on the other side, staring back.

12. Celia will not hang out with strangers.

But did Demetri count as a stranger? She'd met him already, and he was just a boy her age who was probably here because he wanted to apologize for being so rude last night. Maybe he'd been freaked out and now he wanted to say sorry, Celia thought. She decided her parents would like her hanging out with someone her own age, and probably didn't care that much about rule number twelve anyway.

She unlocked the dead bolt, the chain lock, and the normal lock.

As soon as she cracked the door open, Demetri rushed in and slammed it shut. Dark moons ringed his eyes and his skin looked pale and sweaty. Had he slept? His scent of apples and—sunlight? Yep, same as last night—filled the room.

Celia inhaled the lush scent. "What's going—"

"Shhh." He locked all the locks on the door, then ran into her living room. He pulled the blue curtains closed over the bay windows, and the light in the apartment turned from morning bright to underwater blue. Demetri grabbed something from his pocket and tossed it on the floor in front of the windows. When she looked closer, Celia saw it was a handful of robin-blue eggshells.

"What are you doing?" she called out quietly.

Demetri tugged his knotty knit cap down lower on his forehead and wiped sweat from his brow. "Morning, Celia." He spoke softly. Carefully. For a moment their eyes met and he smiled, but then he looked down at the carpet. "I'm sorry I'm here. I needed to hide, and this was the closest place."

"Make yourself at home," she said. "Run inside my apartment and throw eggshells on my carpet. It's cool and not weird at all."

Demetri frowned and bit his lip. He looked toward the door, then at the window. "Sorry, but can you keep it down?"

Celia opened her mouth to speak. Something stomped hard on the roof. It shook the whole apartment. A second later there was a shrieking cry that sounded like a bird. Celia folded her arms over her chest and glared at Demetri. "What's out there?" she whispered.

"Nothing good." Demetri tried to smile. "But it's nothing to worry about, really," he whispered. "This was the closest place I could find to hide. I'll leave soon, I promise." He took out his yo-yo and did a couple of tricks, letting it dance at the end of the string before jerking it back up to his hand.

Celia looked at her front door and then up at her ceiling. Cracks ran across the plaster that hadn't been there yesterday. What would it take for her ceiling to cave in?

"Are your friends safe?"

He shrugged. "Hope so. They left hours ago. I was finishing up something when I got spotted." He rocked back on his heels and looked around. He wore threadbare pants, and his hoodie had a bunch of patches sewn on it to hold it together. His fingernails were black. Not dirty, but painted. "So, it's a nice place you've got here, it's real—"

Celia folded her arms in front of her. "What were you finishing up?"

"Um . . . a magic spell?" He walked to the wall where all the framed photos hung crookedly from the earthquake. He started straightening them.

Celia rolled her eyes. "To keep away the unicorns on the roof?"

Demetri looked confused. "There's no such thing as—"

"Exactly. What were you really doing?" She walked closer to him.

He stumbled backward from her with a wild look on his face, like she had been about to attack him. He moved so that the big blue love seat was between them. He seemed . . . scared of her?

"You know, last night wasn't the first time I've seen you," she said. "I saw you four months ago, when I first moved here. You were acting strange then, too."

"What was I doing?" Demetri walked to the curtains and peered outside.

"You were sitting on a curb, throwing shoelaces into the drain and looking, I don't know, sad?"

Demetri blinked a couple of times and moved farther away from her. He shook his head. "Most people don't notice me." He stared at her like she was something he didn't understand.

"What were you doing?" Celia whispered.

"More spells. To hide from old ladies and . . . kids like you."

Rude. But he said it so softly, like he was choosing each word carefully and wasn't trying to be mean.

The room shook as the thing on the roof stomped around. Celia sank down onto the edge of the orange couch, careful not to step on the broken bowl and gunky chunks of macaroni strewn across the floor. She couldn't tell if she liked Demetri or not, but she was glad to not be alone right now.

Demetri peeked out the window again, then drummed his

hands on the back of the love seat. "So . . . um, what school do you go to?" He spoke like he didn't know how to ask a question like that, as though he didn't live in a world where people constantly asked boring questions. He bent down and picked up a fallen framed picture. Behind the broken glass was a picture of Celia, age five and fearless, with pigtails and a rainbow T-shirt. Demetri stared at it intensely.

"Hamilton Middle. You?"

"I don't. I'm . . . homeschooled." He put the picture back up on the wall, then bent down and picked up another one. This photo showed a sunny day at the beach with her grandpa, a year before he'd died. Demetri ran a finger over the cracked glass surface.

"Oh." Homeschooled. Maybe that explained why he and the other kids had been on the roof? Maybe they'd had some assignment to break into an apartment building right after an earthquake and act mysterious? Nope. It explained nothing. And anyway, was he even telling the truth?

"I've heard that homeschooling is hard because you have to do two hours of PE a day," she lied.

Demetri picked another picture up off the floor and put it on the mantel. "Yeah."

"And it has to be two hours of parkour, where you run around the city and jump off things," she added.

He started to nod and then gave her a look. "That's not true, is it?"

"It's as true as most of the things you're telling me," she replied. "Do you always lie so much?"

"I usually don't talk to people. I've . . . seen you around too. I'm not homeschooled, but I do study things. I watch the city, and I've seen you walking to and from school." He hesitated. "It's not your fault that you're lonely."

The thing on the roof made another thump, and the entire living room shook. Celia stared at the ceiling. How did he know she was lonely? Was it so obvious that everyone who saw her knew? "What do you mean it's not my fault?" Her voice wobbled and she bit her lip. She wanted so much for his words to be true.

Demetri sighed and sat down on the other end of the couch, as far from Celia as possible. He picked up a thick red pillow and placed it between them. "The fact that you don't fit in here? That's a good thing. There's a lot wrong in Youngstown, and even if people don't know what's going on, it twists them. It's not their fault, but it's not your fault, either. A lot of them don't know how to be nice to anyone." Demetri spoke like everything he said was a simple truth. "They've been hurt, even if they don't know how."

The idea that maybe there wasn't anything wrong with her felt like a five-hundred-pound weight pressing down on her shoulders had suddenly lifted. Then again, his words didn't make sense. "Are you lying right now?"

"No."

Celia stared at him for a long moment. She believed him.

Or—she believed that he thought he was telling the truth. "You're a weird one, Demetri."

"Yes."

"Are you hungry? You want some cereal?"

He flinched, even though there was no thump overhead. "Please don't offer me things."

"Right. Because you don't want girl cooties?"

He blinked and looked confused. "That's a . . . joke?"

"Not a funny one, I guess."

He tried to smile.

Something boomed overhead.

Celia hid her shaking hands in her lap. "What's up there?"

"It will be gone soon."

"If you don't tell me what's up there, I'll have to go take a look," she said.

His eyes widened. "You wouldn't."

"You don't know me."

"I do not." His gaze flicked toward her, then away. "But trust me, Celia. You don't want to meet what's on the roof right now."

"Can I guess? Is it a flock of humongous migrating birds?"

Demetri put another pillow between them. It was the embroidered one with a peace symbol that Celia's grandma had made.

"A rival gang of kids who walk in formation? A traveling dance troupe?"

Demetri frowned as the thing on the roof thumped around. Puffs of plaster wafted down from the ceiling.

"A construction crew making repairs? A really angry football player?" Celia spoke faster. The longer it stomped up there, the more Celia felt like this wasn't going to end well. "Am I even close?"

"No."

"But it's going to go away, right?" Whatever it was, and nothing she could think of seemed even a little likely, it had to go away. And soon her parents would be back and everything would be fine, right? She really, really wished the thing thumping around up there would stop. "Everything is going to go back to normal—that's what the mayor said." Celia's voice sounded fluttery and small.

Demetri folded his hands over his chest. "Everything is only going to get worse."

"What?" Celia began picking up broken shards of pottery off the carpet. She laid them in a row on the coffee table. "Why do you think that?"

Demetri didn't answer. He stood and began pacing back and forth along the length of the living room, taking a zigzaggy route to avoid all the fallen things scattered across the floor.

"I'll leave soon," he whispered. "I won't bring trouble here again." He stopped and picked up two fallen hardcover books that Celia had read last summer. "These are good." He placed them on the huge bookshelf that covered most of one wall. "So are these." He picked up two more.

"I know."

"You read a lot?"

"Yep," Celia said. "It takes me away from here."

"Exactly." He grinned. It was a real smile this time, way different than the fake ones.

Celia smiled back. "I loved in that one when they go on the long Appalachian Trail hike." She pointed to the thick book in his left hand.

"And how that mountain lion follows them and you just know they are doomed," Demetri said.

"And you think it's going to try to eat them, but then it becomes their friend and protects them," Celia added.

They talked about the various books in whispered voices as the thudding continued across the ceiling. Talking about books with Demetri felt the same as reading them. Slowly, Celia started to feel less and less freaked out.

"You know, you can stay here," Celia said. "If your parents are away like mine and you're alone. Or if you're in some kind of trouble. If whoever is up there is violent." She pointed at the roof. "When my parents get back, they'll help you."

Demetri flinched and looked toward the door. He seemed scared of her, for the second time.

"I should go now."

"What about . . . ?" Celia pointed upward.

Both of them listened for a long moment. There hadn't been any thuds in a while.

"I am certain it is safer out there than in here. Thank you for giving me shelter, Celia. It was very kind. And despite everything, it was nice to meet you."

Demetri stood and made a funny little bow, the kind her grandpa might have done.

Celia didn't want him to leave. She wanted to talk about more books and maybe go on a walk with him to explore the shaken city. Even if he lied and didn't make sense half the time, she liked him, despite how weird he was. Maybe his strangeness was part of why she liked him so much. She got up and gave him a mocking curtsy in return. Her ankle twisted over a fallen book, and she fell toward him.

Demetri reached out to catch her but pulled his hands away at the last minute. The tip of his finger grazed her cheek as she slammed into the floor. Her knee burst with pain. "Ow!"

Demetri's mouth hung open. He backed away from her toward the front door. "I'm sorry," he whispered. "I'm so sorry."

Celia winced as she got up. Her cheek felt warm where he'd touched it. "I'm fine. Catching my fall would have been nice, but whatever."

Demetri stared at her as he shook his head back and forth. "Forget me," he whispered. "Forget all of this. And Celia?"

"Yeah?"

"If anything . . . feels different, ignore it. I'm sorry." His face froze. He looked like he was crying beneath the stillness of his features. He turned and let himself out.

As soon as he was gone, the pain in Celia's knee faded and the familiar ache of loneliness returned. Only this time, it felt different. Before it was just a blob of hopelessness, but now it had a Demetri-sized shape to it. After so long without making a new friend, it finally felt like she had someone she could talk to: someone who read the same books as her and cared about things. She wanted to get to know him and make him smile some more. She needed to figure out why he thought he had to lie to her all the time. She didn't want just any friend anymore, she wanted Demetri.

4

LIVING WITH WOLVES

Hours passed. Morning turned into afternoon, and there was nothing to do.

Celia tried both phones again. Neither worked. She wanted, more than anything, to hear her mom's voice sounding frantic and funny and telling Celia she would be home soon.

She picked up broken things around the apartment, but everywhere she looked there was more mess.

The apartment felt small and cold, and there weren't any new books to read or anything to watch, of course. She paced around and her mind raced as she thought about the earthquake and the thumping on her roof. Whatever it was, it had scared Demetri enough that he had to hide. She thought and thought, but she couldn't figure out what it might have been. What if it came back and she was all alone? The more she thought about it, the worse she felt. She couldn't stay inside all day with nothing to do but freak out and worry.

4. Celia will not traipse around town like a
   vagabond.

Celia was pretty sure her parents wouldn't want her leaving home, not when there had been an earthquake, but she could walk to the library and back again. The library was always allowed.

As she pulled clothes out of her dresser, Celia studied the knee she'd fallen on. It was already turning a satisfying purple. If something hurts, it should mark you, Celia thought. She put on her favorite wool tights, a gray skirt, a sweater, her tennis shoes, and a down jacket. She added a black knit hat and a red scarf, and slipped the cell phone into her pocket, in case it started working. She made a peanut butter and honey sandwich, filled up a water bottle, and grabbed her bike helmet in case another earthquake happened. The last thing she put into her backpack was her parents' list of rules.

When she left, Celia caught her reflection in the cracked hallway mirror. There was a small red mark on her cheek— right where Demetri had touched her. It was weird that it would leave a bruise as dark as the one on her knee.

The elevator had a handwritten *Danger!* sign taped over the doors, so she took the stairs, running her fingers over the newly made cracks in the walls.

Outside, the air had a dusty taste, and the world looked like a snow globe someone had shaken too hard. Cars sat bumper to bumper. Broken glass lay scattered on the sidewalks. Adults moved with slow, dreamlike motions, stopping and staring blankly before going back to sweeping up or trying to get their phones to work. An old man sat out on his stoop handing out paper cups of hot chocolate from a steaming aluminum pot set on a camping stove.

Celia took one. "Want a sandwich?"

He nodded and said, "Strange days."

"Strange days," she agreed, as she gave him her sandwich.

Celia walked on and wrapped her fingers around the warmth of the paper cup.

On the next block a couple of houses leaned against each other. An old brick building wrapped in bright-yellow danger tape looked like a birthday present no one wanted.

At the corner, someone had spray-painted the word *Doom* in big letters across the sidewalk. Underneath, scrawled in a messy calligraphy, it read:

The city will shake and the girl will be found.

Above the words was a stencil of a sad-looking girl wearing a gray skirt, a red scarf, and a black hat.

Just like what I'm wearing, Celia thought, which was a weird coincidence. She shivered, shoved her hands into her pockets, and walked around the letters, not letting her shoes touch them. She hurried on to the library, half a block away.

The library was old and made of stone. There were twin statues of camels outside, next to the library's open double doors. The inside was lit with gas lanterns, and people filtered in and out. Whenever Celia had a question or needed to find a book, librarians had always been able to help her, so she wasn't surprised to see that they could deal with an earthquake, too. Some stood behind desks manually checking books in and out, while others reshelved volumes that had fallen to the floor.

As she walked up the library stairs, Celia saw a card table set up just inside the doors, stacked with different sizes of brightly colored papers, all handwritten. Some offered sanctuary, others listed addresses for free food and trauma counseling. A single yellow flyer caught her attention and seemed to almost flutter up into her hand.

Who caused the earthquake? it read with scrawling penmanship. *What are they going to do next? What do we have to do to stop them?*

It listed a meeting time and a place—Saint Jude's Cathedral— which was four blocks away. Celia checked her watch and saw that the meeting had started five minutes ago.

The flyer seemed kind of paranoid: nothing caused an earthquake, they just happened. She thought about games kids used to play in Portland where there would be all-city quests and battles and teams on different sides with some kind of silly prize for the winners. Maybe this was something like that. She wanted to go and check it out.

Celia reread her parents' list of rules twice just to make sure she wasn't forbidden to go to church or play games. She put the flyer into her pocket. She turned away from the library and walked toward the cathedral, passing boarded-up stores, crashed cars, and dusty firefighters trudging down the middle of the street.

Celia scratched at the spot where Demetri had touched her cheek. The skin felt rough, like a callus. On any other day she would have obsessed over how that was possible, but today the thought drifted away with all the other strangeness.

Saint Jude's Cathedral took up most of a city block. It was a massive white marble building with a million stained-glass windows. None of them looked broken. Celia wondered what she would find inside. Just a game, she thought. She looked at her list again.

22. Celia will not join a cult.

Celia pulled open one of the tall wooden doors and slipped inside. She smelled beeswax and the faint scent of mold. Beyond the bowl of holy water and rows of lit candles, Celia spied some kids sitting in wooden pews near the altar. A huge round stained-glass window rose up behind it and showered the room in blue and green light. Celia walked down the aisle toward the group. She glanced behind her and saw an upper floor of the cathedral, twenty feet up, with more pews and a big silver organ. When she turned back, all the kids were staring at her.

"Church is closed today," an Asian girl with purple-spiked hair snapped. "We're the only ones allowed in here." She stood in front of everyone else. All the kids, about two dozen of them, looked like they were Celia's age or a little younger.

"But . . ." Celia looked around. "I saw the flyer at the library. This is some kind of game, right?"

"She saw the invitation. She came," a boy with a large nose whispered. He stood and stared at her. "It's the girl from my dreams."

"Are you sure?" a girl with long blond hair asked.

The boy nodded. "She's even wearing the same clothes that I saw." He smiled and said louder, "Come in. Sit down."

Celia didn't move. This was the second time someone had said they dreamed about her.

They stared at her like they'd never seen a thirteen-year-old girl with bad bangs before. Celia bit her lip and took a couple of steps forward, reminding herself that this was all some kind of role-playing game. They probably told every new kid they'd dreamed about her.

The purple-haired girl said, "Sit down already."

A girl scooted over in one of the pews to make room.

Celia sank down onto the cold hard wood.

The purple-haired girl, standing a dozen feet away, put her hands on her hips and said, "Tell us *your* earthquake story, new girl. We're all sharing." Her raspy voice sounded like she'd spent all morning yelling. Her tone of voice demanded an answer.

Celia looked behind her at the doors. Everyone watching her made her feel nervous. She didn't know if part of the game was making up stories, or if they wanted the truth. She decided to keep it vague. "It's been . . . strange."

All the kids nodded.

"Everything feels wrong," she added.

Kids smiled at her.

Celia felt like the question had been a test, and somehow she had gotten the answer right.

"Who are you?" the purple-haired girl asked.

"Celia."

"Hey Celia. I'm Amber," the girl sitting next to her whispered. She had a long braid, thick black glasses, smooth brown skin, and a pretty face. She gnawed one fingernail and watched Celia with owly eyes.

Everyone kept staring at her.

"So, uh, how do you all know each other?" she asked into the silence.

"Not how," the purple-haired girl said. "That's not what you should be asking. The question you should be asking, Celia, is *who*. You need to know who we are."

"Okay . . . who are you?" Celia settled back in her seat, ready to hear some dramatic story that would explain what this game was all about. Because this had to be a game. It just had to. Nothing else made sense.

"We are the hunters. We're the ones who keep everyone in this city safe."

5

LOST HOPE

Hunters? Celia brought her legs up to sit cross-legged on the pew. Perhaps this was hunters versus werewolves, or zombies, or maybe vampires. As long as they weren't too scary, she loved books about monsters. "Hunters of what?" she asked.

"Hunters of the secret city," a girl with long stringy hair said.

"Of the unnamed," a scarred boy added.

"Of the unseen," a girl wearing a black leather jacket whispered.

"You found the flyer. You've noticed strange things happening. That means you belong with us." The girl at the front of the room ran her hand through her purple hair. "I'm Ruby, by the way."

Other kids called out their names. A lot of them had nick-names like Spike, Rampage, and Twinkle Toes.

Celia wanted a nickname, too. Maybe she could be Night-hawk, or Danger Girl.

Amber, the girl sitting next to Celia, scooted closer and whis-pered, "It's really good that you found us before anything else happened. We're going to be friends. Okay?"

"I'd love that." Warmth spread through Celia.

"Enough with the introductions," Ruby barked. Kids turned their attention back to her. The stained-glass window above and behind her made everything look moody and intense. "Let's get everyone up to speed, including Celia. Talk to me, hunters," she ordered.

As people started talking, Celia watched them. The hunters wore clothes made out of leather or thick cloth. Like the kids last night, they looked like they belonged together. But the kids from last night had looked poor, and all the hunters wore really well-made stuff, even if some of it was dirty. They each wore a silver pin on their chest. Celia looked closer at Amber's and saw it was a hand wrapped around a heart. Not the Valentine kind, but the kind that pumped blood.

A boy dressed in a dozen shades of brown leather was saying things that made no sense to Celia. "The Council of Elders met with some of us this morning at their headquarters. They told us the earthquake wasn't natural, but a spell cast by *them*."

"They can make earthquakes whenever they want?" a wide-eyed boy asked. He looked a little younger, maybe eleven.

A girl in all black replied, "Not usually. The Council of Elders thinks they might be working together. But that's not all. They found strong magic stretched across the boundaries of the whole island. Nothing gets in or out. Not people. Not communication. Nothing. Until the doom prophecy ends." Her hands moved through the air like fluttering birds as she spoke.

Ruby scowled. "So we're trapped, and from the sound of it, we may be facing an alliance of Bigs."

Amber, the girl next to Celia, raised her hand and said loudly, "Bigs hate each other. That's one of the only reasons they don't take over everything. What could bring them together?"

Kids rat-a-tatted their hands on pews and shook their heads. Every one of them was so into this game—big eyes, furrowed brows, tensed shoulders. Celia searched for signs that they were acting. She found none. She bit her lip and reminded herself it had to be a game.

"No idea," Ruby growled. She paced back and forth. "What else?"

Silence. A scuffling sound came from above and behind them. Celia looked back but saw nothing. It was probably just a rat.

Amber raised her hand again. "I've spent the morning learning everything I could about the doom prophecy." She pushed up her thick glasses. "I found it written in a couple of different places: a gallery downtown, and in the graffiti flats. It says, *The city will shake and the girl will be found. The city will hiss and the girl will run. The city will fill with silent words and the girl will decide—*"

"*To save the city,*" Ruby said, interrupting her.

Kids across the room looked at Celia, and then away.

The doom prophecy? Celia had seen the first part of it written on the sidewalk next to an image of a girl who looked just like her. What if . . . none of this was a game? She shivered. Her belly clenched.

"We need more information," Ruby said. She pointed at a boy with a scar. "Reach out through the secure hunter network and contact other teams in every nearby city. Someone somewhere has to know what's going on."

The boy frowned. "No electricity and no computers means no communication. Anyway, I was on the network last night before the quake, and things seemed pretty normal. Along the West Coast, some hunters were fighting a leviathan, and in Mexico City some kids got hurt taking down Chupa. That's all."

"Find a way to contact them," Ruby said. "Maybe the Elders can get a spell to help." Ruby pointed at two other kids. "You two grab some hearts and go to the port. Find out everything they know."

Both kids nodded grimly.

"You three take Chinatown and the Salt District."

Ruby pointed at Amber. "You and me? We'll stick with Celia

and tell her what she needs to know." Ruby's intense gaze rested on Celia for a moment.

"Everyone else? Do whatever needs doing, by any means necessary. We'll meet back here tomorrow at sundown. They got the jump on us once. Now we jump back." She ran both hands through her purple hair and flashed a cocky grin.

The kids began to leave the cathedral in twos and threes. Their steel-toed boots thunked against the stone floor as they put on hats and wrapped thick wool scarves around their necks.

They said hi or wished her luck as they left.

Celia watched them go and wondered if these kids were the most hard-core gamers ever. Or, and this couldn't be true, but maybe they were telling the truth? Maybe they knew something that no one else did—something dangerous and strange about something that could make spells and cause earthquakes. A fluttering feeling filled Celia, and she didn't know whether it was fear or excitement. Maybe both.

Ruby's heavy black boots stomped as she walked down the aisle. Her hand touched Celia's shoulder. "Follow me."

Celia stood and walked behind her, past the rows of oak pews and alcove saints. She looked up at the silver pipe organ on the balcony and saw a flutter of movement. She only got a moment's look before he ducked down, but that was all she needed to see the knit cap, the ragged clothes, and a dark flash of sad eyes.

Demetri was up there, spying on the hunters.

6

MORE AND MORE COMPLICATED

Celia didn't say anything about seeing Demetri as she walked out of the cathedral with Amber on one side and Ruby on the other. Why was he there? Maybe he was part of their game, and playing for the other side. The sky spit down cold needles of rain. Celia wrapped her red scarf around her neck and pulled her cap over her ears. She wished she'd worn pants, not a skirt. Cold seeped through her wool tights. All the hunters left in different directions. Amber and Ruby stood on the steps with her, wearing their sleek black raincoats and thick-soled leather boots.

"So what now?" Celia asked.

Ruby shrugged. "We tell you things. You get less stupid."

"Be nice," Amber said.

"Nice isn't going to save her," Ruby growled. She picked at a black leather bracelet around her wrist. She wore a bunch of them.

"Can I tell her the first thing? The big thing?" Amber blinked and watched Celia from behind her thick glasses.

"You sure?" Ruby asked.

"I think so. I've thought about the different variables of possible reactions, and for almost all of them her learning the truth right away is the best way to—"

"You're the doom girl." Ruby poked Celia in the chest with her pointer finger.

"What?" Celia took a step backward and looked at both of them. "What?"

Amber nodded. "Most of the time, when a big magic spell is cast, a prophecy appears that gives clues about what's going to happen. It's like . . . some kind of natural protection against all the mayhem. A prophecy invades creative people's thoughts, and they don't even know what it is. So you see it in graffiti, hear it at poetry slams, and hear people singing about it on street corners. The doom prophecy showed up last night, all over the place, after the earthquake. And this one is all about you."

"But . . ." Celia took another step backward and thought about how people kept saying they'd dreamed about her. "I don't understand . . ."

Ruby looked bored. "*The city will shake and the girl will be found.* You're the girl in the prophecy and we found you. It's not that complicated."

"Actually," Celia said, "I found *you.*"

"That's what you think." Ruby smirked.

Celia spoke in a rush of words. "Is this part of how your game works? Am I the doom girl because I was the last to arrive at the meeting? Or because I found your flyer and whoever finds it and comes to your meeting, they're the doom girl? How does any of this *work?*"

"This isn't a game, Celia," Amber said. She looked up at the gray sky. "I wish it was. But this is real life. Our life."

"And yours now too," said Ruby. "Get used to it."

Celia shook her head. She hadn't eaten much today and her stomach hurt. Cold came at her from all directions. "I don't get you guys at all. I'm going home. None of this is real and you are both . . ." Celia shook her head. She didn't even know how to finish that sentence. Rain dripped down her neck.

Ruby sighed. "You can't run away from this. You're the doom girl."

"Yep. You're prophesized to, uh, save the city," Amber added. "You'll save us all."

They both looked at her like they needed her.

Delusional, Celia decided. They aren't playing a game, they believe all this, somehow. "It's been really nice to meet you, and

I hope you both stay safe until the electricity and all that comes back," Celia said. She took a step backward, forgetting she was close to the stairs. She started to fall down the slick white marble.

Ruby grabbed her arm and steadied her.

"'The doom girl' might sound bad, but it's a good thing," Ruby said. "You get to be the hero. And we'll help you. You don't have to do any of this alone."

Hero. Celia blinked and thought about every movie full of girls saving the day, and what if . . . "Not that I believe you, but what kind of things would I have to do?"

"We don't know." Ruby shoved her hands into her pockets. She glanced up and down the street. People walked by hidden under their umbrellas. "The prophecy will come true, one way or another. We'll play it by ear and figure it out."

"This is the weirdest joke ever, right?" Celia said.

"Bizarre things have been happening to you ever since the earthquake, haven't they?" Amber whispered.

Kids running up to the roof right after the quake and a girl saying she'd seen Celia in her dreams. Demetri hiding in her apartment from something huge that thudded overhead. A callused bruise on her face where Demetri had touched her. A picture of a girl who looked exactly like her above the doom prophecy. Some hunter kid saying he'd dreamed of her. And right here, right now: two girls looking way too serious as they talked about impossible things. "Nothing that strange," Celia lied. She took a step away from them, careful this time not to fall on the stairs.

Ruby gave her a hard look. "If not yet, then soon. Things are going to get stranger and stranger for you. Nowhere is safe. You're at the center of all this. Your normal life? It's over," Ruby said. "At least until the three parts of the doom prophecy have happened. You're lucky we're the ones who found you first." She cracked her knuckles. "Nothing we can't handle. This is bigger than anything we've faced, but we're good at what we do. Amber has more brains than ten kids combined. And I'm the leader of the hunters. Wanna know why?" She thrust out her arm and pointed at all the leather bracelets on it. "I earned one of these for every Big I've taken down." There were dozens of them. "Stick with us and we'll save the city together."

Celia took another step away from them. "I'm just a normal girl."

"Just a girl destined to save the city," Amber said, and smiled with a false, bright smile.

"Just a stupid girl who still doesn't know anything," Ruby grumbled.

Beyond them, a couple of cars lumbered down the broken street and honked at each other to go faster.

"Prove it." Celia's heart beat hard beneath her coat. "Prove anything you are saying is real, or I'm going home."

Amber held out her hand. "You still have the flyer you found at the library?"

Celia took the crumpled piece of paper out of her pocket. Amber took it from her hand, smoothed it out, and dropped it. By the time it drifted to the ground, all the handwriting had faded off it and the paper had gone blank.

Celia blinked. She picked it up, and as soon as her fingers touched it, the ink bled back onto the paper and formed words again.

"The Council of Elders told us we had to try to find you," Amber said. "They got a spell made for us that only the doom girl could read. We put it out at the library, at every food bank, and on lots of street corners. For everyone else, it looked like a blank piece of paper."

A shiver rolled up Celia's spine. She let the paper drop, watched it go blank, and then caught it. Ink swirled back across the paper.

"It's . . . magic?" Celia swallowed hard. "Magic is real?" Half of her still thought this was a joke, but only half.

"Uh-huh." Amber bounced on her toes. "I love studying magic, even if humans can't do much with it. It's my favorite thing to read about."

If humans couldn't . . . then who could? Fairies? Trolls? The cold from the marble steps seeped up through the rubber soles of Celia's tennis shoes. What if magic was real and there was a whole secret world out there? She dropped and caught the piece of paper, loving how the ink faded and came back.

"I'll show you something else." Amber's face went serious as she looked up and down the street, then pushed up her coat sleeve. Thick ropy scars ran down her forearm in angry lines. "That's from Bigs. They attacked and killed my parents, who didn't even fight back because they couldn't see them. They almost got me, too. But then hunters rescued me, took me in, and taught me how to fight back. Without the hunters, I'd be in foster care, probably. . . ." Amber's face went a muddy gray color. "You have to stop Bigs from hurting other families like mine, Celia. You just have to."

Celia looked away from the scars.

Ruby put her hands on her hips. She tilted her head up and surveyed the sky. "The sun sets early this time of year. It'll be dark enough to go hunting in an hour. They leave trails in the dark. Come on—we'll buy you a hot chocolate and explain everything. If, after that, you still want to pretend you're just a normal girl, it's your funeral."

Celia looked at the paper and then at Amber's scarred arm. Part of Celia wanted to hide in her room under all the blankets until normal came back. But another part of her wanted to go to a café with two intense girls who thought that the world had magic in it and that she was the chosen one, and maybe, just maybe, they were right. Celia wrapped her scarf around her neck. "Something warm sounds good."

Celia followed them down to the sidewalk. She checked the cell phone. There was still no reception. Because of a spell, the hunters had said.

They walked down the buckled road, and the gray day grew darker and slicker under a steady trickle of rain. They passed storefronts with displays full of tumbled-down mannequins and others with plywood nailed up over broken windows. Restaurants were closed. Apartments flickered with candlelight. A white-haired woman sat in one of the windows wearing dark glasses and staring out at nothing. Her hair was pulled up in a perfectly round bun at the top of her head. She held so still she looked like a statue.

Shadows lengthened. Thick shards of glass lay scattered across the ground. Amber and Ruby linked elbows. Celia hung back a couple of steps, but Amber turned around and linked arms with Celia too.

"Hunters stick together," Amber said.

Celia almost reminded her that she wasn't a hunter, but it felt so nice to be included.

They walked on through the shaken city. Handwritten signs sat propped outside some high-rise apartment building saying *Repent, The End Times Are Here,* and *The Girl Will Be Found.* The sidewalks were mostly empty, and the few people they passed moved hunched over. People kept pulling out their phones and staring at the screens before slipping them back into their pockets. Celia thought of her parents. A weighted cold settled into her.

Then they turned a corner and saw a place lit up with LED flashlights hanging from a crooked awning. The glowing lights, a spot of cheeriness inside the growing murk, drew them forward.

Amber and Ruby slipped inside. The bitter smell of coffee wafted out the door, mixed with the sweet smell of hot chocolate. Celia's stomach rumbled.

She hesitated on the doorstep. If she went home now, and didn't pay attention to sounds on the roof, or knocks on her door, or pieces of paper that ebbed and flowed with magic ink, would life turn normal again? Would she be able to stay safe and lonely and bored?

Or was normal over from now until the prophecy ended? Doom girl, Celia thought, and wanted to know more about what that meant and what was going to happen. Maybe, even though the world felt chaotic and scary, maybe a bunch of good things could come out of this too. And no matter what, at least it was interesting. Celia was so tired of normal, when all that meant was feeling sad and lonely all the time.

Amber stuck her head back through the door and grinned at Celia.

"Come on," she said, waving her in.

Celia pulled her parents' list of rules out of her backpack. She'd broken way too many of them already.

4. Celia will not traipse around town like a vagabond.
5. Celia will be home every night well before sunset.
12. Celia will not hang out with strangers.
15. Safety first, no matter what.

Celia sighed and turned to the last page. She reread the very last rule.

27. Our amazing daughter has a smart head on her shoulders and she doesn't really need this list because we know she will use good judgment. Celia, we love you and trust you and have fun but not too much fun and call if you need anything!

I love you too, she thought, and rubbed away the tears that welled up in her eyes. If they were here right now, they would say she should go home, lock all the doors, and eat food from cans until they came home. But they weren't here.

Celia stepped forward into the light and noise of the café.

7

SHOULDN'T BE REAL

The coffeehouse was crammed full of people sitting knee-to-knee and talking loudly over the battery-powered boom box that played hip-hop. Tea lights flickered on every table and counter-top, and hurricane lanterns glowed from the corners of the room. Small camping stoves were set up on the counters, heating delicious-smelling drinks.

Ruby ordered for everyone: three hot chocolates with extra whipped cream and a plate full of pastries. The barista, a mid-twenties guy with a ponytail and a patch over one eye, didn't make her pay. He said they were trying to get rid of everything before things went rotten. The three girls wandered to the back of the place and found a small wooden table carved with decades of hearts and initials.

Ruby passed out pastries. Her spiky purple hair had fallen down in the rain and lay limply on her head. She swiped a finger through her whipped cream and licked it. "Shall we?" she asked Amber.

The other girl nodded and leaned toward Celia. "So. Once upon a time, people could be magicians, if they learned the right things, studied hard, and were smart. They could take magic from all living things and manipulate it." Amber took a sip of her drink and gave herself a whipped-cream mustache. "Then, about a hundred and fifty years ago, humans stopped being able to use magic. We can still activate spells, if someone else makes them for us, but that's all. We can't take raw magic and do anything with it."

Celia nodded slowly. "Okay. What changed?" she asked.

"No one knows what happened, but magic closed to us on the same day Littles and Bigs showed up."

Celia dipped bits of cinnamon roll into her cocoa and licked the vanilla-scented icing that dripped onto her palm. With every sip, she felt more awake. She took a deep breath. "So what are Littles and Bigs?"

Amber leaned forward. "We call them that because it's safer than saying what they really are. Some Bigs have really good hearing."

Ruby's hands curled into fists.

Amber's eyes darted around the room. She leaned closer until

Celia could smell the fruity scent of her shampoo. "What they really are is . . . monsters."

Monsters? Celia rolled her eyes and looked from one girl to the other. Neither of them smiled.

They thought monsters were real, and had made the earthquake using magic, and that she was part of some prophecy having to do with . . . monsters? She almost started laughing, except . . . the word did something funny inside her. It made her breath catch and she found herself looking in all directions, as though there might be a monster in this café, which was ridiculous because there was no such thing as monsters. Everyone knew that.

"Breathe, Celia. Just breathe. If there's anywhere safe in Youngstown right now, it's here with us in a loud, crowded place." Ruby grabbed hold of Celia's cold hands.

Celia whispered, "*Monsters* aren't real."

"They shouldn't be real," Amber whispered back. "But they are."

Celia shook her head.

"You've seen monsters. Kids can see them," Ruby said. She ran her hand across the tea light's flame, close enough to leave black marks on her fingertips. "Deep down, if you think about it, you know we're telling the truth. Kids see Bigs and forget about them right away, because our minds refuse to believe it. We glimpse Littles and think they are just dressed funny, even though a part of us knows they aren't real kids. Hunters see monsters and don't forget like other kids, because monsters have hurt us. You'll be able to see them too, now that we've told you about them, but you'll have to work at it at first."

Half memories of shadow-things flickered through Celia's mind. That time she'd been camping in the Cascades and saw something huge and misshapen flapping above the trees. Or how once, at Washington Park, all the shadows had turned strange and it had felt like they were chasing her. And even though *monster* was just a normal word, a word people used all the time, she didn't want to say it out loud, because what if Amber was right and something out there might notice?

Ruby pushed a stale chocolate croissant toward Celia. She touched a star-shaped scar on her neck. "You're going to start seeing stranger and stranger things."

Celia looked at the front door and wanted to run down a dozen streets until she made it home. But what if *they* were really out there, ready to attack her? She took a bite of pastry but didn't taste it. "If all this is true, how come no one knows?" Her voice sounded faraway and small.

"Monsters own magic, so they're good at hiding. They make spells to hide any proof that they exist. And even though no one knows they're real, people can't stop telling stories about them," Amber said.

"Think about all the stories about things that go bump in the night," Ruby said. "Think about how many horror movies there are about monsters. No one knows, but at the same time everyone is obsessed with them because deep down, people sense stuff."

Celia opened her mouth and shook her head. Monsters weren't real. She remembered a lullaby her dad used to sing to her about locking all the doors and lighting all the lanterns to keep safe. She thought about the rows and rows of monster masks at the Halloween store, and all the books about monsters she had read. Celia traced her finger over a carved skull-and-crossbones etched into the table and wondered, What if all this is real? "Tell me more," she whispered, and filled her mouth with the bittersweet taste of cooling cocoa.

Amber took out a pen and started doodling on a paper napkin.

"First you have a Big. That's what we call an adult monster." She sketched a shaggy, gorilla-like creature. "Then you have a Little. A kid monster." She drew a kid with devil horns. "Then you have us. Normal kids." She made arrows between the pictures. "Every Big used to be a Little, and every Little used to be a normal kid."

"What? Monsters are human?"

"Not even slightly. But they used to be," Ruby said.

The tea light flickered. That meant . . . people could be turned into monsters? "How?"

"It's pretty simple," Amber said. "A Little can change a regular kid into a Little by touching them for a while. The second a Little changes someone, that Little turns into a Big. When a Little changes us, that makes them Big, get it? Littles can only change other kids, though: not grown-ups." She redrew her arrows on the napkin.

Celia thought about viruses and how quickly they could spread. "How many millions and millions of them are there?" She looked around the room.

"Not that many." Amber stared into the tea light. "First, because hunters hunt them. And second, Bigs enslave the Littles they make for years and years. But eventually, every sneaky Little finds a way to escape and attack a new kid, and the whole scruddy cycle starts all over again."

"So hunters kill these . . . Littles and Bigs?" Celia hated killing anything, even mosquitoes.

Amber looked startled. "No. Just Bigs. And we mostly don't kill them."

"But you said Littles are the ones who attack kids, right?"

"Sure," Amber said. "But before a Little attacks a kid, they haven't done anything wrong. And some Littles try to be good. They aren't that different than us. They—"

"No." Ruby interrupted her. "However nice they act, Littles always destroy another kid eventually. They can't help it. It's who they are. When we catch a Little, we turn them over to the Council of Elders. They keep them locked up. That's the only safe thing to do with Littles."

"The Elders. They're your bosses?" Celia drank the last of her hot chocolate.

"Sort of. They all used to be hunters. The best and brightest get to sit on the council. The Elders recruit us and train all the kids who've been hurt by monsters. Being a hunter is not"— Amber looked away—"it's not a life anyone would want for a kid, so they only train those of us whose lives have already been ruined by *them*. Kids do the hunting, since we can see them, and the council does everything they can to help us and keep us safe."

Something lurched into the café. Celia tensed but then saw it was just a guy wearing a thick down jacket and furry hood.

"This isn't a joke, is it?" The word *monster* repeated over and over in Celia's head. She felt like throwing up.

"It's the opposite of a joke. Bigs hunt people and eat them. Or they drain them of their life forces until they lose their will to live. Or a million other terrible things, because they are super evil. Imagine being hurt or worse by something you can't even see. Last night they figured out how to make a huge spell that shook all of Youngstown and trapped everyone here. We don't know why, or what they are planning next, but people will get hurt. People will get killed by invisible things they can't fight against. We have to figure out how to stop them. We need your help, Celia."

"I'm good at writing book reports," Celia said. "Riding a bike, being bored, making pizza as long as someone else does the dough. But you know what I'm not good at? Fighting anything, ever." Her voice went higher and higher as she talked.

"We don't know what the doom girl will have to do," Amber said. "Maybe you won't have to fight. There are other ways you can help. Maybe book reports will save the city."

It's time for me to go home, Celia almost said. But what was at home besides loneliness, broken glass, and being alone with way too many thoughts?

The world had monsters in it, maybe. And if that impossible thing was true, then maybe for some impossible reason she'd been chosen to stop whatever they were planning. If she did that, she'd have a whole group of intense hunter friends. They'd have secret handshakes, give her a nickname, and tell jokes that only made sense to each other. She'd be Celia the monster hunter. Celia the brave.

She knew it wouldn't actually be like that, that real life was never how you imagined it, but then again, if there were monsters, maybe there were heroes too.

Celia drank the last of her hot chocolate and sat up straight. "You know you're going to have to prove that monsters are real, right?"

Ruby grinned. She drummed her knuckles over the wooden table. "We thought you'd never ask."

Amber and Ruby followed her as Celia led the way out of the café.

8

THEY CAN SMELL FEAR

Outside, the world was made of rubble and wet concrete, puddles and gray clouds. Everything looked like a huge bruise. Celia buttoned her coat all the way up to her neck. Fingers of cold slipped in though the gaps.

Monsters, her mind whispered. She thought about Demetri hiding in her apartment this morning from the thumps along her ceiling. Had that been a . . . ?

"Keep up!" Ruby barked from a dozen steps in front of her. The hunters scanned the street, like *they* were nearby.

Maybe they were. Maybe they always had been.

Celia ran forward to walk beside them. She took a deep breath and thought about other things that had seemed unbelievable at first. Like how arctic terns flew for three years straight and slept on the wind, or how trees could live a thousand years, or how crocodiles were little dinosaurs. So if monsters were real? Maybe that would seem normal someday too.

"First rule of the hunt is that we stay together. All we're going to do tonight is catch a Little, interrogate them, and then turn them over to the Elders. Easy." Ruby spoke in a low voice as she stomped along the ground in her heavy leather boots.

"What will the Elders do with the Little?" Celia asked.

Amber frowned.

"What they have to, to keep us safe," Ruby said.

"But what will they—" Celia started.

"Cages," Amber said. "It's for the best."

The hunters kicked puddles and sent dirty water spraying across the concrete. Ruby led them into an alley full of garbage cans and a couple of feral cats. She swung her bike-messenger bag around to the front and pulled out an unmarked spray can.

"Right now? Do we have to?" Amber frowned. "We might not find any. We haven't seen any signs of them yet."

"Don't whine. You know how fast things can change in the field," Ruby said.

"Fine." Amber sighed, grabbed the can, and sprayed a white mist over her face, neck, and hands. She passed it to Celia. "It's an aerosolized protection spell. Once it's on, Littles will get burned if they try to change you into a monster. We'll be safe for a couple of hours."

Celia looked at the can. "I thought humans couldn't . . ."

"We can use magic, we just can't make the spells. The Elders force *them* to make spells for us and put it into things we can use," Amber said.

"Put it on already," Ruby grumbled.

Celia closed her eyes, held her breath, and sprayed herself all over. As soon as the mist touched her skin, it itched, especially on the cheek Demetri had touched. The spray smelled like black licorice and vomit. "I'm pretty sure nothing is going to want to attack me with a ten-foot pole, smelling like this," Celia said.

"Yep. It repels rats, bullies, and creepy old men, too." Ruby grinned.

Amber giggled. So did Celia, a moment later.

Ruby sprayed herself, and they walked back to the main road. Dusk had slipped into true night, and the lack of streetlights made every shadow and doorway look like it could be hiding something. Amber and Ruby walked with a predatory grace, scanning everything as they moved. Maybe they were freaking out on the inside, but they didn't look like it.

Celia noticed a group of five men on the other side of the street. They were big and talked with deep voices that echoed down the road. One of them carried a baseball bat.

Celia looked from them to Amber and Ruby. "I wish they were the hunters," Celia said. "They're big and tough. Why does it have to be"—she almost said *us*—"kids?"

Amber spoke in a tone Celia was beginning to recognize as her lecturing voice. "We're the only ones who can see them, remember?"

"I don't get why," Celia said. Celia knew there was always a reason for how things worked in the natural world. Maybe the same held true for the unnatural world, too.

"I have a theory," Amber said. "When magic disappeared for people, it became hard for humans to notice it." She lowered her voice to a whisper. "And since monsters are made by magic, humans mostly don't see them. But who believes in magic, even though grown-ups tell them it's not real?"

"Kids," Celia said with a sinking feeling.

Ruby nodded. "However it works, once you hit fourteen, it's really hard to see monsters, even if you know they are real. You just look past them or forget about them, unless you are super stubborn. Hunters are the ones who can see them and fight them. Kids are also the only ones who can become Littles. Once you hit fourteen, a Little can touch you all they want, and you won't change."

Fourteen? Celia's fourteenth birthday was in two and a half months. She pulled her hat lower on her head. Until then, she might get attacked at any time and be turned into a—

"I have other theories," Amber continued, "like why their hearts are so important and—"

"That's enough," Ruby said, interrupting her. "Look at her,

Amber. Our doom girl is ghost white. We can tell her the rest later."

"But she needs to know about—" Amber started.

"Shut up," Ruby said.

"But—"

Ruby pointed across the street. Glowing orange smoke curled along the ground, floating a few inches above the sidewalk.

They jaywalked across the street. A couple of men, sitting out on concrete steps and holding bottles in paper bags, watched them from a crooked stoop. This part of town looked like it had been falling apart long before the earthquake hit.

"What is that?" Celia whispered, pointing at the smoke.

It swirled and danced across the ground, keeping its shape despite the wind and rain.

"That's their scent. A monster's scent is invisible during the day, but it glows in the dark. Littles smell sweet, Bigs smell sour," Amber said.

Celia knelt, not too close, and inhaled. She smelled caramel and toffee, with a hint of laughter. How could that be part of a smell? Celia wondered. Then again, how could a scent be visible?

"Little," Ruby said. "Just what we're looking for. You ready for your proof?"

Celia's heart thrummed. She stuffed her hands into her pockets, bit her lip, and nodded.

The smoke grew thicker and brighter as they followed the trail down the sidewalk and around the corner. It clung to her ankles and swirled up her tights. The smell reminded her of going to county fairs and eating deep-fried candy bars on a stick. Pieces of trash littered the ground: paper bags, tin cans, and plastic wrap.

"There." Ruby pointed to where orange smoke billowed out from an alley. "We'll catch the Little and tie it up, and then you can come join us. Hang back for now, doom girl. Watch and learn. It's Little hunting time."

Amber and Ruby ran forward, disappearing around the edge of the alley, where cardboard boxes, soggy newspapers, and Styrofoam littered the ground.

Celia walked slower and slower as she neared the alley. Now was the moment when her life would change. When she looked around that corner? She was going to see a monster.

9

JUST A GIRL

At first, all Celia saw was an empty alley with two large dumpsters.

Then she realized the dumpsters were shaking.

Celia's heart pounded. Another earthquake? No: the ground wasn't moving. Just the two dumpsters.

Beyond the dumpsters, Amber and Ruby stood back to back. Ruby threw off her coat and unsheathed two thin swords strapped to her back. Amber reached into a leather pouch hanging from her belt and threw a metal marble into the shadows and darkness.

The marble exploded five seconds later. A howling filled the alley.

Celia's eyes slammed shut. When she forced herself to open them again, she watched the lids of both dumpsters open. Deep laughter boomed out from both dumpsters. It faded into the whistling wind that moved down the alley, blowing trash everywhere.

Every animal instinct told Celia to run. But she widened her stance and planted her feet firmly on the ground.

Shadows grew out of one of the dumpsters and reached toward the two hunters.

Celia blinked. She made herself see what her mind did not want to notice.

Not shadows, but . . . tentacles. Two of them, made out of slimy trash that snaked along the ground. One of the dumpsters sprayed brown liquid at the girls. Ruby and Amber jumped away. It hit right where they'd been standing and splattered the hunters' pants. Amber turned and threw more marbles toward the dumpsters. The lids slammed shut, and the marbles clattered to the ground. They exploded, harming nothing.

The garbage tentacles grew longer and thicker, adding more trash to themselves. They stretched toward Ruby and Amber, who moved deeper into the alley. They girls backed up against a brick wall piled high with overflowing garbage bags.

As Celia's eyes adjusted to the shadows, she noticed something else. Next to the dumpsters sat a small cage made out of rusted metal pipes, shards of glass, and sludgy snarls of string.

A blond boy with green skin that shone in the dim light sat in the cage. Orange smoke pooled around him. He faced away from Celia, watching the hunters. Then he twitched suddenly and whipped his head around to stare right at her.

The boy waved.

Celia waved back, not knowing what else to do. This is all real, she thought. Her arms and legs felt numb.

One of the garbage tentacles was curling along the ground toward Amber. As she lobbed exploding marbles into the dumpster, it struck.

The tentacle wrapped around her ankle and yanked her to the ground. Amber fell, and the other tentacle rose up from the grime and struck her leg.

Amber screamed. A black, tar-like liquid stuck to her leg where she'd been hit. It bubbled and began to flow up her thigh. She grabbed the tar and flung it off her. It landed on the ground and stayed still for a second. Then it wiggled and began oozing back toward her.

Amber scrambled to her feet, and she and Ruby backed deeper into the alley.

Celia tried to make sense of what she was seeing: a small green monster in a cage, and two dumpsters with tentacles undulating out from them.

She was looking at a Big with its enslaved Little, she realized with a sinking feeling.

Ruby cried out as she ran forward. With her thin swords, she tried to slice through one of the monster's tentacles.

It danced away from her and then struck back, whip-fast. It hit her in the middle of her back. A black and oozing mass bloomed where she'd been struck. It throbbed and started crawling up her neck. Ruby screamed and ran to Amber. The other girl pulled it off and flung it against the wall. It splattered against the bricks, then slithered to the ground.

It began crawling back toward Ruby.

Ruby ran forward again. This time, she sliced through one of the waving tentacles.

Hundreds of bits of trash fell to the ground.

Amber threw a handful of exploding marbles at the other tentacle. More trash rained down everywhere.

Both hunters started to run out of the alley, but the pieces of garbage picked themselves up and reassembled, glomming back together in seconds. Tentacles slashed toward Ruby and Amber, hitting them and driving them back.

The girls huddled at the far end of the alley as they tore off the leechlike pieces of ooze that climbed up their bodies and got tangled in their hair.

The tentacles swept back and forth across the width of the alley as eerie laughter erupted from the two dumpsters. More trash flowed out from the dumpster and attached itself to the tentacles. The monster was making itself bigger with rusty nails and broken glass all along its length.

The tentacles couldn't reach all the way back to Amber and Ruby yet, but they were getting close.

A throaty chuckle that sounded like it came from a man who'd been chain-smoking for a thousand years filled the air. The monster spit bile-garbage. It arced across the alley. The hunters dodged away from it.

"This Big is too strong for us. We need more hunters here, now!" Ruby cried out as she swung her swords through the air at the nearest tentacle.

Celia knew the words were meant for her, but she had no idea how to find other hunters. She had no way of helping them. All she could do was stand there and watch. The girls pulled off black tar blotches that ran up their legs and hurled them through the air.

The tentacles swung wide and lengthened. They smashed into the hunters. Ruby flew backward. Amber fell to the ground and rolled away just as the tentacle rose up and smashed into the ground.

"It's not going to let us go. We have to find its heart. That's the only way we get out!" Amber cried to Ruby.

Heart? What did that mean? Celia had no idea.

"Control the heart, control the monster," Ruby yelled, and cast a desperate look to the end of the alley where Celia stood. She ducked beneath a tentacle that thrashed toward her and vaulted over the other one. She sprinted down the middle of the alley toward the dumpsters, a half step ahead of the tentacles that chased her. She leaped into the air and landed in the middle of one of the open dumpsters.

A look of triumph crossed her face. Then the dumpster shook, and the leader of the hunters fell into its garbage-filled depths.

The lid slammed shut above her, as loud as a shotgun.

The monster made a belching sound and laughed over Ruby's muffled screams.

"Ruby!" Amber screamed.

Out of the corner of her eye, Celia saw a frantic motion. The green boy in the cage shook his head and pointed to the other dumpster. *Heart*, he mouthed.

What heart? What did it mean?

Amber fought off both tentacles by herself. They reached all the way into the back of the alley. She ducked, whirled, and threw exploding marbles everywhere. But as quickly as she could destroy them, the monster rebuilt itself. Black goo climbed up her legs.

Ruby's screams grew more desperate from inside the dumpster.

The Little rattled the bars of his cage to get Celia's attention again. He gestured to the dumpster without Ruby in it. *Heart*, he mouthed again.

A real heart, or something metaphorical? She didn't know,

but Amber and Ruby needed help. Someone had to save them.

She turned to look down the main road.

A man in a red jacket was out walking his dog.

"Please?" Celia cried out. "My friends—"

He glanced down the alleyway and then looked away.

Two women walked down the opposite side of the street.

"My friends need help!" Celia yelled, and pointed toward Amber.

One of them frowned. The other squinted. They walked on.

They couldn't see the monster.

No one can see this. No one can help them but me.

A tentacle wrapped around Amber's arm and threw her against the alley wall. Her thick glasses flew off and hit the concrete.

I've never even been in a fight, Celia thought. I don't understand about the heart. There's no way I can fight a big monster.

None of those facts changed what she had to do.

Celia crouched down and ran as fast as she could toward the nearest dumpster.

10

BREATHE

As Celia neared the dumpster, the green boy in the cage gave her a thumbs-up and smiled, showing her his pointed fangs.

The lid of the dumpster was open. Celia jumped and landed inside.

The dumpster shook beneath her feet. The metal lid slammed shut, smashing against Celia's head and pushing her down into the soft muck of garbage. Total darkness surrounded her. A rotten-meat smell was so strong that she threw up in her mouth. Celia crouched inside as bits of trash slithered up her legs and wrapped around her arms. Sticky tar oozed everywhere and clung to her. She slapped it off, but more and more pieces covered her. She screamed for a second but then stopped. She didn't want anything to get into her mouth.

The heart, she thought. I have to find it. It's in here some-where. Probably.

The monster's laugh boomed through the dumpster so loud that it made her ears ring.

The garbage on Celia's arms thickened as she reached through the squishy rottenness around her, searching for something, anything, that seemed heart-like. Bits of trash climbed over her mouth and up her nose. She gagged and slapped them off with garbage-covered hands.

Celia thrust her fingers into the thickest part of the garbage and grabbed hold of soft and rotten things. The heart. The heart. Where was the heart?

Garbage covered her face. She tried to pull it off, but it held on tight. She couldn't see. She could barely breathe. Don't panic. Search, she ordered herself, and thought about all the girls in all the movies who managed to keep going, no matter what.

The muck squirmed around her arms and legs, alive and pushing back. Celia moved in the direction it seemed to least want her to go.

The garbage-mask thickened, and she couldn't breathe at all. She wasted a couple of seconds trying to claw it off with her hands, but too much slimy wet garbage clung to her fingers.

Celia searched faster. The need to inhale built in her chest, and she grew light-headed. All she found was endless soft muck.

The heart. Where was it?

Her arms grew heavy as bricks. A blackness, deeper than the pitch black of the dumpster, grew at the edge of her awareness. Her chest throbbed with pain. Monsters were real, and she was going to die.

The heart.

It got harder to remember to keep going. Her lungs hurt.

The heart, she thought faintly.

Her finger brushed against something firm. She grabbed onto it and felt the vague edges of a cardboard box beneath her coated fingers.

Celia's legs collapsed. She fell forward into the garbage and pulled the box toward her. It seemed to expand and contract against her still chest.

I need to breathe, she thought, and passed out.

The monster's heartbeat echoed around her, shaking Celia awake.

The mask of trash fell off her face, and Celia sucked in air. Nasty dumpster air that smelled like puke and death, but she breathed in great gasps of it as she lay on a mass of rotting garbage, curled around a box that throbbed in her arms.

"I need to get out of here," she whispered with a mousy voice she barely recognized.

The dumpster lid opened above her, and the charcoal sky hanging over the city had never looked so beautiful. She stood up, still clutching the box, and saw Amber lying in a fetal position in the back of the alley, haloed by a circle of fallen garbage. Her arm bled and her pants were slashed open at the knee and thigh. Sticky black tar pooled lifelessly at her feet.

With a growl, Ruby leaped out of the other dumpster and landed in a wary crouch. Every inch of her was covered in wet, moldy trash. She spun around slowly until she saw Celia. Her jaw dropped open as she stared at the box in Celia's hands. In the dim light of the moon, Celia saw it was a pizza box with the words *Pizza My Heart* printed on the outside of it. It was soggy around the edges and looked like anything else you might find in the garbage, except for the way it expanded and contracted and made a soft *lub-dub* sound. Something that looked like pizza sauce dripped out from one corner of it.

"The doom girl saved us?" Ruby whispered. She ran a hand through her slicked-down hair and flung gray goop off her fingers.

"I had to try. There was no one else," Celia said as she carefully stepped out of the dumpster, clinging to the heart box and wobbling on uncertain legs.

"Someone finally found his heart, after all these years," a small voice said beside Celia. "Thank you, thank you, thank you." The Little green monster pressed his face against the bars of his cage. Sores and scars covered his face. He used to be a kid, before a monster attacked and changed him, Celia thought.

"Can I have it?" he asked, and reached a claw-tipped hand through the bars.

"Give the heart to me," Ruby ordered. "We can use it to make the Big talk." One of her eyes had swollen shut, rimmed with a fat, purple bruise that matched the color of her hair. Amber got to her feet, picked up her broken glasses, and limped toward Ruby.

Celia looked down at the pulsing pizza box. For what felt like the millionth time today, she wasn't sure what to do.

"Give it to me. Let me destroy him," the caged boy whispered. "I've earned it. He's hurt me for so long."

A whimpering sound came from the dumpsters.

"Shut up," Celia commanded, still staring at the pizza box.

The dumpster went quiet.

"Give me the heart," Ruby said. "Now."

"Please?" the Little monster asked again.

Celia looked at Ruby and then at the Little in the cage. "You've been his slave?" she asked.

The boy nodded and looked like he might start crying. He might be a monster, but he was also someone small who had been hurt for far too long.

"We need the heart, Celia," Amber said. "We'll explain why. We—"

Celia tossed the pizza box toward the Little's cage.

His clawed hands reached out from the cage and grabbed it.

"No!" Ruby and Amber screamed. Both dumpsters shook so hard they bounced.

The Little pulled his hands back into the cage, taking the box with them. He raked his claws across the surface. Where he scratched, blood pooled up. The dumpsters screamed louder. A wet, squelching sound filled the air as the boy ripped the box in two. Blood splattered across his face and all over the cage.

A deep silence followed.

The Little monster sobbed and tossed the two pieces of the box out of his cage. They landed on the garbage-strewn ground, as lifeless as any cardboard.

Ruby glared at Celia. "That. Was. Dumb."

Celia flicked a blob of wet Kleenex off her shirt. She glared back at Ruby. "I'd do it again," she said. If you were owned by a monster, then you should get to decide what happened to him. Celia might not understand a lot of things, but she knew that was true.

"I tried to explain ahead of time about the heart," Amber said angrily to Ruby. She sighed and turned back to Celia. Her fingers explored her shoulder where her coat and sweatshirt lay slashed open. She picked off a gelatinous handful of black goo and threw it on the ground. "If you have a Big monster's heart, you can control him. We could have used Dreck's heart to learn everything he knew about the earthquake."

"But no, you had to let the Little destroy it," Ruby said.

Celia crossed her arms over her chest.

Ruby exhaled and shrugged. "But whatever, we're alive because of you. With no training, you bested Dreck, one of the oldest Bigs in town. There's only one way to control or kill a Big, and that's to get their heart. You did it."

"You're sort of amazing, Celia." Amber squinted through the broken glasses that hung crookedly on her nose. "How did you know what to do?"

"I told her to go into the dumpster," the Little said. "We're on the same side about most things. I don't get why hunters never see that."

"The same side until you destroy one of us," Amber said.

Ruby ignored the Little and kept her somber gaze on Celia. "Amber and I should both be dead." The leader of the hunters pulled a black leather string out of her pocket, grabbed Celia's wrist, and tied it on. "You got your first monster. Welcome to the hunters, Celia." She hugged her, crushing Celia against her banana-splattered shoulder.

Amber hugged her too, and Celia stood in a hunter sandwich for a long time, feeling their warmth before they let her go.

"Let's bounce, unless you two want to hang out in the nastiest alley ever," Ruby said. "We'll walk you home, Celia."

"Are you kidding me?" the Little called out from the cage behind them. "You can't just leave me here. You have to let me go."

11

NOTHING COULD HURT HER

"We're not leaving you," Ruby said over her shoulder. "We'll have the Council of Elders pick you up and take you in."

The Little pressed his miserable green face up against the cage bars and said, "Let me go. I promise I'll never hurt another kid. I told her the heart was in the dumpster. I saved you. You have to let me go."

Amber and Ruby wouldn't look at him as they walked toward the front of the alley, but Celia watched him. Amber had said the Council of Elders took in Littles and put them in cages. How was that better than what Dreck had done to him?

"Come on, Celia. Remember what he is," Amber said, calling back to her from a dozen feet away. "The second he's free, he'll attack some kid and turn himself into something as evil as Dreck. They always do."

"I won't." The boy pressed his face harder against the jagged bars. "My name's John, and I'm a kid, just like you, or I was until I got attacked by a monster."

Celia looked from him to the two hunters waiting for her at the front of the alley. The Little did look like a kid, if you ignored his green skin, claws, and sharp teeth.

"Please?" he whispered.

Celia kicked at a rotten orange on the ground. Now that the fight was over, she felt tired and empty and didn't want to have to think about anything besides getting home and taking a shower.

"You did tell me to search for the heart in the dumpster," Celia said.

"I've never hurt anyone. Not once," he said.

"Come on, Celia," Ruby called back to her.

The cage didn't have a lock, just a clasp that he couldn't reach from the inside.

The Little saw her looking. He moved away from the door, pressing himself against the back side of the cage.

Celia darted forward, flipped open the catch, and moved back.

The door of the cage flew open, and the Little jumped out. He wore a huge smile and twirled around with his arms out and his head flung back. "Thanks so much!"

"Sure," Celia said.

"Get away from him!" Ruby cried. The hunters walked back down the alley toward her.

Celia stood between the Little and the hunters. She stepped back.

The Little whipped his head around to stare at her. "I can feel the air move when you move. I can smell you, and it's the most beautiful thing. It's like"—he paused and his smile grew wider—"ice cream on the hottest day of summer!" Something glittery and unsteady danced in his eyes.

"You said you'd be good," she whispered. "You promised."

"Run, Celia," Amber called out.

The Little moved so fast that Celia didn't remember him pushing her, her falling to the ground, or his coming to be crouched on her torso, staring at her with wide, unblinking eyes.

He looked confused too. "Oh no," he whispered. "I didn't mean to. I only touched your coat. No skin. I promise. Sorry!" He scrambled off her and backed away.

"I'm sorry," he repeated. "It's just . . . you smelled too good."

Ruby barreled toward him with her blades out.

He danced away from her and ran, twice as fast as any human, out of the alley.

Ruby tucked her blades back into the holstered sheaths she wore crisscrossed on her back. She helped Celia up. "You always do the opposite of what people tell you?"

"Sort of. I don't know?" Celia sighed, thinking about all the rules she'd broken today, and all the things her parents hadn't even known to put on the list but would have been forbidden if they had.

"Fabulous. The Bigs are banding together and the doom girl at the center of the prophecy has a rebellious streak." Ruby scowled. "Whatever. You get a pass today, Celia, because you saved us and you don't understand what we're up against. But from here on out, you have to listen to us."

Celia gave her a nod-shrug. She'd listen to Ruby, but she wasn't a hunter. She didn't have to obey anyone.

"Come on. We'll drop you off on our way home," Ruby said.

"You two live together?" Celia asked.

Amber nodded. "I needed a place to go, after my parents . . ."

"And I needed a place when my mom found my weapons and kicked me out. She wouldn't believe me that my best friend had been killed by monsters, and that I hunted them. No one believes us. Most hunters are orphans or runaways."

Celia thought about not living with her parents. That idea made her so sad.

Amber smiled at Ruby. "No grown-ups, but sometimes Ruby acts like a really bossy older sister, even though we're the same age."

Ruby rolled her eyes and stuck her tongue out at the other girl. "And if I'm lucky, Amber acts like a professor of boring-ology and can talk at me for hours."

They grinned at each other.

"I call dibs on first shower, by the way," Amber said. "I have rotten sausage juice in my ear."

"Yeah, well, I'm pretty sure I have a moldy cockroach in my hair," Ruby replied.

"I've got you both beat: rotten eggs down my pants." Celia giggled. So did the hunters.

They walked side by side down unlit roads. Everyone they passed carried flashlights and moved away from them, disgusted by the sight and smell. Celia loved the cold wind that blew through her clothes and shivered over her goose-bumped skin. She loved the broken glass on the sidewalk that glittered like tiny diamonds in the moonlight. She loved, most of all, the simple pleasure of breathing.

She'd survived. She'd saved two girls. Two friends, maybe.

The three girls laughed about the battle, retelling every awful moment and turning it into something funny. They told her about how Dreck had ruled the Five Point neighborhood for decades and used magic to keep everything dirty and run-down. He stole people's happiness to make himself powerful, and filled people's houses with garbage and despair.

"Tell me about other Bigs," Celia said. The darkness didn't scare her anymore. The rain didn't chill her. There were monsters in the world, and she had destroyed one of them.

They told her stories about Splintered, two twin Bigs who

deepened and extended winter every year on the South End, and made roads and sidewalks extra slick in order to cause car wrecks and break people's hips. Or Gootcha, who lived under the Peralta Bridge and whispered to wayward travelers that they should give up and jump so she could capture them and put them to work in underground caverns, mining emeralds and peridots. They listed half a dozen more.

Amber worked on picking out clots of chewing gum from her long braid as they walked. "The only good thing about Bigs is they hate and destroy each other. But if it's true they're working together right now . . ." Her voice trailed off. "It means something really big is going on."

They got to Celia's dark apartment building.

Amber carefully hugged Celia goodbye, avoiding the goopiest parts of her clothes. "I'm so glad we found you. You're the best, doom girl."

Ruby rolled her eyes. "The best at smelling nasty. We'll see you in the morning?"

"Yeah." Tomorrow, she would hang out with her friends. That fact felt almost as impossible as everything else that had happened today.

Celia climbed the dark stairs to her apartment on legs that felt so exhausted they could barely carry her weight. She tried to turn the lights on once she got inside, forgetting that they didn't work. She found the flashlight and took a garbage bag with her into the bathroom. Celia peeled off her clothes and put them in the bag, then turned the water on extra hot to spray the oily stickiness off her body. She ran a bar of soap over every inch of her skin, grateful that she lived in an old building with an oil-fired water heater.

Today I fought a monster, she thought. It wasn't on the list of things her parents didn't want her to do, but . . . Celia heard the strange choking sound of her own laughter. It was too much. Way too much, and also, she sort of loved it. Not almost getting killed, but the whole strange day of learning about monsters and doom girls. Doom girl, she thought again and again. I'm going to do something important. It didn't feel real. She washed her hair multiple times with lavender shampoo, and scratched her nails through her scalp, rooting out every last bit of rot. She touched the leather string on her wrist, over and over again, liking how it felt.

What would Mom and Dad think, she wondered, if they knew that monsters were real? She thought about her mom teasing her that the tooth fairy loved to eat her teeth. Or how her dad swore he'd met a talking toad when he was three. She'd always thought they were joking, but what if part of them knew something?

She stood under the stream of hot water and let it wash over her until it went lukewarm. After toweling off, she found an un-labeled tube of ointment in the bathroom cabinet that smelled medicinal. She rubbed it everywhere. Her ribs felt bruised where the Little had jumped on her. The flashlight confirmed purple-black marks on her chest.

She worried about that monster somewhere out in the world, and what he was doing. Not attacking a kid. Not turning evil, she hoped.

Celia put her pajamas on and meant to find some food to eat, but her bed felt so soft and the idea of lying down, just for a moment, seemed more delicious than anything.

The next thing she knew, pale morning light streamed in through the window and she heard something walking around in her apartment.

12

THE LAST ONE ANYONE SHOULD TRUST

Celia's first thought was that it must be a burglar. Then she remembered the monsters and how they were real and she was the doom girl.

Someone or something was in her house.

Celia pulled her faded purple comforter over her head, like if she covered up every inch of her body, she'd be safe. I destroyed a Big, she thought, touching her leather bracelet and willing herself to do something.

She peeked out from under her blankets.

Demetri, tiptoeing past her open bedroom door, froze. He turned his head slowly and looked at her. He winced. "Sorry," he whispered.

Celia sat up. No one should break into someone else's house, but she was so relieved it wasn't anyone dangerous. Besides, she wanted to ask him about why he was at the cathedral and what he knew about magic, prophecies, and monsters. But the first thing she said was "What are you doing here?"

He shoved his hands into his pockets. "Sorry," he said again. Demetri wore the same ratty clothes and bumpy knit cap as yesterday. He rubbed the dark half-moons under his eyes. "I had a bad dream about you getting hurt. I wanted to come here and leave some protection spells. You are okay, right?" He stared at her intensely.

"Yeah. Kind of?" Celia yawned and scratched the itchy spot on her cheek. Her ribs ached.

"I should leave."

"You can leave," Celia said. "But not until you answer some questions."

Outside the morning light tinged the clouds pink and blue in the east, but darker clouds stretched above them, covering most of the sky. Demetri took his yo-yo out of his pocket. "How's your cheek?" he asked as his hand moved and flowed around the yo-yo. The plastic circle danced for him.

She rubbed it. "Fine. Itchy where you touched it. Why is that?"

He looked at his spinning yo-yo. "Leave it alone and it will go away."

Celia checked her alarm clock to see if the electricity had come back. Nope. She grabbed the cell phone to see if it worked. Nope. She glanced around her room, wondering what Demetri would think of the usual mess, with clothes and books strewn across the floor, along with a broken lamp and some broken glass near the window. "You want some breakfast? I've got chocolate wafers, or cereal."

"Do not offer me anything. It sets a bad precedent and makes me think I can take things from you." Demetri snapped up his yo-yo and stared at the ground. "I told you that already."

His words made her nervous. "I forgot you're some kind of klepto or something." Celia slipped out of bed and padded into the kitchen, wishing she wasn't wearing the hearts-and-rainbows kiddie pajamas her grandma had sewn for her when she was eleven. Demetri followed, keeping his distance. She filled the kettle with water for tea but then remembered she had no way of heating it. She poured herself a glass of water instead and added a spoonful of melted cranberry concentrate from the freezer. Demetri stood in the kitchen's doorway. There were so many things she wanted to ask him, but she didn't know where to start.

"So why were you at the cathedral spying on the hunters?"

"To learn things."

Celia rolled her eyes and drank some juice. "That explains nothing."

"You should stay away from the hunters." He looked toward the front door like he wanted to leave.

"Did you hear about the battle or something? Is that why you're here?"

"Battle?" He played with the silver salt and pepper shakers on the counter.

Would talking about it betray the hunters? They hadn't told her to keep anything secret, and Demetri was part of all this, somehow. She touched the small callus on her cheek. "The hunters told me about"—her voice dropped to a whisper—"monsters. I needed proof, so we went hunting and fought Dreck."

Demetri's eyes widened. "Dreck? He's really powerful." His knuckles whitened around the shakers.

"And stinky," Celia added.

"They should not have taken you with them. They put you in real danger."

"It was an accident. We were only supposed to be hunting Littles."

Demetri's eyes narrowed to slits. "And did you terrorize any Littles before fighting Dreck?"

"What? No. I helped Dreck's Little. I let him out of his cage. He seemed nice."

Demetri nodded. "They're just kids, you know."

"Yeah. But then he did attack me a little bit."

Demetri groaned and closed his eyes. "I came here to make

sure no monsters take notice of you. Stay away from all of this, Celia."

She shrugged. "I'm not sure I can. Anyway, I might be really good at fighting monsters." She gulped down more cranberry juice. Too warm, but the sourness tasted good. "Dreck almost killed us, but then I ended up finding his heart and destroying him."

Demetri blinked. Then his lips ticked upward. "*You* found his heart?"

Celia grinned and sipped more juice. She tried to look tough but had no idea how to. "Yeah. I sort of loved it, in a weird way. Maybe because I'm the doom girl."

Demetri let out another soft groan. "Why would you say that? You must not become part of this world. It is made of sadness and tragedy." He looked down at his black-nail-polished fingernails, and Celia thought he might start crying. "If I dragged you into it somehow, I'm so sorry."

"You didn't," she said. "It's not your fault." Celia crunched on a handful of dry cereal. "Your friend and one of the hunters dreamed about me before the earthquake. The hunters put out a magic piece of paper that only the doom girl could find, and I found it. You didn't make the prophecy." She paused. "Did you?" There was so much she still didn't understand.

"Nobody makes prophecies," he said. "They are hints about what's coming. Like a map, to anyone who knows what to look for." He frowned. "A really unhelpful map that never makes sense until it's all over, usually. Whatever anyone tells you, they don't know anything for certain. You don't have to be a part of this."

"Amber and Ruby say trouble will follow me until this is over. Do you have any idea about what I'm supposed to do?"

Demetri shook his head. "Stay home and not think about monsters."

Celia shrugged. "I can't. That's not how brains work. Besides, the hunters say they'll help me, and if there's a way I can do good, I . . . I want to do something good." She chewed on another handful of cereal.

"It's not safe."

Yesterday, Celia had almost run home a half dozen times. But she hadn't, and she'd saved people and been almost like . . . a hero. "The hunters say I have to save the city."

Demetri stared at her for a long moment. "They are excellent at twisting the truth."

"At least they tell me stuff and don't act all cryptic." Celia swallowed down some more cereal and then opened a drawer to grab some nuts. A glass jar had broken inside, and she carefully retrieved a plastic bag of almonds amid the shards. "So you don't like the hunters?"

He shrugged and shoved his hands into his pockets. "Their world is black and white. Not gray. Maybe they're right. Who am I to judge? I'm the last one anyone should trust."

But anyone who said that seemed extra trustworthy, just by saying it, Celia thought. Only honest people admitted they weren't perfect. She breathed in his apple-and-sunlight scent as she chewed on some almonds. "Tell me stuff, Demetri. I know there's a doom prophecy. I know monsters are real. What else?"

He looked back at the front door.

"If you're not a hunter, how are you involved?" She remembered him feeding shoelaces into a drain when she'd first seen him. And on the roof he'd been chanting and playing with his yo-yo. "You use magic, just like the hunters, don't you? They force monsters to make spells for them. Is that what you do?"

"My methods are different, but . . . yes."

"Really?"

"Yes."

Celia smiled. Something inside her relaxed. Demetri was into magic, just like Amber. Maybe it didn't have to be any more complicated than that. "Is your yo-yo full of magical spells? Is that part of how you do it?"

"You think I'm that good with a yo-yo?"

Celia rolled her eyes, wishing he would give a straight answer.

"It's just a yo-yo," he added softly. "It helps me concentrate." Demetri went still and light pulsed out from him. For an instant, he glowed like the sun.

Celia blinked. "Whoa. What was that?"

"You saw? Most people are blind to magic."

"Was that your aura?" Celia had an aunt who could see auras. She said Celia had a lavender and green one.

"No. My wards. I wear protection spells, and I made them visible to check their strength. I keep having the feeling that they're weakening, especially around you. But they're intact."

"Like the spray the hunters use to keep Littles away?"

"Their spray stinks and burns any Little who touches them. My wards work a more subtle magic: they make it so no one knows I even exist."

"Why do you need wards?" Celia picked up some shards of glass and put them in the garbage under the sink.

"To make it hard for them to find me."

"Who?"

"Monsters."

"Oh." Celia paused. Of course. "Can I have one?"

Demetri crossed his arms over his chest and frowned.

"Is that rude? Does it break some magical code of conduct? Sorry. I just thought, since I'm the doom girl and all . . ." She wished she wasn't always saying the wrong thing around him.

"It's a good idea. But it comes with a complication."

"What?"

"Since it's my ward, I'll always know where you are if you wear it." He looked like he wanted to tell her more, but he didn't.

"So, you'll have magical GPS to find me?" She gulped down the last of her cranberry juice. "That seems fine."

Demetri slipped a silver necklace over his head. A granite stone pendant hung down from it. At least seven other necklaces peeked out from beneath his ragged hoodie. He placed it on the formica counter between them.

Celia's fingers tingled when she touched it. The chain was warm from his body heat, and the ward felt heavier than it looked. She held the gray pendant in her palm. It was flat and oval shaped, with a hole bored into the top of it. "How was it made? Do you know?" He had said he had different methods than the hunters, but he would still have had to get a monster to make it.

Demetri touched the other necklaces around his neck. "Spells take sacrifice. This one took the memory of fireflies."

"So now that monster can't remember fireflies?"

Demetri shrugged. "The memories are still there, but what they meant and why they were important fade to gray. Keep the ward on, Celia. It is my best one: grounded and stable."

"Seriously? I can give it back if you need it." She ran her fingers over the smooth stone.

"Take it. These are uncertain days. For you, especially, doom girl."

She slipped it over her head. The necklace felt like it belonged there.

"You could leave Youngstown and never come back, you know," he said.

"Aren't there monsters in other cities too?"

"More or less. In some places, a lot less. And the prophecy only extends to the borders of Youngstown."

"But I have to wait for my parents to come home. Besides, the ferry dock and airport are messed up. The bridges are out."

"If you get the chance to leave, consider it."

She shrugged and then nodded, but what planet did he live on where a kid could go and do whatever she wanted? And anyway, how was she supposed to save the city if she bailed?

Demetri watched her with his sad face. "How's your cheek, really?"

"I can feel where you touched me. Did some magic you have from a spell leak into me? Is that why?" She ran a forefinger over the rough skin.

"Yes." Demetri stared at her cheek. "I'm sorry."

"Does it look that bad?" Celia walked out of the kitchen. Demetri pressed himself to the side of the doorway as she passed. She went into her parents' room to look at her cheek in the mirror. She could just make out a faint pink mark the size of a fingertip, but if she hadn't been looking, she wouldn't have noticed. "With everything that's going on, it seems like the last thing to worry about," she called back to him. "So tell me about how you learned about magic and monsters. I keep wondering about you."

"Of course you do," he said, so quietly she wasn't sure she'd heard right.

Celia walked back to the kitchen, but Demetri wasn't there, or in the living room, or even in her bedroom. She found a note taped to the front door, above all the locks. It read, *Forget me and everything that's happened since the earthquake.* The note had his sunny apple scent on it. His handwriting looked shaky.

But what if she didn't want to forget everything? And why had he shown up at all if he didn't want anything to do with her? Why would he care enough to set up protection spells and give her a ward? And why, even after talking to him, was she still so full of questions?

Celia slipped his note into her pocket and walked into the kitchen. She tried the landline and the cell again. Neither worked. She turned on the radio, but it was all talk about people trapped in rubble and gas leaks. She turned it off.

A knock came from the front door.

Demetri was back? She ran to it and flung the door open.

Ruby and Amber stood dressed from head to toe in black.

"Hey Celia! Ready for hunter training?" Amber asked, and gave her a quick hug.

Ruby walked past Celia and went straight into the living room. She took it all in with one sweeping glance before flopping down on the couch.

Celia searched the room to make sure there wasn't any evidence Demetri had been there. She saw a new houseplant on the mantel and a bright-red mug on the coffee table that hadn't been there before. He had said he was here to leave protection spells: maybe these were them. No one but her would notice they were new.

She wanted to keep Demetri secret. He didn't like hunters very much, so who knew what they thought of him, or if they even knew he existed?

Ruby raised one eyebrow. "The earthquake wrecked your place."

"I haven't had time to clean up yet."

"Ruby made us clean up our apartment before it even stopped shaking," Amber said. She wore a new pair of black-framed glasses, identical to the ones that had broken the night before. "She's the worst about cleaning."

"And Amber thinks doing the dishes once a week is over-kill."

Ruby popped up from the couch and walked into the kitchen. She came back a second later with the box of raisin bran. She jumped over the back of the couch and landed in a sprawl on the cushions. "Let's get moving, doom girl. We're taking you Little hunting in the underground; then we have a hunter meeting tonight. We'll wait while you gear up."

Little hunting? Did Celia want to do that? What would Demetri think about it? But whatever. He'd run off without even saying goodbye. "I don't want to hurt anyone," Celia said.

"Not a problem, my tender-hearted friend," Ruby said.

Her purple hair rose up in spikes across her head. "It's a catch-and-release mission today. We're on council orders to move quickly, question as many as we can, and not bother taking any Littles in to headquarters to be locked up."

Amber stood near the bay windows, staring down at the shaken city. She opened her messenger bag, took out a pile of black clothes, and held them out toward Celia. "I brought hunter clothes for you. I think we're about the same size?"

"Thanks," Celia said. As she took the clothes to her parents' room so she could see how she looked in the mirror, she noticed no part of her hesitated or thought about telling them no. She wanted to be out in the world today, learning things, doing stuff, and maybe, if she did everything right, saving the city. Excitement buzzed an inch beneath her skin.

The black wool pants felt scratchy as she pulled them over her legs. They fit perfectly. The two thin, black sweaters hugged her frame and warmed her upper body. Her Demetri necklace made a bump beneath them. The wool coat she put on had lots of pockets and seemed thick enough to keep her dry. Last, Celia pulled up silky black socks and tied on heavy black boots. They were good shoes to run in. She imagined herself chasing monsters.

When she stared at herself in the mirror, she didn't look like the sad girl anymore.

13

FORTUNE FAVORS THE BOLD

"So, are you okay and all right and all that from yesterday?" Amber asked. "I kept thinking about you and how last night was so bananas. It was a hundred times too much for your first day out." Amber and Celia walked side by side down the sidewalk, easily matching each other's strides. Icy flecks of rain fell. They followed behind Ruby. The girl's purple hair was already starting to droop in the rain, but she still walked with a perfect "don't mess with me" swagger.

"Am I okay?" Celia ran her hand across her torso, where her ribs were bruised and sore. A memory of being trapped in the dumpster throbbed through her. Then she thought about getting Dreck's heart and controlling him. "I'm fine. I mean, I think

I might have broken a nail, so that's upsetting, but otherwise . . ."
Celia made herself grin at Amber, just like she thought a real
hero might. She looked down at her hand and saw that there was
a sliver-moon of blood beneath her pointer fingernail. She picked
at it, but it didn't go away.

"You did so good. For the first six months I was a hunter, I
never even got near a Little," Amber said. "Does the city look
even worse today than yesterday?"

They jumped over a hole in the sidewalk. The cracked ground
seemed to have widened in the night. Pale tree roots reached up
through the concrete as though they'd had a sudden growth
spurt.

"Huh," Amber said. She knelt down at one of the fissures in
the sidewalk. "Ru, hold up." She ran her hand over the pale roots
poking up from the inside. At the end of each grew a fingernail.

"What . . . is that?" Celia said.

"The Roots of Coltus," Amber whispered.

Ruby walked back to them and knelt down. "Weirdest Big
ever. He just messes up roads. Slowly."

Celia touched one of the hard, smooth roots and flinched. It
was warm and felt like skin.

They kept going and passed adults who moved hunched over.
They wore pinched and worried looks on their faces.

"Why is that Big a bunch of roots?" Celia asked.

Amber grinned. "I love having someone new to explain things

to! So. Littles can change color, or grow horns, tails, claws, and spikes. Sometimes their eyes get weird or their feet become hooved, or sometimes they don't look that different at all. But that's nothing compared to Bigs." Amber bounced in her steel-toed boots.

Ruby had taken the lead again and looked back at them. "Keep up," she ordered.

"Yes, ma'am," Amber shot back. "So when Littles become Bigs"—her voice dropped—"some aspect of them becomes really strong. Like maybe someone hated spiders and became a huge spider, or maybe the Roots of Coltus had a phobia about trees or something."

"Or garbage," Celia whispered back. "Maybe Dreck had to take the garbage out as a kid and hated it." The memory of dark muck and not being able to breathe overwhelmed her. She stumbled forward.

"You okay?" Amber asked, putting a hand on Celia's shoulder.

"I'm fine. I was just thinking about how sorry I feel for any Bigs we might meet today."

Amber linked elbows with her and rolled her eyes. "So tough, doom girl. But we are going to stay far away from Bigs today, okay?"

They jumped over more cracks in the sidewalk and passed a graffiti mural spray-painted over a caved-in wall. *The city will hiss,* it read.

That was the next part of the prophecy, wasn't it? Celia thought.

Ruby took them to stairs that led down to a subway stop. It was covered over in yellow tape that read *Danger: Do Not Enter*. Ruby didn't even slow down as she ducked beneath it and skipped down into the darkness.

"Down there?" Celia asked, staring at the stairs that led into pitch black.

"Yep," Amber sighed. "But Ruby and I will keep you safe, as much as possible. Ruby feels terrible about what happened yesterday."

Yesterday. Celia chewed her lip and looked into the darkness. I got a monster's heart. I saved everyone, she reminded herself.

"You kind of have a psycho look on your face," Amber whispered. "I can't tell if that means you'll be the best hunter ever, or just sort of unstable."

Celia took a deep breath, ducked beneath the yellow tape, and ran down the steps. Amber followed behind her.

Someone from the street yelled down at them, "Get out of there. It's not safe!"

Ruby's chuckle rose up from the darkness.

"It is safe though, right?" Celia asked. "I mean, it won't cave in, will it?" She held on to the rain-slicked handrail as she walked down. A cold, rotten-smelling wind blew steadily up the stairs. Celia walked slower the darker it got.

Ruby said from the darkness below, "*They* use the subway tunnels. They wouldn't destroy them."

Celia bit her lip. That information only swapped out one fear for a bigger one. She took another step down, but there weren't any more stairs and her foot hit the ground, hard.

"Can I turn a light on, Ru?" Amber asked.

"Fine."

Light bloomed behind Celia from an electric lantern. It made a small, bright circle along the subway's dirty tiled floor.

Ruby stood a couple of feet away. She squared her shoulders and jutted her chin out. "You ready for this, O prophesized one?"

Celia nodded.

They sprayed each other with the terrible-smelling protection spray.

"When I first got to the city, I liked to imagine that mole people lived down here and built the tunnels," Celia said.

"No such thing," Ruby replied.

"I know, but it's funny, right, that in reality there are . . ." Her voice trailed off as Ruby walked to the edge of the subway platform. She jumped off the ledge and disappeared into the darkness.

"I wish there were mole people, instead of *them*." Amber walked to the edge and fell into the darkness, taking the light with her.

Celia chewed on her lower lip as she followed. There were signs all over the subway warning people to stay away from the electrified rails. It was at least five feet down to the subway tracks, Celia saw, as she looked at the two girls below, standing in a small circle of light. Her parents hadn't written, *Celia will not get electrified*, or *Celia will not chase after monsters in dark subway tunnels*. But that was only because who in their right mind would need to be reminded not to do that kind of thing?

"Come on, little doom girl. Fortune favors the bold and all that," Ruby called up.

Celia closed her eyes, jumped, and landed a moment later on the hard-packed dirt between the tracks.

"This way." Ruby started walking away with long strides.

"*They* use these tunnels?" Celia asked.

"It's mostly just Littles running errands." Amber's quiet voice echoed in the tunnel. "Some Bigs, too. But don't worry. We know the tunnels well, and what to avoid."

Ruby added, in a louder voice, "There's Dax, a huge bat-guy who hangs out at an unused station under Twelfth Street. And Smotherer. She's on the A line, usually. Oh, and Spooks the Clown. But we probably won't run into any of them."

"Usually, probably," Celia whispered, not liking those words.

The darkness seemed to fill up with monsters, always fading just out of sight as they walked deeper and deeper into the subway tunnels. Whatever boldness Celia had woken up with faded away.

She forced herself to breathe as they walked between the lines of the silver train rails.

"Smell that?" Ruby asked.

"Chocolate and whipped cream," Amber whispered. She clicked the light off for a second. In the pitch blackness, a line of glowing orange smoke led into a side tunnel.

Amber clicked the light back on.

"I'll take the lead," Ruby ordered. "Celia stays back. Keep her near escape routes, okay, Amber?"

Amber nodded.

The hunters made no sound as they started running into the tunnel. Their feet barely seemed to touch the pebbled ground. Ruby sprinted forward into the darkness.

Celia ran clumsily beside Amber, desperate to keep up with her so she wouldn't fall back.

The curling wisps of orange smoke grew thicker. The air smelled more and more luscious.

"Lights off," Ruby whispered from in front of them.

Amber's lamp clicked off.

Celia stumbled, every step suddenly uncertain. Her eyes teared and blinked in the darkness, not accepting that there was nothing to see. Amber's warm fingers slipped into her hand and pulled her forward.

"No!" a boy's voice yelped in front of them.

Celia and Amber moved blindly toward the sound. At first she thought her mind was making up the dim shadows, but as she kept going down the curving tunnel, she could see more and more.

A hand gripped her shoulder, and Celia would have screamed if another hand hadn't clamped over her mouth.

Ruby's face materialized in the gloomy gray light, inches away from them. She removed her hand, put a finger to her lips, then pointed down the tunnel. She grabbed onto Celia's free hand with rough, callused fingers.

The three of them walked slowly forward. A faint muttering grew into voices. The air smelled like a mixture of chocolate and sour oranges. Ruby inched them forward more slowly, until they could see two people standing inside a gray circle of light at a crossroads in the tunnel. Glowing orange smoke pooled over the ground. A Little stood frozen, staring up at the Big monster who loomed over him. Celia froze too, as any thought that she was a girl who could fight monsters fled from her. Cold terror took its place.

14

INTERROGATE, INTIMIDATE

Celia pressed her back against the wall of the tunnel and went motionless as she tried to make herself small and unnoticeable. She watched the scene between the two monsters a hundred feet in front of them. This was supposed to be safe. There weren't supposed to be any Bigs, she thought as her heart pounded. She was starting to suspect that what the hunters wanted to happen versus what went down were two different things a lot of the time.

"If they notice us, we run," Ruby whispered, putting her mouth up against Celia's ear. She pointed across the tunnel toward a dark hole. "Within ten feet it gets too small for the Big to follow."

Ten feet and we'll be safe, Celia thought, and wondered when her definition of safe had become a narrow black-holed tunnel beneath the city.

In front of them, the two monsters faced each other. The Little looked like a kid a couple of years younger than Celia, except for his yellow skin and blue horns that jutted out from his hairless head. He stood with his neck craned up at the Big.

She towered over him, standing on bony, birdlike legs. She wore tattered red shorts and a black tank top. Spikes and thorns jutted out from her arms, torso, and head, like a porcupine's. They were bone colored and looked sharp. Her small head was dominated by a long beak. In one spiked hand she held a lantern. With the other, she dangled her fingers over the Little's head.

"Speak the words!" the Big hissed and squawked. One of her spiked fingers sliced through the air and hit the Little's head.

He yelped as blood trickled down the side of his face. "Your will be done. Complete obedience, always and forever, of course," he stuttered.

The Big twitched her fingers, and a glowing red ball appeared in her hand. She dropped the orb of light onto the top of the Little's bald head. It flared and broke like an egg. Magic ran down his face in a goopy mess.

The Little stumbled back, wiping away the magic with his yellow fingers. "Ow! That really hurts, Master Aruna. Like a hundred bug bites! Ow."

The monster threw back her quilled head and laughed with a hacking bird sound.

The Little howled. He stumbled to the ground as he kept trying to get the magic off his face.

"Know the cost," the big said in her raspy bird voice. Her spikes bristled and stood up all over her body as she leaned over him, opened her beak, and bit his ear.

"Ow!" he screamed. He put his hands over his head. "I said I'd obey. I'm bound to my word. Why'd you have to put another binding spell on me?"

"Everything moves." She hissed and shifted her weight from one bone-thin leg to the other. "Everything tilts. The great spell is afoot." Her thorny fingers wrapped around him and lifted him off the ground. She held him up, inches from her face. "Obey!" She flung him hard against the tunnel wall.

He fell to the ground and lay there for a long moment. Then he sat up and drew his knees to his chest. "I always obey," he whined as the last of the magic faded around him. "I was out running messages for you, like you asked."

The Big leaned over him and bit his other ear. She laughed, a wild bird-of-prey sound, and turned and started sprinting down the tunnel, in the opposite direction from Celia and the hunters. She took the lantern with her and left blackness behind.

In the sudden darkness, the only sound was the Little's soft sobbing.

Ruby's hand slipped out of Celia's. Celia breathed into the inky darkness, trying to imagine what it would be like to be that boy. That Little.

A couple of long moments later, Ruby called out, "Lights."

Light bloomed beside Celia, blinding and bright until her eyes adjusted. Amber held up the lantern and walked forward. Ahead of them, Ruby pinned the yellow-skinned monster against the tunnel wall with one gloved hand. She used her other hand to cover his mouth. Plumes of orange smoke fell out of his sleeves and pants cuffs as he struggled to get away. The chocolate and whipped-cream smell intensified as Celia trailed behind Amber.

Amber stopped and whispered, "Everything we do, we do it because we have to. Remember that."

When they got near, Ruby glared at the boy and hissed, "Tell us what you know." She spoke like each word was its own sentence. "What are they planning? What does your master want?" Slowly, she took her hand off his mouth.

He inhaled sharply and shook his head from side to side. "Leave me alone," he whimpered. "They never tell me anything. I have messages to tell other Bigs, but they're all code words that don't make sense to you or me. I don't know stuff. Why would I know stuff? I'm just a Little." He rubbed the tip of one blue horn and sniffed the air. "All I know is they're freaked out about something, and are trying to catch someone. But if you wanted, all four of us could try to find out together. We could be friends."

His eyes went big and glassy as he turned to stare at Amber. "You smell so good," he added. "I promise I won't hurt you."

Amber walked right up to him. She stood less than a foot away.

A dreamy look came over his face as his hand reached toward her.

Amber leaned closer to him.

His smile widened. He licked his lips. His yellow fingers floated up toward her face. They darted forward and touched her chin.

A hissing sound filled the air. He gasped and pulled his hand back. Red welts rose up on his fingers as he howled.

"It doesn't matter how nice they seem—they always try to attack us," Amber said, looking at Celia in the dim light.

The Little started crying. He touched the cut on his head that the Big had given him. He stared at his wounded hand. "Just leave me alone. Why can't everyone leave me alone?"

Ruby's gloved hand kept the Little pinned to the tunnel wall.

Celia stood with her hands on her hips and tried to look tough. They weren't really going to hurt him. Amber had promised that.

"Talk," Ruby ordered.

"You want to know what I know? Nothing. Everyone's losing it since the earthquake," the Little said. He scrunched his eyes closed, like he could make everything go away by not looking.

"Poor Little monster," Ruby taunted. "If you can't tell us anything, you're going to the cages."

He started crying harder. Fat tears rolled down his yellow face.

Celia chewed the inside of her cheek. This is part of hunting. Part of being the doom girl, she thought. Even if I don't like it, we do need to learn stuff.

"You think we're mean?" Ruby winked at Celia over the Little's head. "Our friend destroyed Dreck yesterday on her first mission out. She's got a taste for it and wants more."

The boy's yellow-sheened skin went lemon-lime as he looked at Celia.

Celia glared back at him.

He jutted his chin out. "Good. I hated Dreck. I hate them all. We're on the same side, you know? And even if I knew something, even if I accidentally overheard something I wasn't supposed to, you think they'd let me just tell you?" He started coughing.

"Useless," Ruby growled. "Utterly—"

"Wait," Amber said. "You mean you can't tell us, don't you?"

He nodded and coughed harder.

"He must be hexed," Amber informed Celia. "That coughing is from a spell that keeps him from saying something."

"No!" he yelped. "I'm definitely not hexed." He coughed some more.

"How do we break it?" Celia asked.

"We don't." Amber opened her bag and pulled out an old Ouija board with frayed edges. She laid it down on the uneven tunnel floor and held the piece of plastic in her hand that could spell out words or answer yes-or-no questions. She sat down cross-legged in front of it.

Ruby let go of the Little. "Sit. If you try to run? Try anything, and a hex will be the least of your worries."

He sank to the ground on the far side of the Ouija board. Celia sat down beside Amber. The monster watched them miserably.

Ruby stayed standing above them, playing with a small, sharp knife that she tossed between her hands.

"Did you overhear a plan?" Amber asked the Little.

He shook his head.

"A spell?" Ruby asked.

"Nah."

"A name?" Celia guessed.

"No! Definitely not a name!" he yelled, and then smiled a little.

Celia smiled back. Up close, it was hard not to stare at his blue horns and shiny yellow skin.

"A name. Okay." Amber placed the plastic piece on the Ouija board and moved it around the alphabet.

"Not that way! You definitely don't want to go there. No! That's not the first letter!" he yelled. "Go the other way. You've got it all wrong! Go back!"

The plastic piece circled the letter *K*.

"No," he growled, "that's the most wrong you could possibly be." He gave them a small smile and a thumbs-up. "No, not that way!" he started up when Amber began moving the plastic piece again.

They got four more letters—*R, A, W, L*—before the Little relaxed back against the walls of the tunnel.

"Krawl?" Amber whispered.

The word sent shivers through Celia. What was a Krawl?

"You heard some monsters talking about Krawl?" Amber whispered.

"Absolutely not. That's the one name no one has ever said in front of me!" he said.

"Who's Krawl?" Ruby asked.

Amber shook her head. "I'll tell you later." She focused on the Little. "Does Krawl have something to do with the earthquake?"

"No! A hundred times no! That is absolutely not true!"

Which meant yes.

"Can you describe what Krawl looks like?" Amber asked.

The Little relaxed. "No idea."

"Anything else?" Ruby asked.

The Little shook his head and closed his eyes. "That's all. Honest. I want you guys to destroy them. I hate them just as much as you do. Will you leave me alone already?" Sweat rolled down his face next to the lines of dried blood where his master had cut him.

"Promise you'll never turn a kid into a monster," Amber said.

"I promise."

"Littles lie." Ruby took something out of her pocket and held a piece of foil-wrapped chewing gum up toward him. As Ruby peeled off the wrapper, the green piece of gum caught the light and shone bright for a moment.

The Little whimpered and pulled his knees up to his chest. He pressed his mouth closed and shook his head.

"What's the matter?" Ruby mocked. "You promised."

The boy shook his head again.

"It's a spell that makes him hurt every time he thinks about touching a kid," Amber told Celia.

The Little turned his face to the side. "I'll never do it, but it's not like I can control all my thoughts. I helped you. Please. Leave me alone."

They know what they're doing, Celia thought as she folded her arms over her chest and watched Ruby pry his mouth open and slip the piece of gum into his mouth. A cold wind blew down the tunnel and right through her. She pretended his choking and whimpering sounds didn't bother her.

Finally, Ruby let him go.

The Little scrambled up to his feet. He turned and ran down

the tunnel, calling back, "I hate hunters!"

"That was good, Ru. Textbook interrogate and intimidate," Amber said. She looked pale and uncertain in the lamplight. Her voice sounded small and breathy.

Ruby nodded and looked down at her gloved hands. For a second she looked young and lost, but then a hardness settled over her. "Tell us about Krawl, Amber."

Amber shook her head. "Not down here," she whispered, and peered over the top of her glasses into the darkness. "Not until we're somewhere safe and surrounded by other hunters. Come on. Let's go find more Littles."

Celia wanted to leave the tunnels and go up into the light of day, but they trudged deeper into the darkness. She kept thinking about that Little. She wondered how lonely it was to be him. *Why didn't I tell them to stop?* "How long does it take?" Celia asked. "When they attack and change a kid, how long do they have to touch you for?"

"Ten seconds and you're gone," Amber whispered. "Sometimes they get a couple of kids to hold hands, and then they can turn more than one."

Ruby added, "The more Littles they make, the more powerful they are as Bigs." She strode through a puddle in between the train tracks, splashing water everywhere.

"There's no way out," Ruby continued. *Littles don't change. They don't age.* "Even if that Little back there tries as hard as he can? Even if he goes for decades without hurting a kid, that only makes things worse."

Celia looked behind her into the darkness. "Worse?"

"The longer they stay Little, the more powerful it makes them as Bigs. I know that kid back there looked pitiful, but what he is, Celia, is a ticking time bomb."

The world shouldn't be like this, Celia thought. Someone should do something about it.

"I'd rather be dead than be a Little," Ruby said bitterly as she stomped through another puddle.

I might be the doom girl, but the Littles are actually doomed, Celia thought as she rubbed her cold arms. She thought about being a creature destined to destroy someone else. "Me too."

"Good." Amber grabbed Celia's hand and squeezed. "I knew you would make a good hunter. You are so brave for just learning about *them* yesterday."

Celia smiled into the darkness.

They walked on and on through intersecting tunnels, until Celia lost all sense of how far they'd gone or where they might possibly be beneath the city. They found an abandoned subway stop that had walls thick with black and green mold. Pink-eyed rats as big as dogs hissed and squeaked at them from the platform. They walked through tunnels that dripped water from the ceiling and grew forests of white and brown mushrooms in between the unused train tracks. They walked and walked but didn't see any other trails of sweet-smelling orange smoke.

Ruby passed out granola bars and small cans of energy drinks that made Celia's heart race. They rested, perched on the cold metal subway tracks. Celia felt exhausted. She didn't want to complain.

"Can we go up now, Ruby? Please?"Amber asked.

Ruby checked her watch and nodded. "Hunter meeting is starting soon," she said. She led them down a different tunnel, then stopped and pointed up to the ceiling.

Metal rungs were cemented into the side of the tunnel wall. They climbed up and pushed open a metal circle on the ceiling that was a manhole on a side street in Chinatown. The sun had already set, but the air felt full of light compared to where they'd been.

15

WHO UNITES THEM

They walked along the edge of Chinatown, with its brightly painted dragon sculptures that wound around the telephone poles. They stopped at an earthquake relief tent handing out hot buns, seaweed-wrapped rice balls, and soy hot chocolate. Ruby spoke rapid-fire Mandarin to the gray-haired woman handing out food. They trudged on through the north edge of downtown, where gray skyscrapers loomed and shattered glass sat in jagged piles on the sidewalk.

Celia looked everywhere for signs of monsters but didn't see any. She felt tired but at the same time like she might never sleep again. Amber and Ruby walked on both sides of her, linking elbows with her.

"Slumber party," Amber said. She rubbed her eyes. "When this is over, I want to eat takeout Indian at our place and watch a million movies. You have to come, Celia. The council always gives us downtime after things have been intense."

Ruby nodded, scanning the street for trouble. "I'm going to play video games for three days straight."

Amber rolled her eyes. "Ruby relaxes by killing imaginary monsters instead of real ones."

"Amber nerds out and reads spell books and history books that weigh twenty pounds each," Ruby shot back.

"And then they make you fight monsters again?" Celia asked. "How did the hunters and the Council of Elders get started in the first place?"

Amber shrugged. "I've tried to research it. Not all histories get written down. As far as anyone knows, hunters started when kids fought back against *them*. When they grew too old to see them, they trained younger people and taught them everything they had learned. The council passes down hunter lore and gives us spells."

"How old are they?" Celia asked.

"The Youngstown council?" Ruby paused to think. "The youngest is eighteen, and the oldest is in his nineties or something."

Even if they couldn't help fight monsters, at least some grown-ups somewhere were helping, Celia thought. They trudged on through the city. When they finally got to the cathedral and opened up the heavy doors, they were the last hunters to arrive.

The hunters inside waved and called out hellos that echoed through the massive church. Oil lanterns smoked and burned bright along the outer edge of the room, lighting up the stone faces of saints. The three of them walked in, past the holy water and all the burning beeswax candles, each one lit with a prayer.

Celia glanced up at the balcony behind them. No sign of Demetri.

Amber and Celia slid into the same pew they'd sat at before.

Ruby walked down the aisle and took her place in front, standing tense beside the pulpit that held a dozen burning altar candles. She ran a hand through her hair. "Report back. Tell me what you got."

A boy with dreadlocks raised his hand and cleared his throat. "Pips and I went hunting along the docks. We followed Wolfjack into Magog's territory. They sent a pack of dogs after us, then a swarm of locusts, then cats."

A girl sitting next to him with short blond hair nodded. "Squeak distracted them with fish. We listened in on two Bigs scheming. We heard they've got thirty Bigs working together."

Gasps followed her words. Celia shifted where she sat as she remembered Amber saying the only reason Bigs didn't take over everything was that they never worked together.

"Good job," Ruby said.

The scarred boy cleared his throat and raised his hand. "I rigged a ham radio up to a satellite dish and was able to get a weak line out. Nowhere has been hit besides Youngstown. Other hunters have been trying to get here to help. No one has found a way in past the border spells."

"We heard rumors from four different Littles that the next part of the prophecy will hit soon," a small girl, who couldn't have been older than ten, called out. Her leather jacket was ripped open at the shoulder.

The boy sitting next to her added, *"The city will hiss and the girl will run."*

Kids turned and stared at Celia. She chewed on a hangnail and looked up at the stained-glass window, pretending not to notice. Celia couldn't imagine running anywhere. Now that she finally got to sit down and be still, she never wanted to move again.

"What about you? What did you find, Ruby?" a girl with messy ponytails called out.

"First, we killed Dreck last night." Ruby tried to look indifferent, and held it for a moment before she grinned. "Turns out that one isn't as useless as she looks." Ruby pointed at Celia.

All the hunters stared at her again with wide eyes and open mouths.

Amber slung an arm around Celia's shoulders.

"What intel did you get from Dreck?" a girl wearing a wool fedora asked.

"Nothing. His heart got destroyed. By accident," Ruby answered.

Amber sat forward. "And today we found a hexed Little. We got a name off him. Krawl."

"Krawl? Who's Krawl?" a boy called out.

Amber swallowed. Her eyebrows pulled together as fear flickered across her face. She took a deep breath.

"There's monsters and then there's monsters." Her fingers twisted around in her lap. "Krawl used to rule Youngstown, from back when monsters first showed up until, I don't know, sixty years back? Of any Big I've ever read about, she was the best at magic. Spell casting was her game. She would set fires in classrooms and lock kids in just to make a sacrifice for a spell she was doing. She poisoned a cloister of nuns and set lions loose at the zoo. Back when she was the biggest Big in town, the council and the hunters spent all their time trying to stop her. They never even came close. No one even learned what she looked like. Then, one day, she was gone. Some people say that something banished her, or that she ran from something. Rumors of her popped up in Ukraine next; then she caused the Bermuda Massacre and moved on to Rwanda."

"Why did she leave? Why is she back?" a boy with long hair whispered.

No one had an answer to that. Everyone took turns shrugging and looking scared.

"She sounds powerful enough to force a bunch of Bigs to work together," a girl with a pixie cut called out. "She sounds powerful enough to know how to make an earthquake."

Everyone went quiet, and Celia felt a rising panic fill the air. A boy with curly black hair wearing a faded leather jacket raised his hand. "We got something else. You might not want to hear it, Ruby."

"Speak." Ruby paced back and forth, stomping her boots.

The boy bit his lip and looked at the ground. "We swung by council headquarters and got the Grogan's heart, so we could give it a squeeze and he would have to obey us and tell us everything he knows."

Something thudded against one of the cathedral's doors. Everyone turned to look.

"Just the wind. Keep talking," Ruby said.

"The Grogan told us that the new Big in town—he must have meant Krawl—is back to find someone. Someone who all Bigs hate."

"Who?" Ruby asked.

"We squeezed his heart good. The Grogan didn't lie to us."

"Who?" Ruby growled.

"Demetri."

Demetri? Celia jerked up in her seat.

Ruby frowned and rolled her eyes. "Yeah, right."

"That's what he told us," the boy countered.

"Who's Demetri?" Celia asked.

"No one." Ruby crossed her arms over her chest and glared at the hunters—at anyone daring to contradict her. "He's a stupid fairy tale that Littles tell so they can sleep better at night."

"The stories say he's good at hiding," Amber called out. "Maybe the reason we don't think he's real is because he doesn't want us to think he's real."

Celia swallowed and thought about all the wards Demetri wore. She touched the one under her clothes.

"No," Ruby said. "There's no way Demetri can be real."

Celia was just about to ask why, when something touched her ankle. She looked down.

A thin green snake wrapped itself around her leg. It raised its head and hissed.

16

AND THE NEXT WILL HISS

Celia screamed and kicked her leg forward, flinging the snake off her foot. It went sailing underneath the pews. She jumped up into a crouch on the pew. Behind her, hundreds of snakes slithered in through the front doors. Others dropped down from a cracked stained-glass window twenty feet up. They moved swiftly and silently, S-curving along the cathedral's stone floor. They came in all sizes and colors, with diamond patterns, hooded heads, and rattles.

The other hunters pulled their legs up onto the pews too.

Ruby drew her thin swords out from underneath her long wool coat and yelled, "Hunters, get behind me!"

The hunters began jumping from pew to pew before leaping

off the benches and onto the raised platform Ruby stood on. They spread out in a V shape behind their purple-haired leader. Amber and Celia were the last to get there.

More snakes poured into the cathedral through the front door. They spread out and covered the ground as they slithered toward the hunters.

Ruby turned to Amber. "Take Celia and find a safe place to hide! We'll hold them back."

"No," Amber said. She stared glassy-eyed at the snakes. "I'm not going to leave you here, Ru. There's too many of them."

All around them, the hunters faced the snakes and prepared for battle. A wild-haired girl opened her messenger bag and pulled out two coiled whips tipped with steel points. The scarred boy took out a bow and arrow from his backpack. Other hunters grabbed spray-paint cans, tennis balls, throwing stars, and baseball bats. Amber reached into the pouch she wore on her belt and took out a handful of exploding marbles.

Ruby glared at Amber. "Leave now with the doom girl. You know what our orders from the council are. Keep her safe."

Amber tugged on her long black braid and frowned. "Promise me you'll run when they get too close. Promise me you'll keep safe and—"

"Go!"

Amber stood her ground, hands on her hips.

The snakes slithered closer.

"I promise," Ruby growled.

Snakes wound around the front edge of the platform the hunters stood on. They hissed and struck at each other. Some of them raised their heads and flicked forked tongues into the air, tasting the hunters' fear.

Amber grabbed Celia's hand, and they sprinted through a maze of dark hallways until they came to a door with a battery-lit exit sign. "There's a safe house a couple of blocks away. We'll go there," Amber said, and opened the door.

Amber gasped. Celia stopped breathing for a second.

The moonlight shone down on a sea of snakes moving along every road and sidewalk, for as far as they could see. Snakes slithered through the trees, climbed fire hydrants, and wound themselves around telephone poles. There were thousands of them: tens of thousands. A musky scent filled the night air.

Celia and Amber slammed the door shut and stood in the dark hallway. Screams echoed from the front of the cathedral where the hunters fought. They breathed hard.

A soft hiss came from their left. The shadowy shape of a massive snake moved down the hall.

They ran in the opposite direction, sprinting left, then right, and then up a spiral staircase, taking two stairs at a time. They ran up to the balcony with the pipe organ. There didn't seem to be any snakes up there. They paused and looked down at the hunters.

The kids made a tight circle on the raised platform. Thousands of snakes circled them. One hunter used a slingshot to lob bouncy balls at the snakes. When the rubber balls hit the ground, they exploded with a bang, sending snakes flying. Weapons danced through the air, striking at the reptiles. A kid sprayed black spray paint on the ground, and the snakes hissed and moved away from it.

A flick of motion out of the corner of her eye was all that warned Celia. She jumped right just as the striking head of a huge cobra whipped by with bared fangs. It was seven feet long and as thick as her leg.

Amber stood wide-eyed on the far side of the snake.

The cobra rose up. Its diamond-shaped head wobbled from side to side as it stared at Celia. It licked the air and fixed her with yellow eyes before swinging its head around to look at Amber.

Both girls began backing away from the snake and widening the distance between them. The snake swayed and watched Amber.

"There's another staircase behind the organ! I'll meet you upstairs," Amber whispered. She turned and bolted away.

Before Celia could do the same, the cobra swung its gaze back to her and hissed, showing off glistening fangs. Celia took two more steps slowly backward under the snake's watchful stare. Its forked tongue flicked through the air. Snakes couldn't smile, but it looked like it grinned.

I can't do this, Celia thought. I'm just a kid and I can't—

The cobra pulled its head back, readying to strike.

Celia turned and ran. She flew past the silver pipe organ. Fangs nipped at her ankle. She ran faster. The snake bit into the leather of her boot. The sudden weight of the snake pulling back on her foot almost made her fall. Celia kicked back, as hard as she could. She got free from the snake and ran toward the staircase.

Her legs pushed her up and up the dark stairs, running past moonlit stained-glass windows. She kept running until she came to a trapdoor in the ceiling and couldn't go any higher.

She pushed on the trapdoor with her shoulder as hard as she could. It didn't budge.

Celia pounded her fists against it. Nothing.

Please don't be there, she thought. Please don't let that huge snake be right behind me. Slowly, she turned around.

The cobra wound its thick body up the last couple of steps, taking its time now that Celia was trapped.

She crouched in the space between the trapdoor and the top stair and kicked at the snake. It swayed out of her reach. The snake opened its mouth and hissed around fangs dripping with venom. It pulled its hooded head back.

As soon as it strikes, I'll move left and throw myself down the stairs. I'll get past it and run, she vowed, eyeing the slim space that she could maybe, just maybe, get through.

The cobra flared its hood wider and leaned farther away from her.

Any second now, and it would strike.

Celia's heart felt like it was going to explode.

The trapdoor popped open above her. Hands reached down and yanked Celia up just as the snake struck.

17

SOMETHING STRANGE

The trapdoor slammed shut behind Celia. A metal bolt slid into place a moment later, locking it. Amber must have made it up before me, Celia thought.

The hands let go of her. Celia scooted away from the trapdoor, back and back until she leaned against a cold stone wall. The room was dark, lit only by a sliver moon. Everything was blurry as hot tears ran down her face. Celia didn't want Amber to see her crying. She buried her head in her knees. I should be dead right now, she thought. I was almost dead a second ago.

"Sorry," Celia whispered. "Why didn't you let me up sooner?"

"Because I wasn't sure I should," said a boy's voice with a soft accent.

"Demetri?" She kept her head buried. She didn't want him to see her crying either. "You rescued me? Thanks." Her voice cracked. "The snakes—"

"We're safe from the snakes—we're at the top of the cathedral and there's no other way in. They can't climb up the sheer walls," he said.

Something thumped against the trapdoor. Celia yelped. She imagined the cobra hitting the other side of it. "My friend Amber is out there," she stuttered. "Did you see her? She ran in the other direction and we were supposed to meet up and—" What if Amber was alone and surrounded by snakes?

"She's a hunter?" Demetri asked.

Celia nodded.

"Hunters are resourceful. This kind of magic is too strong to last. The snakes will be gone before dawn."

"But . . ." Guilt flooded Celia. She was up here while her friends were down there fighting hundreds of snakes, and she should . . .

"You getting bitten by a cobra won't help anyone," Demetri said.

A dull thumping on the far side of the trapdoor accentuated his point.

He was right. She didn't like it, but he was right. Celia wiped her snot- and tear-covered face with her sleeve, took a deep, ragged breath, and raised her head. Demetri stood at the opposite end of the small round room, as far away from her as possible. He stood at a stone window, watching the city.

There was something strange about him, and as soon as she saw it, Celia looked away. It was too much. Everything was too much.

Screams rose up from across the city, far enough away that they could almost be mistaken for crows or sirens.

Celia took a deep breath. She looked at Demetri again and inhaled his apple and sunlight scent. Demetri stood in the shadows. His shirt sleeves and the cuffs of his pants leaked smoke. *Orange* smoke. She hadn't seen it when she'd first met him, because her mind hadn't let her see it, back when she didn't know about monsters yet. And after that, she'd only seen him in daylight. "You're a Little," she whispered. She realized that a part of her had already thought that might be true.

He sighed, turned toward her, and sank toward the ground. "I am, and I'm sorry to say that you're stuck with me for the night." Demetri pulled off his knit hat. Underneath it, horns wound around his head where a normal boy would have hair. They were brown and thick, like a goat's, and lay in spirals against his skull.

They would have been pretty if they hadn't meant he was doomed, Celia thought, and had an urge to brush her fingers over them. She pressed her back against the wall. "Why do you keep following me? Are you trying to turn me into a monster?"

"No," he whispered. "Celia, I would never do that."

Which was the same thing every other Little she'd met had said. "Then why were you on my roof? Why did you come to my apartment, twice?"

He shook his head. "After the earthquake, magic flooded the streets and I needed to get elevation to see what it was doing. We picked your building at random."

"The thing thumping on the roof, it was a Big, looking for you, wasn't it?"

Demetri nodded. "You shouldn't have pointed out where you lived."

"I didn't realize at the time that you were a child-destroying monster." She sat up straighter.

"I'm not. I . . ." Demetri sank to the ground and hugged himself. "Believe what you want, but I'm not going to destroy you. I don't know why, but we keep ending up in the same places."

Celia watched him and thought that, despite what he was, she didn't think he was lying. "Maybe it's because of the prophecy. Maybe there's something we have to do together to save the city."

Demetri's fingers played with the edges of the trapdoor, like the huge cobra waiting on the other side of it might be a better fate than hanging out with her. "Maybe, or maybe after tonight we should never see each other again."

Celia brought her knees up to her chin. "Ten seconds. I can't believe that's all it would take for you to turn me into a monster."

How could it be that easy? She rubbed her cheek.

Demetri watched her. "You fell. I didn't mean to touch your cheek. It was only for a second, not long enough to hurt you, and I won't do it again. I never want to see you again. But"—he scowled—"I have a feeling we will run into each other again and again."

"If it's not something either of us is doing, maybe it's some kind of spell," Celia said.

Demetri looked thoughtful, then shook his head. "I'm warded. If no one can find me, they can't put a spell on me." He ran his black-tipped fingernail over the horn that curled around his ear. It's not fingernail polish, it's a claw, she realized.

Celia stared at him, wishing there was more light to truly see all his strangeness. "Before the snakes came, the hunters said you were a myth. They said you didn't exist, Demetri."

Demetri laughed. "Good. They must never realize I'm real."

"Why?" she asked.

"We have a sanctuary. I'd rather they didn't find us and attack us."

"It's a . . . sanctuary for Littles?"

He nodded. "For those who have escaped from our masters. We live free there. None of us attack kids. We've made a vow." His smell took on a bitter edge. "The hunters think that's impossible."

"But . . . you will attack a kid someday, right? The hunters said

Littles always . . ." She stopped talking as his eyes narrowed and his hands turned into fists. Howls and screams echoed through the city outside the window. A cold wind blew through the room. "I'm just repeating what they told me," she added.

Demetri nodded. His face softened. "The hunters only know one story, but the world is made of many stories."

Celia smiled and pulled her knees closer. "I like that. Tell me more."

"Tell you what?" Demetri asked.

"Anything. What it's like. How did you become . . . what you are?"

He sighed. "I'll tell you, Celia, but only as a story that happened to me. It will never happen to you, okay?"

"Deal." His words made her feel safe.

"Once upon a time," Demetri said, "my mother died. My father would visit me once a month at the orphanage. He and my mother were Russian immigrants, and back then, in their culture, a father didn't raise a child alone."

Back then. "How old are you?"

"Thirteen." He let out a long sigh. "Always thirteen, no matter how many years pass. Always stuck here." He looked down at his body and then tapped his head. "And here. I can't grow up in my body or my mind." Sadness filled the room, as real as his orange smoke. "One day I met a girl named Kristen at the muddy park next to the orphanage. She was small and sickly, and smelled like honey and rainwater. All the kids from the orphanage liked her. She was pale, wore leather gloves, and would bring her small red rubber ball to the park to play with us every day. It must have been terrible."

"It doesn't sound bad."

Demetri sighed. "I mean for her. My kind's longing? It gnaws into us when we are near you. She smelled wonderful and seemed sad, but when I made her laugh, it felt like everything bad in the world went away. She never mentioned what she was, or why she, a girl who dressed so nicely and brought us boxes of boiled sweets, would spend her days with twelve dirty orphans."

"She was a Little?' Celia asked.

"Not exactly. I like to think Kristen didn't know what would happen when she touched us."

"She would have to know, though, since someone did it to her, right?"

Demetri frowned and shook his head. "No. Kristen was different. She had been . . . changed by her father. He was a powerful magician who wanted to use her to stop all other humans in the world from using magic. That is a huge spell, a world-changing spell, that requires great sacrifice. So he sacrificed his daughter to the spell."

"Why did he want magic to go away for humans?"

Demetri gazed out the window and shrugged. "Power. There have always been men who would do anything for more power.

He must have thought he could make this spell, control Kristen, and rule the world. For years he worked magic on his own daughter to make her powerful enough to survive his spell. He worked to turn her into a vessel who could hold all of the world's magic. He put spell after spell in her and used dark magic to shape her. But, when the time came, the last part of his great spell, where all magic would bind only to her, it did not work. He could not, for a long time, figure out what had gone wrong. When his daughter, who had grown deathly pale and whose fingers had turned to wood, told him that she was filled with a hunger to play with other children, he grew angry at her and at how she was still nothing more than a child. When she told him it gnawed at her and she could smell them from the bedroom she was never allowed to leave, he understood why his spell had not worked. A great spell needs a great sacrifice, and more children needed to be destroyed before his spell worked."

Celia swallowed and gripped her own hands. She knew what must have happened to Demetri, and anyway, this was a story from a long time ago. Even so, she bit her lip and hoped she was wrong.

"Kristen taught us a game one day, *Ring a ring o' roses*, where we held hands and ran around in a circle until we grew dizzy and fell down. She looked small and near death as she slipped off her gloves and joined our circle. Her smooth wooden fingers gripped my hand. We touched and magic surged through me for the first time. Magic thundered and exploded through the world as it changed and came to us and only us. It sparked and crashed into our circle in that small and muddy park. That much magic is not easily controlled, not even by a magician as great as Kristen's father. It went wild. It took what we were and amplified it."

"I was ever lost in my head, so I grew horns. Janice had always loved to run. She sprouted wings. Liam ate constantly, and got a wide mouth with fangs. All of our bodies twisted and changed. And deeper than all of that, it made us need to hurt other kids, just like we'd been hurt. Because Kristen had accidentally done an evil act, the magic erased what she'd been and remade her more powerful than any of us. She became purely evil, like every Big since. All goodness in her got erased."

"That's how it started," Celia whispered. She realized this wasn't just a Demetri story but the first monster story.

Demetri nodded. "Kristen became the first Big, and all of us became her Littles. Her father had been a fool: nothing could control what she was, even though he'd tried to weave into his spell a way of controlling what he had made. She hated him. There was no way she would ever let him get close enough to find her heart."

"So that heart outside the body thing, that was made to control Bigs?"

Demetri nodded. "Kristen's father made the heart spell to control his daughter."

"And all of you were the very first monsters? Every other monster comes from all of you?"

Demetri nodded again. "Youngstown is our birthplace. Monsters are everywhere, but they started here. They are particularly nasty and plentiful in this town. All the other Littles Kristen made became Bigs. They have created domains across the seven continents and are the worst and most powerful monsters in the world. They put evil thoughts into the hearts of dictators, cause famines and floods, steal people's happiness, and create misery wherever they go."

"But not you. You didn't change."

He nodded.

"And you help other Littles do the same, even though all the time all you want to do is touch a human kid?"

Demetri sighed and nodded again.

"But . . . isn't there an easier way? Can't you come up with a spell to not feel those urges?" she asked.

He didn't answer for a while. The snake thumped its head on the other side of the trapdoor.

"Magic can't change everything," Demetri said softly. "It can't change what you are."

Celia pulled her legs closer and leaned back against the cold wall of the room.

She remembered Amber telling her that the longer a Little stayed little, the stronger he would become as a Big. "You'll be powerful if you ever change."

"When I change, as everyone is so sure I will, I'll be horrible. With my longevity, and my skills as a magician." He shook his head. "I shudder to think of what I will be capable of."

"And right now, being in this room with me, you want to attack me?"

"Yes, but I decided I'm less of a threat than the snakes," he said.

Celia heard the smile in his voice and relaxed.

"But it's not easy, since I touched your cheek." His ragged breathing filled the room.

I should be scared, Celia thought. "I promise I'll push you out of the tower if you try to touch me."

"How kind," Demetri said. "I promise I will fall. I'm truly sorry, Celia. You shouldn't have to know about any of this."

"Me too. I mean, I wish you didn't know any of it either. I wish no one did, and that that Little girl Kristen hadn't known either."

"It's hard for me to feel sympathy for her. She owned me and hurt me for a long, long time," Demetri said softly. He rubbed the tip of one of his horns with his thumb.

"But she was your friend. There had to be some of that left. Was she nicer than the other Bigs?" Celia asked.

"No. Crueler."

"But maybe, deep down, there was a part of her that—"

"No," Demetri interrupted. "I tried for years to make her

remember, to make her come back a little, but . . . Kristen died the day she became Krawl."

"Krawl?" Celia shivered. "Krawl is your maker?" She took a deep breath. "Um, so did you know that she's back and is probably uniting Bigs and making the earthquake? And the snakes too, I bet."

"She can't be back," Demetri whispered.

Demetri stood and paced across the room. He leaned out of one of the windows. "The biggest spell I ever made was to banish her from Youngstown. It almost killed me. I set up spells across the city to keep her out. Why didn't I feel her break them and enter? It's all this magic everywhere." He sniffed the air. "Are you certain?"

Celia inhaled the inky darkness. "No. But a hunter heard she's here because . . ." Celia paused. She didn't want to say the next part. "Because she wants revenge on you. I'm sorry."

Demetri laughed, ragged and bitter. "Revenge? Then it's revenge she will get. It's all starting to make sense, Celia." He turned toward her. His dark outline stood silhouetted in the window. His eyes pulsed bright with magic. "This doom prophecy? This quake and snakes? It's one enormous spell she must be weaving. Krawl is conjuring something huge to hurt me, and she doesn't care if she wrecks the whole city in the process."

"How do you know that?"

Demetri turned and stared out the window. "She owned me

for years. I know her. From the very beginning, she always loved the big, complicated, multiphase spells."

"Great," Celia whispered.

"So she starts this spell with an earthquake and follows it with a plague of snakes. Why? And what about the third part of the prophecy, *the city will fill with silent words*? There are dozens of spells she might be building." He sniffed the air. He leaned out into the emptiness of the night air. His lips peeled back in an ugly grin. The sad boy disappeared, and someone else took his place.

"Come find me, Maker Krawl," Demetri growled. "Come find the boy you owned. Wherever you are, whatever you're planning, I'll be waiting for you. And I will destroy you."

18

RAINBOWS AND UNICORNS

Time passed in the dark room that sat above the city. Celia tried to lie down on the stones and sleep, but the world was full of wind and snakes, and she had no idea if her hunter friends were okay, and anyway, going to sleep around a Little was probably the worst idea ever.

Demetri sat perched in one of the stone window frames, gazing out at Youngstown. "I won't harm you. You should sleep," he said.

"I keep thinking about that cobra almost biting me," Celia whispered.

"You should rest while you can," Demetri said. "More bad things will be coming."

Celia hugged herself and shivered. "What could be worse than snakes?" Then she added, "I read this book once about a ship that took a thousand years to travel to another planet from Earth, and when they got there, the planet was full of monster snakes. I guess that would be worse."

"What happened next?" Demetri asked.

Celia told him the rest of the story of how the human colonizers had gone to war with the snake monsters and were losing until they realized they could destroy them by teaming up with this sentient green algae that grew everywhere. Demetri told her about a book where humans traveled to a planet full of robots who kept getting confused about human emotions and killing anyone who felt sad in order to alleviate suffering. They talked on and the conversation shifted from books to music, back to books again, and then Celia found herself telling Demetri about her parents and how much she missed them. The light in the cold room slowly shifted from gray to a pale blue as the night ended. Celia's eyes became heavier and heavier, and she couldn't stop yawning.

Celia woke with a start. Sun shone on her face as the rays of dawn flooded the cathedral's turret. She blinked and sat up. Demetri was gone. The air held his lovely, fading scent. She stretched and stood. Demetri had said the snakes would be gone by morning. Please let him be right, she thought.

Celia went to one of the open windows and leaned out. She searched the road for snakes but didn't see any. White strands of trash littered the ground, unidentifiable from up here. Nothing slithered around that she could see. But what if the snakes were still down there? What if they were always part of the city from now on, and the weather reports would become snake reports, and restaurants would only serve snake meat, and everyone would have snakes for pets?

She went to the trapdoor at the center of the room. It lay bolted shut. Demetri must have used magic to lock it behind him. Celia took a deep breath, unlocked the door, and opened it a quarter inch, ready to slam it shut if the cobra still waited for her. Nothing. Celia opened the door another inch.

Slowly, with shaking hands, she raised the door and lowered herself down to the stairs. She took three steps down before she saw it: a white, empty husk of snakeskin coiled on the steps.

She hurried past it, skipping down the staircase that she'd fled up yesterday. The only sound in the whole cathedral was the thump of her feet.

Had the hunters survived the night? Celia hoped that everyone was all right.

More white snakeskins wound around the banister and littered the hallways. At the bottom of the stairs the skins lay inches deep. Celia strode through them, heading to the main part of the cathedral, where she saw two people huddled together near the pulpit. Above them, dozens of snakeskins lay wound around the hanging crucifix.

As she got closer, Celia saw it was Amber and Ruby. Even though they looked nothing alike, the way they sat close to each other and held each other made them look like sisters. Celia ran to them and threw her arms around both of them.

"I'm so glad you're both alive." She spoke in a river of words. "Is everyone okay?"

"Amber got bitten," Ruby said. She pulled back from Celia and wiped a tear off her face.

"Are you okay, Amber? Do you need a doctor?"

Amber gave her a pale smile. "Fine." The back of her hand was swollen up around a purple bruise with a fang bite at its center. Her lips were blue.

"Where were you?" Ruby asked. "Why didn't you help her?"

"It's not Celia's fault," Amber whispered. The girl's skin looked ashy and gray. "I found a room I thought was empty. Two vipers attacked me. I killed them, but . . ." She touched her puffy hand. "Most snake venom isn't fatal, even if it may cause vomiting and hallucinations."

"I'm sorry," Celia said. "That cobra chased me. I ran all the way up to the top of the cathedral. The snakes couldn't climb up there, so I was safe." No part of her even paused for half a second to consider telling them about Demetri.

"At least someone was." Ruby glared at the snakeskin littering the room.

"Are you sure you're okay?" Celia asked again.

"Yeah. Fine. Hey, so there's not a snake goddess hovering above that pew, right?" Amber's eyes widened behind her thick glasses. "I might be hallucinating."

Ruby scowled at the snake bite on Amber's arm, as though her anger was a venom antidote. Her spiky hair rose up in wild purple clumps. "I should have kept you both with us. We killed a lot of snakes and then camped out in the refectory. We were fine. The rest of the hunters are out searching for Krawl this morning."

"Good," Celia said. She wanted to find Krawl too. Maybe the doom girl was the only one who could defeat her.

"Why do you have a snake tongue, Ruby? It's freaking me out." Amber squinted and leaned away from Ruby.

"Hallucinations," Ruby reminded her.

"Maybe Amber should stay here while we search for Krawl," Celia said.

"No. We aren't looking for Krawl."

"But she's behind all this, right, and if we find her, maybe we can—"

"We have a more important mission. We're hunting Demetri."

Celia's cheeks flushed. "He isn't real. You said he was just a story." She thought about how hunters liked to put Littles in cages.

"Yep. But"—a wolfish grin spread across Ruby's face—"he's supposed to be powerful and nearly as good at magic as Krawl is. If we find Demetri, we could use him to fight Krawl."

"He doesn't sound real," Celia said quickly. "And anyway, I can't go hunting with you today." No way and nohow would she ever help them put Demetri in a cage.

"Why not?" Ruby asked.

"I . . . have to go to school?" Celia said. "It's Monday. I—think I still have school."

"Are you kidding?" Ruby said. "You think schools are going to be open today? Besides, how can you think about school at a time like this?"

"I just . . . need to go home and clean up, or go on a walk by myself, or whatever." Celia chewed on her lip. "I'm not a hunter. Maybe I need a little downtime." She stood up. Maybe she should try to find Demetri somehow and tell him to watch his back.

"But we're in the middle of the doom prophecy. We have to make sure nothing bad happens." Amber shivered.

Celia silently agreed with her. That was why she wasn't going to hunt Demetri. "You really look like you need a doctor, Amber."

"I feel good. Sort of floaty. I'm not floating, am I? Anyway, I'm pretty sure every hospital is going to be out of snake antivenom today," Amber said.

"You have to come hunting with us, Celia. You left Amber alone and she got bitten. You owe us," Ruby said.

"I owe you? I almost died. I had to run and—" Celia stopped talking. Let Ruby think whatever she wanted. Hunters didn't understand lots of things: that was what Demetri had said. Ruby and Amber were her friends, but that didn't mean they were right about everything. Celia began to walk out of the cathedral.

"Where are you going?" Ruby snapped at her back. "It's not safe out there. Bigs will be looking for you."

"I'm not hunting today." Then she added, because a part of her, no matter how much she didn't like what they did sometimes, still wanted to be their friend, "I'll see you soon."

"*The city will hiss and the girl will run,*" Ruby called out as Celia walked away. "See? It's all coming true!"

19

LIKE A NOBODY

Outside, snakeskins blew down the road. It was early enough that not many people were out. They were probably still barricaded behind doors, dreaming snake nightmares, Celia thought.

She scratched her cheek as she walked down the road. My Demetri mark feels less itchy today, she thought, and wondered what she should do now. She had no idea how to find Demetri and warn him about the hunters. Maybe, since she was the doom girl, just walking around would make something good happen that would help save the city, like the prophecy predicted.

A boy walked down the sidewalk carrying some handwritten papers tucked under his arm. They said hi to each other in a friendly, "glad we're both alive" kind of way. He handed her one of the papers.

At the top of it was a pressed seal of the city and at the bottom was the mayor's signature.

The first paragraph, written in a hurried scrawl, said that the zoo had gotten a new snake shipment in, but unfortunately the shipping crate had been damaged in the earthquake, and the snakes would be contained soon.

Did the mayor believe that? How could anyone think that many snakes could be caused by something normal?

The next paragraph said that everyone should remain calm and indoors, and everything would go back to normal soon.

Celia took out her cell phone and saw that, of course, it still didn't work. As she walked, she couldn't stop glancing around and checking to make sure there were no more snakes. She half expected to see them S-curving down the road or dropping down from tree branches. An old blind woman half a block back used a white cane to tap along the sidewalk. She wore a shawl draped across her shoulders, the same color as her white bun. Celia thought about turning around and asking if she needed help. But the woman was walking fine, and Celia thought it might be annoying if you were old and blind and everyone was always asking you if you needed help when you didn't.

Celia turned a corner and saw a dog park in the middle of the block. People stood alone and in pairs, watching as their dogs ran around and sniffed at the snakeskins. A bunch of the dogs sat together and looked alike. Celia blinked and saw it wasn't just that they all looked alike, but that they all wore black leashes that led to the same man in a hooded trench coat who stood beneath a tree. There was something strange about him. The dogs were strange too. They were connected to the man on long flickering leashes and were made of . . . smoke? As soon as she saw it, she couldn't unsee how unnatural and monstrous they were.

On some invisible command, the smoke dogs ran forward. Their leashes stretched as they started chasing real dogs. The smoke dogs moved swiftly over the muddy grass, and the dogs ran from them. Celia watched as one of them pounced on a smaller schnauzer and lowered its slobbering muzzle toward the dog's body. The dog barked and writhed as it tried to get away. The owners looked on, unable to see anything that was happening. The schnauzer managed to squirm out from under the bigger dog and run. She looked away and saw the man with all the leashes watching her with glowing red eyes. Beneath his hood, there was only more smoke.

Celia turned and ran, fleeing from the sounds of panicked and barking dogs. She ran down a block, and another one, breathing hard and not looking back, sure the smoke dogs would be chasing her. And if they were? No one would help her. No one would even notice.

Celia glanced back. Nothing followed her. She slowed to a

jog on the third block, and on the fourth she paused to catch her breath. Nearby there was a community center with a sign out front saying they were open. The outside of the front window was covered over with a large white poster. Someone had written on it with a fat black pen, *What Is Going On? Does Anyone Know?*

Hundreds of handwritten notes were written across it. *It's just a coincidence* and *The government hates us and is experimenting on us* and *BAD LUCK!*

Everyone's world has changed, Celia realized. Everyone in the city, even if they don't know what is going on or why, is living in this topsy-turvy world. It's not just me and the hunters against the monsters.

Someone had written, in small letters at the bottom of the poster, *It's invisible monsters. They're everywhere.*

That little bit of truth, easy to miss with all the other guesses, seemed like the least likely possibility.

Next to the poster was a hand-printed sign saying anyone in need should come in and get help. Celia peered in through the glass door and saw candlelit lanterns lighting the boxy room. It was crowded with cots, people, boxes of food donations, and a mishmash of furniture. A couple of girls from Celia's school sat on a couch. She imagined walking inside and having them smile and hug her. *Are you okay?* they'd ask. One of them would tell Celia she could stay at her place until Celia's parents came home, and then they'd eat breakfast together.

Except . . . they don't know me. They've never been nice to me, Celia thought. She was surprised to realize that fact didn't hurt her like it would have before the earthquake.

She opened the door and stepped into the dim room that smelled like cooked cabbage and stinky socks. Faded motivational posters with curling edges were tacked onto the walls. *Failure is when you give up* and *Live every day like it's your last.*

"Are you here to write a letter?" a man with a Spanish accent and white hair asked.

"Letter?" Celia asked.

"To our loved ones outside the city. To tell them we are okay."

"I guess so," Celia said. She was pretty sure they wouldn't be able to get the letters out of the city, but maybe something had changed.

He led her to a table full of pens, papers, and envelopes. Celia sat down on a wobbly wood chair and wrote her mom's name on an envelope, along with her grandma's address. Then she chewed on the plastic pen cap and stared at a blank piece of paper.

Dear Mom and Grandma,

There was so much they didn't know, and so many things she'd done that she wasn't supposed to. More than that, there was so much they wouldn't believe.

I'm fine. I'm good. I miss you. Don't worry about me, she wrote, with a shaky penmanship that her parents might not even recognize. She wanted to tell them true things, but didn't want to make them explode with worry. So she wrote LOVE in big letters, signed her name, and folded it into the envelope that tasted like moldy peppermint when she licked it shut. She handed it to the man. "How is this supposed to get out of Youngstown?"

"We have a mailman who's going to try to take a rowboat today." He frowned. "Don't know if he'll make it—there are stories that it's . . ."

"Dangerous," Celia said. "Maybe he shouldn't try. Maybe he should wait until this is over."

The man smiled and pushed his glasses up with a thin pointer finger. "Why don't you let the adults worry about that?"

Because I'm one of the few people who know what's really happening, Celia thought.

Someone tapped her shoulder. "Hey, don't I know you?"

Celia turned and looked at the two girls from her school—Ella and Teal. Celia knew their names because everyone knew their names. They were popular. The exact opposite of me, Celia thought. "Hi."

"Hey. Can you believe it about the snakes last night?" Ella said. She looked Celia up and down, taking in her slept-in hunter clothes and dusty boots with a dismissive look. "It's such bad luck: an earthquake and then the snakes. At least we weren't stupid enough to be outside last night and get bitten."

Both girls laughed.

Teal examined her chipped pink nail polish. "Both our houses got damaged in the quake and we have to stay here. We'll get to go back home soon though. Some people's houses collapsed." They giggled again, like that was funny too.

Two days ago, Celia would have been over the moon that they were talking to her. Back then she'd been so sure something was wrong with herself, but now she could see that Demetri had been right. Growing up in a place like Youngstown twisted you. Maybe half seeing monsters and living in fear had made them mean. She didn't envy them or wish they were her friends: all she felt was sorry for them.

Celia looked past them toward a table full of bagels and cream cheese. I should take a couple on my way out, she thought.

"What about you? Where are your parents? They allowed you to go on a walk by yourself outside?" Ella asked. She twisted her long brown hair around her finger.

Celia shrugged. "They were out of town the night of the earthquake."

"That sucks," Teal said. They both laughed again.

Celia looked at them. Beneath their smiles, she saw fear. "Don't worry. This will end soon. It can't last." Big magic didn't last long, Demetri had said.

"Like *you* know anything. What's your name, anyway?" Teal asked.

"Celia."

"You're new, right? Real quiet?" Ella said.

I wouldn't be if anyone ever talked to me, Celia thought. "Yeah."

"We're so bored here," Teal said. She put her hands on her hips. "All everyone does is come up with theory after theory about what is going on."

"People make up stories when they don't know the truth," Celia said.

"Tell me about it. No one knows anything," Ella said.

Two days ago I held the beating pizza-box heart of a monster in my bare hands, Celia thought, and touched the mark on her cheek. "I know."

They laughed at her some more.

Celia walked over to the bagel table.

The girls followed.

"What do you think you know?" Ella asked.

Celia looked out the window at the leafless skeleton trees covered with hanging snakeskins. The bagels were hard. The cream cheese had a bad smell to it.

"What could you know? You're just a weird girl," Teal added.

Celia nodded. Truer every day. Maybe knowing the truth would help them understand all the weird things in their life. "It's a magic spell being cast by monsters. They're working on a huge spell to do something, but I don't know what."

"Are you kidding? How mental are you?" Ella asked.

Both girls were rolling their eyes at each other when someone rapped hard against the community center's glass door.

Celia tensed.

Outside, two hunters peered in. One of them was a girl with a shaved head, the other was the tall boy who had dreamed about Celia. They gestured for her to come outside.

"You know them?" Ella asked. Both girls stared at the hunters, who wore leather from head to toe. The girl carried a baseball bat. The boy had a black eye.

Celia looked at the two girls and knew she could stay here and try to become friends with them. But she walked outside instead.

20

THE GIRL WHO DECIDES

"Hi, Celia." The boy's eyes flicked up and down the road as his fingers massaged the bruise that circled his eye. "I'm Rampage. We haven't had a chance to talk one on one, but, like, heya and how you doing?"

The short-haired girl leaned against the brick wall of the community center with her hands folded across her chest. "Hey, I'm Trix."

"I thought all the hunters were supposed to be hunting Krawl," Celia said. "Did something happen? Is everything okay?"

"Okay?" The girl laughed and shook her head.

"Not even close, not even a little bit." The boy looked behind him, eyes darting everywhere before he fixed his gaze on Celia.

"But last night I dreamed you'd be on this road, and we have to tell you something."

"Road's empty, Rampage. Make it quick," the girl whispered. She stepped onto an overturned planter box and stood a couple of feet above them, scanning the road. A shivery wind blew snakeskins past them.

Celia bit into the stale bagel and chewed while she listened to them.

"Yeah, so Celia, so um, there's this thing Ruby doesn't exactly want you to know." The hunter spoke fast and his words blurred into each other. "It's like, when I dream, I sometimes get tiny glimpses of the future. Like, not that I'm magic, and it's nothing useful, mostly, but . . ."

"We haven't got all day, Rampage," Trix reminded him.

"Yeah. So. The thing I keep dreaming about is . . . you."

Celia shoved her hands in her pockets and shifted her weight from foot to foot. "Do you know what I'm supposed to do?"

"Nah. If I knew that, I'd win the prize for best hunter in the world if there was that kind of prize. All I know is that your face is plastered all over the future, and a lot of terrible things might happen. Like destruction and death and stuff. And there's something we think you should know, doom girl."

"Get on with it," the girl said, and ran her hand through her stubbled hair.

He nodded and licked his crooked teeth. "Yeah, so Ruby told

all the hunters that you had to think being the doom girl was a straight-up good thing. She said you had to learn the doom prophecy a little wrong, so you would choose right. The real prophecy says, *The city will shake and the girl will be found. The city will hiss and the girl will run. The city will fill with silent words and the girl will decide.* And that's it. That's all."

"Get it?" the girl asked. "Ruby added on the last part about how you would *decide to save the city.* The real prophecy doesn't say anything about *what* you'll decide. So don't go thinking you can't mess things up, or that you're destined to be a hero or something."

Celia blinked. Her world tilted and moved, but this was no earthquake. She took a step back from both of them. Saving the city had felt like way too much, but at least it was a good thing. And now, maybe she would decide something right or maybe she would get it all wrong?

"You're the girl who decides which way things go. You'll choose good, now that you know it's a choice, right? Trix and I got worried that since you wouldn't know, you would just stumble into doing bad." He bounced up and down in his thick leather boots as he spoke. "We tried to talk to Ruby about it, but she doesn't like it when people disagree with her."

"But you won't, right? Not even if the hunters lose track of you and we aren't there to make sure you do the right thing?" the girl added.

Celia's eyes narrowed into slits. "If they lose track of me?"

Both hunters suddenly got very interested in studying the ground.

"You mean the hunters were ordered to babysit me so they can force me to do whatever they think is the right thing?" Celia's stomach clenched and twisted. Amber and Ruby don't like me. We're not friends. I'm their job, same as hunting Littles, she thought.

The boy whispered, "Sorry."

Trix jumped down from the planter box. "What'd you expect? The world isn't made of fairies and Care Bears. We have to do everything we can to stop the Bigs. The monsters are the bad guys. The hunters are just trying to do what's right. You get that, don't you?"

"Right," Celia echoed. Except when the monster was a sad boy who fought against his own nature to watch out for her. Except when the good guys lied to her and pretended they liked her.

"What are you thinking, doom girl? About all the ways you're going to save people, and not destroy them, right?"

Celia shoved her cold hands into her coat pockets. "What would Ruby and Amber do if they thought I was about to choose the wrong thing?"

"Hunters got to do what we got to do," Rampage said, and shrugged. Behind him pigeons and crows pecked and squawked at each other.

"Time to bounce," Trix whispered. She ducked down like she was tying her shoes. "Hunter girls at two o'clock."

Celia scanned the road and saw Ruby and Amber over a block away.

"Tell me what they'll do to me if they don't like the decisions I make," Celia said again, but the two hunters had already disappeared into the community center.

Amber leaned against Ruby as they walked down the street. I'm not their friend. I'm nothing to them, Celia thought. All of that was a way to trick me.

"Celia!" Amber cried out. She grinned with a phony, pretend-friend smile. "I'm so glad we found you."

21

ARTIFICIAL LOVE

"Sorry about this morning. Everyone was exhausted and crabby," Amber said. Her skin still had a gray sheen, but she looked better. She held out her arms to hug Celia. "Can we start over?"

"How did you find me?" Celia stepped back from Amber. She was their assignment. They weren't her friends. She crossed her arms over her chest.

"We tracked you. Hunters stay together." Ruby kicked at a crack in the sidewalk. "Who were you just talking to?"

They don't like me. I'm their job. It felt so obvious, now that she knew it. How could I think they'd want to be friends with me? "Some workers at the community center came out to ask me if I needed anything," Celia answered.

Ruby narrowed her eyes and watched Celia for a long moment. She nodded once. "Let's get going and head north. There are some warehouses where Demetri might be hiding. Not that we're likely to find anything."

"No. I already told you no." She remembered how Demetri had kept watch all of last night as he sat curled up like a gargoyle in the window. At least he likes me, she thought, and then pushed down hysterical laughter at the thought that the only kid in town who liked her had to fight his own nature to keep from turning her into a monster.

Ruby, using her bossiest leader-of-the-hunters voice, said, "I've already talked to you about this. The three of us are hunting Demetri today. That's our job." She stood, hands on her hips, expecting to be obeyed.

"Go away," Celia said. She knew they wouldn't. She knew they would follow her no matter what, since their real job was watching her.

Amber frowned and shook her head at Ruby. She threw an arm around Celia's shoulders.

Celia shook her arm off.

"What's wrong?" Amber looked concerned. Fake, Celia thought. She was so good at faking things. "Maybe we could all use a break?" Amber added. "I've stopped hallucinating, but now I've got a killer headache. Let's go find some breakfast. Maybe we're all just hungry."

"I'm not hungry," Celia said flatly. She took an angry bite of the hard bagel.

Amber frowned. "Did something happen?"

"Do you even like me a little bit?" Celia asked. She wanted to sound like she didn't care, but it came out high-pitched and shaky. She already knew the answer. They didn't. She started walking away from them.

They followed, of course.

Celia rubbed angry tears out of the corners of her eyes.

"Do we like you?" Amber asked. "Of course."

Ruby added, "Why do you ask, doom girl?" Her voice held a quiet threat.

The city, full of hard angles and broken roads, stretched out in every direction. Celia walked faster and didn't need to glance back to know that both girls followed a couple of steps behind her.

"We'll forget hunting Demetri." Ruby spoke to Celia's back. "We can head over to the graffiti flats. It's nearby, and one of the places where prophecies always show up. So many artists go there all the time that at least one of them will have caught the prophecy in a dream. We might be able to find some new clues there."

"Okay," Celia said through gritted teeth. The girls would find a way to follow her, no matter what, and if she could keep Ruby and Amber from hunting Demetri, that was a good thing.

Besides, if there was more to learn about the prophecy, she wanted to see it for herself, and not be fed more hunter lies. "They just write the prophecy all over a wall, not knowing what it is, right?"

Amber nodded. "It comes to creative people, maybe because they are a little more open to magic? It's like a song you get stuck in your head. It's itchy for people, until they express it."

Ruby walked up beside Celia and flashed her a grin. "So you'll come?"

Celia glared at her and kicked a stone that went skittering over the sidewalk.

Amber walked on her other side and tried to link up elbows. Celia didn't let her.

The city looked even more broken today. Side streets were barricaded with piles of rubble. Snakeskins drifted along like tumbleweeds. Everyone they passed walked in protective groups of twos and threes, talking in whispers about the snakes.

Amber tried to keep up but couldn't even walk in a straight line. Sweat rolled down her face.

Celia slowed her pace. "I'm sorry you got bitten."

"I'm happy that cobra didn't kill you. It was so huge. Hey, is something wrong, Celia? You can tell me." Amber pulled at her long black braid and looked at her from behind her smudged glasses.

"You've got a job to do," Celia said coldly.

"Yeah, we both do," Amber said. "You, and me."

Celia slid her cell phone out of her pocket and turned it on. Still no reception. She wanted to talk to her mom or dad so bad that it hurt. Maybe my letter will reach my grandma's house in a couple of days, she thought. But even if it did, a lot could have happened. Would she still be okay by then?

Amber pointed at the phone. "When your parents come back, are you going to tell them everything or try to hide it?" she asked.

Celia thought about her parents' list of rules. Most of them seemed so tame compared to what she'd actually done. "I'll tell them everything. That's just the way my family works: we tell each other the truth."

"They might throw you out," Ruby said. "Mine did. If they do, the hunters will take you in. We'll take care of you, if you need us." She said it like she meant it.

She's just saying that to manipulate me, Celia reminded herself. All of this is pretend to them.

"My parents will love me no matter what," Celia told her.

Ruby kicked at long strands of snakeskins as she walked. "Maybe. Or maybe your parents will abandon you and you'll hunt monsters, see horrible things, and have to do stuff you never wanted to. Things that no kid should have to do." The way she said it, Celia knew Ruby was talking about herself.

Ruby turned toward a rusted door that looked like any other on the block. She kicked it open and disappeared inside.

Celia slipped in behind her and stepped into a world of huge murals and bright colors. The building had no ceiling, and the concrete walls rose two stories high. Every inch of the space was filled with a jumble of art, words, and symbols. A twenty-foot-tall painting of dancing robots covered one wall. Beneath it was written in swirly letters, *Artificial Love*. Next to it was a smaller mural of kids throwing rocks at an old lady.

On another wall a huge octopus with golden tentacles floated over dozens of smaller pictures. Everywhere Celia looked, she saw colorful murals and words. She had to blink a lot to take it all in.

They walked through the first room into another room jammed full of art.

"I love prophecies," Amber said. "It's like there's some secret force that wants to help us out whenever *they* use a lot of magic. I just wish they were more useful. They always make sense once the big spells are over, but they usually don't help while it's going on."

Especially if you lie about what they say, Celia thought. They passed a stenciled picture of a girl who was dressed just like Celia had been on the day after the earthquake. The girl's face was drawn anime style, but even so, Celia felt like she stared into her own face. DOOM was written in block letters beneath the image. They stopped and searched the picture, but it didn't say anything else.

They passed the word *Hate*, written in thick black letters that went all the way up to the ceiling. In smaller print, written thousands of times inside those letters with bright-red paint, was the word *Sad*.

"That's Little art. The prophecy is this way," Ruby said. She led them down a series of long, paint-drenched hallways. Because there was no roof, it felt like the corn maze Celia always used to go to outside Portland.

They passed a white wall with a sprawling mural of a snarling blue man who had bat wings and bear legs. He stood beside a winged unicorn, painted so realistically it looked like it might jump off the wall. Over their heads hung a messy ball of spray paint in every color and shape.

Ruby led them through two more rooms; then they turned and found themselves facing a painting of a black dragon, soaring above the city with his claws out and his lips curled back into a snarl.

Ruby let out a low whistle. "That's new." She pointed to the dragon. Words were scrawled beneath his claws.

Ruby walked up to the picture and ran her finger over the words. At first Celia thought it was written in a language she couldn't understand, but the longer she looked, the more she could decipher the letters drawn in a distorted way.

"*The city will fill with silent words and the girl will decide.*" Celia read the last part of the prophecy out loud and looked toward the two hunters.

"The part about you saving the city must have gotten erased," Ruby lied.

"Yeah, I'm sure that's what happened." Celia folded her arms over her chest.

"Look, there's more," Amber said. She pointed at some words written below the prophecy. "*He will fall,*" Amber read slowly. "*She will rise.* That gives me shivers, even though I have no idea what it means."

"Who's he? Who's she?" Celia asked. Someone else had scribbled ugly neon-orange paint beneath those words. Then she saw it wasn't scribbles but a word, written over and over again, dozens of times. "*Celia,*" she read.

Her name was spray-painted all over the wall.

"He will fall. She will rise. Celia, Celia, Celia," Ruby whispered and shook her head. "But what does that mean?"

Celia moved forward and traced her fingers over the orange paint and the rough concrete beneath. The air around her seemed to grow a couple of degrees colder.

"Sometimes you can see things from farther back that you can't see up close," Amber said as she walked to the far side of the room.

Celia walked to Amber and then turned to study the whole wall.

"You see it?" Amber asked.

Celia didn't.

"The whole shape of it," Amber said. "The dragon and every-thing."

Celia looked at the dragon wings and the words scrawled beneath and saw how, all together, it took the shape of letters. She peered more intently. It read—

"*Demetri*," Ruby whispered.

The leader of the hunters breathed in sharply as she raised her hand and pointed at the doorway near the mural.

Two towering figures entered the room, silhouetted in the dim light. The first was a tall, skeletal man wearing a white top hat and a tight white tuxedo. His ice-blue skin stretched over his gaunt features. He puckered his lips, and when he breathed out, a blast of icy-cold air hit the girls twenty feet away. It felt like standing inside a walk-in freezer. He smiled, showing off icicle teeth. "Look what we've found, sweet Snedronna. Hunter chil-dren."

"Bigs," Ruby growled back.

"Hunters and one very special doom girl, I believe, dear Sne-dron," the other monster replied. She had the same pale skin the color of a white-blue iceberg, and long white hair that twisted in intricate braids and knots down her back. She wore a skintight white dress that clung to the sharp angles and bones of her body. Her high-heeled shoes were made of ice. She blew a kiss at the girls. White clouds blew through the air, which chilled another ten degrees.

Ruby reached beneath her coat and pulled out the twin swords that she wore strapped to her back.

"Two of them, three of us. Bad odds," Amber whispered as she zipped open the pouch she wore at her belt. "If we fight them and lose, they'll take Celia. It's not worth it."

Ruby glared at the two Bigs and slashed her thin swords through the air. The Bigs watched her, amusement playing on their glacial faces. Ruby let out a low growl.

"Ruby," Amber whispered. "There's the whole prophecy to think about. It's your call, but I think we should—"

"Run," Ruby ordered.

The girls turned and fled out the nearest doorway.

22

MY MIND CANNOT MAKE A MEMORY OF YOU

They sprinted past a thousand angry red spray-painted images of kids with horns and claws poking out from beneath their patched hoodies. Gusts of cold followed behind them, along with a bitter scent of lemons.

"Which way?" Amber cried out when the hallway forked.

Ruby led them left. Amber and Celia followed a footstep behind.

"Run, run, little hunters!" the ice woman called out. Her shoes *click-clack*ed against the cement floor.

They ran through a room painted with a floating ball of arms, legs, eyes, and mouths all stuck together. The spray-painted eyes seemed to watch them as they streaked past.

Celia glanced behind her and saw the two Bigs less than ten feet away. The monsters took such long strides that they seemed to glide over the ground. Their bones jutted out at sharp, odd angles as they moved.

"In here!" Ruby turned right, through a doorway. Amber and Celia followed a second later.

Ruby slammed the door shut and grabbed a long chunk of concrete. She wedged it beneath the door handle. An instant later, the Bigs pounded and pushed on the other side of the door.

Celia breathed hard. She looked around for where they should run now.

The room had four tall walls and one door: the one Ruby had just barricaded. There was no way out.

The pounding on the door increased. The door shook.

Celia swallowed hard. "You two have some kind of weapon to stop them, right? Or some way to climb out of here, or call the hunters, or . . ."

"I'm all out of spells. I used them to fight the snakes last night. You?" Ruby asked Amber.

Amber shook her head. "Marble bombs, half a dozen left, and that's all. We should have gone to headquarters and grabbed more spells. But . . ." Both girls glanced at Celia and away.

But they had to follow me and make sure I didn't get away, Celia thought bitterly. And now we are all going to get attacked by Bigs.

There were images of monsters spray-painted on every wall. All of them seemed to snarl and glare at the girls who stood in the center of the room.

The pounding on the door grew louder.

"Those two out there? They're called the Splintered," Ruby told Celia, gesturing to the door. "Even on our best day, even with all our gear and spells, we'd need five good hunters to take them down. There's only one thing we can do now." She and Amber exchanged a long look.

The door shook harder. The piece of concrete wedged beneath the handle wobbled but held. Please let them have a way out of this, Celia thought. Everywhere she looked, leering images of monsters watched her.

Ruby turned away from Celia and rummaged through her bag. When the purple-haired girl turned back around, she held a penny that was painted bright red. "I'm sorry." Her lips were set in a thin line. "I didn't want it to come to this." Ruby stepped toward Celia.

Celia moved away from her until she found herself backed up against the hard wall. "What's that do?" she asked. There was nowhere to run.

"You have to swallow it."

Celia remembered Ruby force-feeding the spelled chewing gum to the Little in the underground. "No I don't." Celia looked up. The walls were twenty feet high. Way too tall to climb. She glared at Ruby and Amber.

The whites all the way around Ruby's eyes showed as she stalked closer.

"We can't let the Bigs take you, doom girl. The Council of Elders said we had to do this if you were about to be caught. For the greater good." Ruby's hand started shaking, but she still held the penny out toward Celia. "Eat it."

Celia slid along the side of the wall, keeping her distance from Ruby. "What kind of people betray each other like this?" Celia heard her voice rising and felt her hands curl into fists. "What kind of kids pretend to be someone's friend just to use them? Liars. Traitors." She glared at both of them. "Not that I care. I never liked either of you."

Ruby flinched. "We have to do this."

The monsters pounded and shook the door.

Amber whispered, "It will make you sleep, that's all."

"For how long?" Celia asked.

"Long enough that you can't help the Bigs if they take you," Amber said. The pounding on the door grew louder.

Ruby moved closer to Celia, cornering her next to a pair of pastel-colored blob monsters.

"How long?" Celia asked louder. "Days? Months?"

"We do what we're told. Open your mouth." Ruby stood in front of her and held the coin up toward Celia's face.

Celia shoved her away, hard.

The hunter danced back a couple of steps before coming

close again. "Just do it, Celia, please. Don't make this harder than it has to be." The battering on the door almost drowned out her words.

"I don't know how I could have ever thought you were my friends." Celia pushed her away again.

"Be quick, Ru." Amber came to stand next to Ruby.

Ruby pushed the penny toward her mouth again. Celia punched out at her, but Ruby ducked. Celia used the moment to run to a different corner of the room. "You have no idea how long it will make me sleep for, do you? Do you even care if I ever wake up?"

Ruby's mouth dropped open. "Of course we care. But . . ."

Amber grabbed the penny out of Ruby's hand. "But if the Bigs take you, they could use you to get everything they want. You're the one who matters—you're the doom girl who decides. People could die. The whole city could get destroyed if the monsters take you." She ran toward Celia and tried to push the coin past Celia's clenched teeth.

Celia shoved her away. "How does this make you any better than the monsters? I hate you. Both of you!" How was this happening? She kicked at Amber to keep her away. The hammering on the door, like the hammering of Celia's heart, grew louder.

"Grab her," Amber said. "Do it, Ruby. Fast."

Ruby stalked toward Celia, but when she got close, she dropped her hands to her sides and shook her head. "I . . . can't. I just can't."

Celia moved away from her, scooting along the edge of the wall.

An explosion of shattering wood and blurred movement filled the room.

The monsters rushed in on their long, icy legs. They grabbed Amber and threw her against the far side of the room. Ruby followed an instant later. The girls smashed against the hard wall and fell to the ground like rag dolls.

Cold hands gripped Celia. They yanked her up and threw her over an ice-hard shoulder. The ice man laughed as his freezing arm clamped over her legs and held her in place. Celia kicked and punched, but she was helpless as a numbness spread into her where her body touched his.

The ice woman walked toward Amber and Ruby on skittering heels. She waved her long, white-blue fingers through the air and stormy gusts swirled off them. "Little girl hunters, how cute you both are. I'd love to see you blue with frostbite. I'd love to see your hands and feet frozen through." Ribbons of icy air flowed off her, swirling around Ruby and Amber. "Aren't they adorable, dear Snedron?"

Ruby raised her swords, but her arms shook so much with the cold that she could barely hold them. Amber threw a handful of exploding marbles at the ice woman.

The woman laughed as snow and sleet flew from her outstretched palm. The marbles hit the cold and fell to the ground with a frozen thunk.

Celia punched the man's shoulder with all her strength. He didn't seem to notice. "Let us not tarry, my sweet Snedronna," he said.

The ice woman ignored him and windmilled her arms, throwing dark clouds into the air. They flew across the room and hovered above Amber's and Ruby's heads, raining down a steady stream of ice and sleet on the two hunters.

"Snedronna, let us leave now," the ice man said. His voice filled the air with a bitter cold that burned Celia's skin. "Remember this mission. Remember the big spell, and how our very existence rests upon our success. We must bring the doom girl to Madame Krawl."

"Just a moment—it won't take long for me to freeze them, sweet Snedron. A mere minute or two."

Amber and Ruby tried to scramble away from the deluge of freezing water, but the cloud moved where they did. The monsters blocked the door. The hunters gave up and huddled against the wall. Ruby was trying to open her bag, probably to get some new kind of weapon out, but she shook too much from the cold. Both girls gave up and hugged each other instead.

Snedronna laughed as she wiggled her bony fingers in their direction. Sharp, pointy icicles began to grow out of the wall, jutting out in all directions above the hunters' heads.

Celia tried to tell herself that Amber and Ruby deserved this, but a whispery voice filled her saying she had to find a way to save them. To try. Even if they had lied to her. Even though they'd just tried to hurt her, it didn't matter.

"Stay here," Celia whispered loudly. She closed her eyes and pretended she was saying a prayer out loud. "We have to stay here just a little longer. More hunters will be here any second," she lied. "Don't leave before the other hunters come," she whispered, and hoped the monsters would notice.

The iceberg arm wrapped tighter around her. "Come now, sister. Snedronna, come! Enough delicious fun. Madame Krawl awaits. We are not safely away yet."

The ice woman scowled. She threw gusts of icy air at Amber and Ruby, then swiveled away on her teetering heels and walked out of the painted room. "A pity—a minute more and they would have been Popsicles."

The ice man followed in her wake. Celia raised her head and watched Ruby and Amber from the vantage point of the monster's shoulder. The two girls sat motionless, drenched, shivering, and staring at her like they'd be haunted by the sight forever.

I saved you, she thought. You lied to me about being my friends. You attacked me, and I saved you anyway. I'm better than you are, she thought, but it held no satisfaction. All it did was make her colder.

The ice woman walked beside the man and studied Celia with her cruel light-blue eyes. "Madame Krawl sent everyone out looking for you today, doom girl, yet no one could find you. The others were too dumb to think to follow the hunters, but not us. And here you are, wearing a ward."

"It's a good one," the ice man added. "Clever. My mind cannot make a memory of you. I can't remember what you look like the moment I look away. But who needs memory when we have your body? Well done, Snedronna."

His sister laughed. The white puffs of her breath turned into ice crystals that fell with a tinkling sound to the ground.

"No, no, no," Celia whispered through chattering teeth as they stepped outside and carried her out into the street.

"Help! Someone help me!" Celia cried out.

They passed four adults who looked right through her. One of them crinkled up his forehead for a moment, squinting as though she was almost visible.

"Help!" she screamed louder.

He looked away.

No one cared. No one even saw her. To see me they'd have to see the monsters, too, Celia thought. She screamed even louder, just in case she could somehow break through their blindness. A kid, no more than eight, stood on the far side of the street and looked right at her. He turned and ran in the other direction.

"Quiet the doom girl. Her screeching makes my head ache," the ice woman hissed.

Bony hands clamped over her mouth. Celia's mouth went numb.

She felt her body being carried down stairs and looked up to see they were descending into the subway. Soon enough, darkness enveloped her.

23

THE LAST BIT OF WARMTH

The good part about the darkness was Celia didn't have to see the monsters. She could almost pretend she was somewhere else. Siberia. Antarctica. Outer space.

The bad part was the way it pressed in around her and felt like that nightmare where you were being chased and were just about to be caught. Except she was already caught, and the nightmare was strong and held on so tight that struggling was useless, begging did nothing, and there was no one to hear her scream. All she could do was wait for it to be over. Would it end soon? Or was this just the beginning of everything being terrible forever?

The monsters moved through the inky darkness of the subway tunnels with swift forward motion. They shed cold, and the shivering air sank all the way through Celia. Warmth felt like something that used to exist.

"Where are you t-taking me?" Celia asked through chattering teeth when the silence grew too huge.

"To Madame Krawl's domain. She's been looking forward to meeting you." Tinkling ice shards fell to the ground as the ice woman spoke.

"Why?"

"Orders," the ice man answered.

"Why do you t-take orders from her?" Celia asked. Bigs weren't supposed to get along. The hunters said they never worked together. "You l-let her boss you around?"

The ice man growled. Ice crystals blew against her numb cheek. "She will lead us to our triumph."

"You should be in ch-charge. Not her," Celia stuttered.

"Quiet, girl. You are the pawn—don't act like the queen," the ice woman snapped. "Perhaps we should maim you as a gift to Madame Krawl. A doom girl has no need for all four limbs, I've always thought."

A sharp sound echoed through the tunnel.

"What was that, my dearest Snedronna?" the ice man asked.

"Nothing, I am sure, yet let us hurry on to our destination and glory, sweet Snedron."

They moved swiftly on their long legs. Something else thudded through the tunnels, closer this time. Was the sound coming from up ahead or behind them? The echoing tunnels made it impossible to tell.

The monsters ran faster.

Celia stared into the darkness, seeing nothing. She wondered what they might fear. What could be worse down here than *them?*

Something hit the back of Celia's legs where she hung over the ice man's shoulder. All motion stopped with a lurching halt.

The ice man snarled. His muscles hardened beneath her as he tried to push through whatever they had hit. It didn't break but seemed only to tighten around him the more he struggled. He growled and tried to back away, but he couldn't do that, either. Despite the numbness in her fingers, Celia felt something sticky and warm. Once she touched it, her fingers adhered to it, strong as superglue. The more she moved her fingers, the tighter they bound. Before long, she couldn't move them at all.

Blinding white lights turned on, beaming from a subway train not ten feet in front of them. They lit up the white netting that lay stretched across the tunnel in a shimmering, complicated pattern. Celia followed the pattern and realized they were trapped in what looked like a huge spiderweb. Celia and the two monsters hung immobilized in it.

Celia squinted into the light and saw two figures standing near the train. The light made it impossible to see who or what they were.

Maybe being attacked by lying friends and kidnapped by ice monsters isn't going to be the worst thing that happens today, she thought. Celia tried to think of a way to escape, but she was too cold, and her mind felt slow and hopeless.

"Madame Krawl?" the ice woman called into the bright light. Her voice squeaked with uncertainty. "We were bringing the doom girl to you. We are your obedient servants. Always."

"Guess again," a girl's voice said with a giggle.

Celia gasped as the air grew suddenly colder. Sharp ice crystals poked the corners of her eyes.

The figures walked forward on the far side of the web. The bright lights blurred their features. One of them held an ax.

"You!" The ice woman hissed, "You'll suffer for this with unimaginable pain. We'll destroy you."

One of them—Celia thought it was a boy—muttered a couple of words and threw something on the ground. It flared with a brightness that fizzed across the tunnel floor.

The grip on Celia's body relaxed as the ice man sagged forward. His limp body was held up by the web. Celia lay trapped on his shoulder. The ice woman drooped and went motionless too. The air grew a tiny bit warmer—still frigid, still arctic, but better.

"You don't get to destroy anyone ever again," the girl whispered. "No more masters!" She ran forward with a serrated kitchen knife and started cutting the netting around the ice man's frame.

The boy used his ax to cut down the ice woman.

Celia squinted, but the light from the subway glowed behind them, and all she could see were dark silhouettes. They were kids, but that was all she could tell about them. Maybe, just maybe, this would turn out okay. That thought felt like the last bit of warmth, and if it went away, she'd die. She flinched as the girl started sawing through the webbing near her body.

"Careful," the boy growled.

"Chill," the girl said. "She's your special human friend, I get it."

"Shut up!" the boy snarled.

He sounded sort of like Demetri, but Celia wanted so badly for it to be him that she didn't trust herself.

The girl leaned close enough to Celia that she could finally make out some of her features. The girl's face was covered in black and white squares in a checkerboard design. She slashed her knife through the net and the ice man fell, along with Celia. She yelped, but her body was so numb with cold she could barely feel it. He lay across her, trapping Celia's legs beneath him.

"I'm Daisy," the girl said, kneeling down beside Celia. "We met before. On the roof. I dreamed about you. Remember? Hi."

"Hi," Celia said to the Little. This girl could destroy her in ten seconds. But if she wanted to do that, it would have already happened, right? Besides, she seemed to be saving Celia, not destroying her.

"Hold still. The last thing I want to do is touch you by accident," Daisy said.

Daisy held a plastic spray bottle up to the net. Wherever she sprayed, the stickiness melted away. In a couple of seconds, Celia was able to scoot out and away from the ice monster.

Celia got up with shaking legs. She turned to the boy. "Is that . . . are you . . . Demetri?"

"Of course." He tugged off his hat, and the outline of his horned head was silhouetted in the light. "We got to you as soon as we could."

"You saved me," Celia whispered. I shouldn't feel safe. I shouldn't trust them, she thought, as relief flooded her. The Littles probably just wanted to use her, like the hunters did.

Demetri finished tying up the ice woman's hands and feet with thick ropes. "The hearts, and then we get out of here," he said.

Celia swayed and shivered where she stood. She wrapped her arms around herself and felt fuzzy from all the cold.

The checkerboard girl knelt and ran her hands over the tied-up ice man's bony body, prodding and poking him. All she wore was a holey T-shirt and patched jeans, but the cold didn't seem to bother her.

Demetri did the same to the ice woman.

Celia rubbed her arms to try to bring warmth back into them. I'm going to be okay? she wondered. I'm going to be okay. Maybe.

Daisy yanked one leg of the monster's white pants up to his knees. Midway up his calf lay a pulsing bulge taped to his leg. The Little cut it off and held up a glass globe full of swirling flecks of snow on the inside. It throbbed in her hand.

Demetri searched the ice woman: turning her over on her side, looking in her shoes, and checking her hair. Nothing. Then he opened her white leather purse and found a matching throbbing snow globe.

Daisy handed him the ice man's heart, and Demetri held both of them, one in each hand. His fingers, tipped with black claws, squeezed them. Both Bigs let out gasps. "Neither of you will hurt anyone. Neither of you will tell anyone anything about Celia, Daisy, or me. Both of you will be bound to complete silence until I tell you otherwise."

The two monsters didn't wake up but muttered in their sleep, "Yes, master. Your will be done."

Demetri put the two matching snow-globe hearts in his backpack.

He stood and started walking back to the subway train, but Daisy stood over the ice man, staring down at his long, unmoving form. "He was Arcadio's maker. He froze off his toes, one by one."

"We have their hearts, Daisy. I'll make sure these two never harm anyone else," Demetri said.

She nodded but didn't move. "Is that enough? Shouldn't they suffer more?" She kicked the ice man hard in the side.

The ice monster growled but didn't wake.

"It's never enough," Demetri whispered. "You know that. But we need to get gone."

Daisy kicked the ice man again. "I hate him. And the monster who made him, and whoever came before that, and all of them all the way back to all the first monsters and Krawl." She wiped tears from her black-and-white face. "You'll let me squeeze their hearts, right? Whenever I'm in a bad mood, D?"

"Of course."

She kicked the ice man again and said to his limp form, "I plan on being in a bad mood all the time." Daisy turned and ran past Celia and Demetri. The Little swung herself up into the subway train.

Celia followed. Demetri walked beside her. His horns curled around his head. Half of his face was lit, the other lay in shadows.

24

INTREPID HEROES

Celia pulled herself up into the subway car and sat down on a plastic seat across from Daisy. The cold ached through every bit of her. She couldn't stop shaking. Demetri walked past them and disappeared into the cabin. The train rolled in the opposite direction from the tied-up ice monsters lying on the tracks.

Soft yellow lights shone along the subway's ceiling as the familiar motion of a train picking up speed took them through the tunnels beneath the city.

I got rescued, Celia thought, letting it warm her. She looked out the window and into the darkness. "How is this train moving?"

"Magic!" Daisy said. She jumped up and swung around one

of the poles, holding on with one hand and leaning away from it. Her checkerboard face grinned and showed off a set of black and white teeth rimmed by a white upper lip and a lower black one.

Celia hugged her knees to her chin and rubbed her hands together to warm them.

Daisy stopped spinning. "I've been dreaming about you, Celia. Every time I close my eyes." She stared at Celia's forehead as though it were filled with interesting things. "Weird, scraggly dreams."

Celia sighed and inched her knees in even closer. "Any idea what I'm supposed to decide?"

She shook her head. "In my dreams, you're always chasing me and you've got some serious speed. You run track or something?"

Celia shook her head.

"It's probably symbolic. Your destiny looms," Daisy said, and laughed like she'd told a joke.

Celia shivered some more. She had the feeling that if she thought too much about how she was supposed to be the one who would decide how all this turned out, then she'd break into a million pieces from the pressure. She decided not to think about it.

"So how'd you find me?" Celia asked. If they hadn't, maybe Krawl would have her by now.

Daisy pointed toward Celia's chest.

"My heart?"

"Your ward."

"Oh. Right." Celia pulled out the granite ward from beneath her clothes and ran her fingers over its smooth surface.

"Demetri felt your fear, and we followed it. It wasn't very specific: we had to guess which tunnel they'd take. We only had one stick-web. Good thing we guessed right, huh?"

Understatement of the year. "Yeah. Thanks." Celia thought about why they would go to the effort of saving her. No one is my friend. No one likes me, she reminded herself. "Good job catching the doom girl. Now you can use me however you want."

"Um . . . what?" Daisy asked.

"You want to control me, right?"

Daisy flopped down onto the seat across from Celia. "No. You were in trouble. So we helped you out." She shrugged and looked down at the ground. "People always think Littles are monsters, but we didn't choose to be this way. We can't help it. Sometimes we do something just because it's the right thing to do." Daisy wouldn't look at Celia. She played with her shoelaces, tying and retying them.

"Sorry," Celia said. "I didn't mean . . . it's just . . ." She swallowed. "It's hard to know if anyone is my friend or if all they care about is the doom girl thing."

"Demetri wants to help you. He doesn't want you hurt by all of this. Did you know he's been a little happier ever since you met? I didn't even know that was possible. It's nice to see him a little less sad."

Celia looked at the closed door to the cabin. She smiled, then shivered and frowned. Where was any of this going to end up?

"You're shaking all over. Because you're terrified of me? I won't change you. Promise. I'm all about the self-control." She put her hands in prayer pose, breathed deeply, and made an *om* sound.

"I'm really cold."

"Oh. Right. I can make a spell to warm you up, if you want. I bet I could figure out how."

Celia imagined spells catching on fire, exploding, or going wrong a dozen different ways inside the small train. "No thanks."

"Cold is all those two monsters can do, but they rock it, right? One time they froze my girl Spelunk all the way through, and we had to be careful when we thawed her."

"She didn't die?"

Daisy shook her head. Her short black-and-white hair spun out in a wild halo. "Littles don't get sick. Or age. Or die. Cut off an arm, and we'll regrow it. We're kind of awesomely invincible. Except for kids. Kids are our kryptonite. You smell, by the way."

Celia blushed. She probably reeked from being so scared.

"Like vanilla and moonlight," Daisy added.

Celia laughed. "You smell like saltwater taffy and the beach on a hot day," she admitted as she touched her own cheek. Her monster mark felt warm, despite the chill in the rest of her. "The ice monsters told me all the Bigs were searching for me."

"We've heard that too."

"So where are you taking me to keep them away from me?" Celia asked.

"Your home," Daisy said. "It's not the best, but no place is the best right now. We're going to set out a watch and try to keep anyone from finding you."

"Home?" If the Littles were planning on taking her there, they really weren't trying to control the doom girl. They were just trying to help her be safe. But then Celia thought about her apartment. The hunters knew where she lived. A Big had been on her rooftop. Demetri had left protection spells there, but it still didn't feel safe. "Home isn't where I should go," Celia whispered.

Daisy tilted her checkerboard face to the side and blinked. "There's not a lot of options: everyone is looking for you."

"If I need to stay hidden, there's one place the Bigs and hunters have never found, even though I bet they've been searching for it for decades."

Daisy blinked her large eyes and shook her head. "Is that a good idea?"

Celia breathed warm air into her hands. "I'm right though, aren't I? It's the one place I'll be hidden."

Daisy shrugged. "It has thousands of wards and spells to keep it hidden, but do you really want to be the first kid to ever go to the sanctuary of the free Littles? You understand what we are, right?"

It wasn't a great option, but it seemed better than all the others. "You are Littles, but you're all more than that. Right?" Celia said.

Daisy sat up straighter. She grinned. "We are. We so are. Okay, I'm going to go tell the boss there's a change of plans!" She bounded up and ran into the cabin.

The train kept moving underneath the city as Celia ached with cold and listened to the sound of Demetri and Daisy arguing. She couldn't hear most of their words, except for Daisy saying over and over again that Celia should be able to make her own decisions.

The train slowed with the hissing and screeching of brakes. The doors slid open and a musty rodent smell filled the air. Daisy and Demetri came out of the cabin. Demetri was scowling, but Daisy flashed Celia a thumbs-up. The Little took a flashlight out of her bag, and the beam of light danced over the tiled floor and benches of an empty subway stop.

"I don't think this is a good idea, Celia," Demetri said.

"It's the best place to hide," Celia countered.

Demetri sighed and nodded.

Celia followed them off the train. She recognized this subway stop. She'd been here before, on a day when she and her mom had gone to meet her dad for lunch. It had been filled with office workers and street musicians playing violins. Now the only sound was the *scrick-scrack* of rats crawling up the walls. At least

Celia hoped it was rats. When does life get to be normal again? she wondered as she peered into the darkness.

They followed Demetri to the elevator. He took out his yo-yo and pulsed it up and then down, closed his eyes, and whispered a word Celia couldn't hear. A throbbing purple light brightened the station for a moment before flickering out. Demetri pressed the elevator button. It glowed green. The doors pinged and swung open. "The spell will make the elevator work for about a minute, even though there's no power down here."

They got in. Celia stood against the back wall of the small metal box, keeping as far away from the Littles as she could.

Daisy pressed the up button twice and then the close-the-door button four times. The buttons flared with another purple light.

The elevator carried them down.

"Down?" Celia asked.

"We spent forever digging a hole beneath the elevator and swapping out some gears and pulleys to get it to do this," Daisy explained.

"One, two," Demetri counted in a quiet voice.

"Three, four," Daisy added. "Five!"

Demetri hit the red emergency button and the elevator came to a lurching halt. He worked his fingers in between the rubber stops of the doors and muscled them open. A squawking alarm sounded as the doors opened to a dirt tunnel dug through the earth. An underground breeze that smelled like dirt and metal blew at them.

"It took a long time digging this tunnel too," Daisy said.

Celia sighed. Another pitch-black tunnel. This one was about six feet tall and had uneven dirt-and-rock walls. A trickle of something wet dripped down from the ceiling as they stepped out in a single line. Daisy went first, dancing her flashlight around so Celia could see where they were going.

Demetri was the last one out. He reached around and pressed the emergency button again. The alarm stopped, the doors slid closed, and the elevator climbed silently upward.

"The secret tunnel of the Littles, in which our intrepid heroes rescue the doom girl from a fate of torture or worse," Daisy said, and giggled.

Demetri stayed silent, like a cold wind at Celia's back. She walked in between the Littles, and the fact that both of them longed to touch her and turn her into a monster loomed. Was this the right thing to do? She had no idea.

The uneven ground of the tunnel lay full of baseball-sized rocks, perfect for twisting ankles. Celia did her best to keep up with Daisy, who walked like the tunnel was as smooth as a sidewalk. The walls were slimy and gross, and Celia's hands got covered in mud every time she put out a hand to steady herself.

"You can't tell any of the Bigs about our tunnel, okay, Celia?" Daisy said.

"I never would."

"Or hunters," Daisy added. "Demetri said you like running with them. Why? I mean, it's good they fight the Bigs, but I guess you don't know what else they do, or you wouldn't hang with them, right?"

"I don't want anything to do with hunters ever again," Celia said. She remembered Ruby and Amber attacking her. The fact that they had done that ached through her, just as real as the cold. "I won't tell anyone anything, ever. I promise." Of everything she'd learned about the monster world so far, Demetri and his friends were the only ones who tried to never hurt anyone else. Besides, Demetri had saved her life twice now: once from the snakes, and most recently from the Bigs. She would never do anything to harm him.

The tunnel twisted and turned so many times that Celia lost all sense of direction. Finally, it ended at a brick wall with a metal ladder going up it. Daisy pulled herself up and disappeared through a small hole overhead. Celia followed and climbed. Soon the narrow hole surrounded her, scraping at her back.

"Keep going, Celia," Demetri whispered beneath her. "We're almost home."

25

THE SECOND RULE

Celia pulled herself out into a world of cement, light, and greenery. She blinked and squinted as she tried to make sense of this place. Warm, sweet air enveloped her.

"Our sanctuary," Demetri whispered, coming up and standing beside Celia. He chewed on his lip as she looked around.

It was the inside of a warehouse, with corrugated aluminum walls peeking out from beneath the thick vines that grew everywhere. Kiwifruit vines climbed up the walls next to fat pink hibiscus blossoms and red bougainvillea. Across the warehouse, garden plots grew where concrete chunks had been cut out of the floor. The bright orange of pumpkins grew next to stalks of corn and bean bushes. Up near the ceiling was a row of windows that streamed in weak winter light. It didn't seem like enough to grow the plants, not this time of year. Surrounding each garden plot sat little shacks and tents. Dozens of Little monsters worked at tables, walked along different paths, and watered plants.

Then the Littles, all across the warehouse, froze. They raised their heads and sniffed the air. Their heads swiveled, and each of them turned to look at Celia. They stared and smiled, because of what they were, and because of what she was. They all kept sniffing her scent as their smiles grew.

They stood and started coming closer over pathways covered with scraps of carpet and worn Astroturf.

Why did I think I should come here? Celia wondered. She stepped behind Demetri and eyed the passageway she'd climbed up.

They closed in on all sides. They had horns, claws, and fangs, or swirling skin and misshapen skulls, or forked tails, or bright-red skin. A few looked like Demetri—90 percent normal except for feathers for hair, or skin with a dusty metallic sheen. About a hundred of them gathered, and the air filled with a heady, impossibly delicious smell. Nothing that smelled that good could hurt her, right?

No. That idea could destroy me, Celia thought, even as all of her senses told her she was safe. She breathed in the summery-feeling air and noticed she had finally stopped shivering.

"You found the doom girl," a short Little with bright-pink eyes and pinker skin said into the growing silence.

"Yes. And all of you are tasked with keeping her safe. You can do this." Demetri gave them stern looks.

Some of the Littles looked down. Others licked their strange-colored lips.

"Of course we can do it," Daisy said. "Like the time Demetri took us all out on Halloween to test us being around kids."

"That was the best," said a girl with tentacles sprouting out of her head. "Remember how all those people gave us tons of candy because they said they'd never seen such great costumes before? Everyone could see us because they expected to see kids dressed up as monsters. It was fun, until . . ."

"Until Wallace attacked a boy," Demetri said. "He gave in and became evil." He looked out at all of them.

Celia watched a Little touch the sharp edge of her fang, and another pull his sleeves down over his bearlike claws.

A horned boy lisped, "We can put up a tent for her as far away from everyone else as possible. We won't hurt her."

All the Littles nodded.

Demetri looked at all of them for a long moment before nodding. "I will be watching each and every one of you. You all know the kind of magic I can do. Do not think you will go unpunished."

"We got this, D," a Little called out. The rest of them murmured and nodded.

Demetri looked toward Daisy. "You'll keep watch as well?"

"Of course."

Demetri walked to the highest hill in the warehouse, which was surrounded by grass and had a scraggly green tree at the top of it. He sat down and leaned against it. It was high enough that he could watch over everything from there.

"Class dismissed." Daisy made shooing motions toward all the Littles with flicks of her black-and-white fingers. "Let's get food," she said, turning her mismatched eyes toward Celia. "I could eat a hundred horses."

The Littles walked away along the dozens of paths that wound through the warehouse floor. Every single one of them kept glancing back at Celia with hungry eyes.

Celia followed Daisy down a carpeted path to a rickety picnic bench. Flowering nasturtiums grew up one side of it. A couple of Littles brought them bowls of food, and Celia had a moment's panic, wondering what monsters ate. She relaxed when she saw mashed potatoes, beans, and brown rice. Littles hovered around the table, pretending to be busy but obviously wanting to be near Celia. She glanced toward Demetri, who sat stone-still under the tree. He won't let anything bad happen to me, she thought. The last cold that had been lodged deep inside her belly began to thaw as Celia swallowed mouthful after mouthful of warm food. She scanned the warehouse, knowing this wasn't a place she could ever let her guard down.

Celia and Daisy ate, and Littles brought them more food—

caramel apples, fresh-baked bread, and a beet salad. Every time Celia looked around, Littles across the warehouse looked away. "Is this what you always eat?" Celia asked. Everything was fresh and homemade.

"This is our normal. We grow most of our own food, and Demetri makes us all be vegetarians. We've all taken oaths not to hurt anything ever, as much as possible. We have to learn to never take lives."

"Demetri says it, and everyone just obeys him?"

"Are you kidding? Littles travel from all over the world to meet him. Demetri's done what every monster and hunter says is impossible. Bigs don't own us, and we don't change kids. We're free." Daisy shoved a big spoonful of greens into her mouth.

"Free," Celia echoed. She wished everyone would stop looking at her like she was what was for dessert. "What else, besides being vegetarian?" Celia asked as she ate some beets.

"The first rule is that we run and hide from all Bigs. We all want to get our revenge on every single one of them, but we stay away. Fighting them almost never goes well. We're weaker than they are."

"But today . . . ," Celia began.

"Today was special, and we got to fight them to rescue you. I loved every second of it." Daisy spooned lentil soup into her mouth. "The second rule is we always help other Littles out, no matter what. We always rescue them when we can. We always share what we have and watch out for each other."

Celia liked that rule. She wished real kids had a rule like that.

A couple of demonic-looking Littles laughed nearby as they planted a row of seeds in dirt.

"And the last and biggest rule"—Daisy blinked her large two-toned eyes—"is we don't touch kids, not ever. Even if every cell of what we are tells us all the time that's what we have to do, we don't. Even when the urge to do it gets so big that it feels like the only thing in the whole world that we can do, we don't." Daisy's breathing went ragged.

Celia looked into the girl's eyes, and it felt like gazing down a thousand-foot well. The Little smiled and reached toward her.

Celia inhaled her beautiful smell and found herself leaning toward the other girl.

Daisy blinked and jerked away from her. She yanked her hand back. "Careful, Celia. Remember what I am."

Celia scooted away from her and nodded.

Daisy licked her lips and tried to smile. "So, it's neat here, right? When I first got here, I couldn't believe it existed. I couldn't believe I got away from my maker."

Two Littles with overalls and long messy hair that looked like seaweed walked past them. One had gray skin, and the other was covered in purple boils.

"Were you with your maker for a long time before you got here?" Celia asked.

Daisy stared into her empty bowl. "Yeah. My maker kept me on a short leash, for years. Like, an actual leash." She touched her neck.

Celia looked at Daisy's black-and-white checkered face and saw past the strangeness to a girl her age who'd been a slave.

"I'm . . . so sorry."

Daisy shrugged. "You want to know the worst part of it? For the first five years, I loved it. There's this yucky thing where at first all you want to do is serve your maker. But that was long gone by the time Demetri rescued me and brought me here. He almost got killed doing it, but Littles help Littles. I'm one of the lucky ones."

Celia looked over to where Demetri sat watching the world. He was a Little, but he was more than that too.

"So no one was free before him?"

"Sometimes, here and there, one of us would run away from our maker and not change into a Big. But no one knew how to make wards back then, so it was harder to hide. Bigs would always find the runaways. We're hard to kill, but it's not impossible." Daisy stared past Celia at some unseen memory.

"The world shouldn't be like this," Celia whispered. All around her, Littles who used to be kids sniffed the air and tried to pretend they didn't want to attack her.

"Right?" Daisy said. "And don't you wish you could go back in time and change the one moment that led to all this? It always starts with one thing going wrong. If I could go back . . . but there's that stupid rule of the universe that time only moves in one direction."

The one moment that changed everything? Celia thought about the piece of paper that had lured her to the hunters. But that hadn't been the beginning. No. The first thing was when she saw Demetri going up to the roof after the earthquake. If she hadn't seen him and followed, she would still be the old Celia, maybe. The lonely, bored, and safe Celia who spent all day at school wishing someone would notice her. Now the hunters wanted to control her, every Big in the city was hunting her, and she sat in the middle of a Little sanctuary where none of the monsters could stop staring at her.

Even if she could go back and redo the moment she made the choice to go up to the roof, she didn't know if she would. Life felt bigger now. Monsters were real, but so was magic. There were girls who pretended they were her friends, but there were also Littles willing to battle Bigs to rescue her. Monsters who vowed to go against their very nature, just to keep her safe. "Will you show me around the warehouse?" Celia asked. "This whole place seems really amazing."

Daisy grinned. "Sure thing, doom girl."

26

FILLED WITH PLAGUE

"Over there," Daisy said, and pointed. "That's our main money-maker."

Celia sat cross-legged on the picnic bench and felt the weight of food and warmth settle in her stomach. She looked at the table full of Littles working with screwdrivers, sandpaper, and saws. Celia couldn't tell what they were making. A tall boy with orange teeth smiled at her and put one of the objects on the ground. It began to roll toward Celia on long swirls of octopus legs that ended in wheels. It tipped over just before it got to her and lay toppled on its side with its wheels spinning helplessly in the air.

"It's a windup toy," Daisy informed her. "We make them and

sell them to fancy toy shops on the wharf. The money lets us buy the things we can't grow or make ourselves."

Celia grabbed it and looked at its underside. Its body was smooth, and she liked running her fingers over the curved dome of the glass top. As she inspected the strange object, Daisy explained how they made each one. The Littles took wine bottles from recycling bins, cut off the bumps on the bottom of them, and sandpapered the edges so they weren't sharp. Then they cut thin strips of sheet metal and wound them tightly together. The legs were made of thin wire from a straightened metal hanger. The wheels were pieces of cut-up bike tires melted back together. All of it was made from things they found around town.

Celia stroked the top of the toy like it was a puppy, then wound it up again and sent it back to the table of Littles working on them.

"Come on, I'll show you the rest," Daisy said. She stood and pointed to all the garden plots across the warehouse. "We use grow spells to have lots of veggies all year round."

Celia followed Daisy. They walked by the table where the Littles worked on the rows of windup sea-creature toys, and maybe Celia imagined it, but they seemed to lean toward her as she passed by. She held her breath as she moved as far away from them as she could without stepping into a vegetable patch.

Daisy led the way down a zigzag path made of red carpet remnants. They passed some Littles gardening, and others cutting up vegetables and throwing them into a pot hanging over a wood fire.

One Little wandered toward them, staring at Celia. He smiled and lunged toward her. Two other Littles ran at him and tackled him to the ground before he could reach her.

It all happened so fast that it was over before Celia could feel scared. A moment later panic flooded her. He had almost . . . he had wanted to . . .

She looked toward the hill where Demetri sat. He stood and glared across the warehouse.

Daisy gave Demetri a shaky thumbs-up.

The Little who had tried to touch her lay on the ground curled up around himself. He mumbled, "Sorry. So sorry. I didn't mean to. I wouldn't . . ."

The two Littles who had tackled him sat cross-legged on both sides of him.

Daisy took Celia on a wide path around him. A dozen steps later, Daisy whispered to Celia, "Don't worry about him. Nazreal's new and a little feral. He'll stay in his house the rest of the time you're here. If he tries anything again, he'll be kicked out."

"What would happen to him then?"

Daisy shrugged. "Let's not talk about the bleak stuff. Over here is our salvage." She pointed to a bunch of trash. It was the opposite of Dreck's filthy garbage. This pile was full of blue bottles, porcelain sinks, used clothing, and showerheads. Everything was arranged in tidy heaps. "We scrounge a lot to get by.

Everyone has to spend five hours a day working. Right now we all have to work ten hours a day, because of the spell."

"The spell?"

"It's really big. We'll get to that."

They walked by some rusty playground equipment: a swing set, a teeter-totter, and a merry-go-round being spun by some of the younger Littles who could run faster than normal kids. They screamed and held on as their legs and bodies spun out from the whirling center. Behind them sat a large metal cage, the size of a bedroom, with an open door and a thick lock.

Daisy stopped in front of the metal cage and hugged herself. "Sometimes some of us have to lock ourselves up when we're feeling weak. But unlike the hunters, we always let each other out. Anyway, check out Minerva's tail. Neat, huh?" Daisy pointed at a girl who hung on to the merry-go-round with her monkey tail. "Lucky."

"I'd want to glow in the dark," Celia said.

"No you wouldn't. George glows, and he was almost impossible to free because he's so bad at hiding. And anyway, don't ever wish you're one of us, Celia."

"I wasn't. I wouldn't. I meant, if I had to choose . . . it's kind of like that game where you pick what superpower you'd want."

Daisy frowned. "It's the opposite of having superpowers."

They walked by a Little with thorns growing out of her hands. She had a black eye.

"Hunters jumped her two nights back," Daisy said.

The words hung in the air as they walked around the edge of the playground toward the largest garden in the warehouse. It had long rows of vegetables and a grassy patch at the center. In the grass, a group of Littles sat lotus-style with their eyes closed in meditation. They chanted together. One girl's eyes snapped open and she stared right at Celia. She smiled with fangs jutting out of her mouth.

Daisy pointed out an area where three Littles sat listening at different tubes and pipes that came out of the wall. "We have spells to listen in on places across the city," Daisy explained. "And Bigs can talk to us through them, if we have their hearts."

They passed a row of tents and came to a place along the wall where at least forty Littles were hard at work building some kind of giant statue made out of chicken wire and papier-mâché. It was shaped like a man and rose up almost to the ceiling.

"Our big spell," Daisy whispered. Awe filled her voice. "Demetri's had us working on it ever since you told him Krawl was back. He says, if we do it just right, it will break the prophecy and destroy Krawl. I can't wait for it to be done."

That might make the doom prophecy go away? Celia stared up at the massive lumpy effigy. It stood on crooked legs and looked like it might fall over if you bumped into it. Ten Littles ran laps around its feet and touched the big toe on the right foot each time they passed. Others folded up newspaper squares into origami cranes and threw them into a hole in the statue's shin. Another crew of Littles stood on rickety ladders and painted symbols on its knees and thighs.

Celia was about to ask questions about how the spell worked, but she was interrupted by someone playing the drums. In one corner of the warehouse a girl with purple and pink skin held drumsticks and sat behind two five-gallon plastic tubs. She banged out a fast beat.

Two Littles ran over and grabbed more plastic tubs. They began playing too: not matching each other's beats exactly, but somehow sounding in sync. Celia found herself bouncing up and down to the rhythm.

A girl with bright-blue horns and a red dress joined them. She tucked a violin under her chin as she raised her bow and began playing fast and hard. Even her squawks sounded good as she filled up the spaces in between the drumbeats. Another boy joined with an old black-and-white accordion strapped to his chest; then a tree-gnarled girl with a large guitar sauntered over. All the Littles stopped what they were doing and moved toward the makeshift band.

Daisy swayed from side to side. "We do this every night. It helps keep us from . . . you know. We need it, tonight especially, to deal with you being here. Stay back," Daisy said, and walked toward the music.

Celia kept her distance as all the Littles gathered in a circle around the band. She walked to a small zucchini-covered plot where she could see them better. Demetri stood and came down from his hill to join them. Maybe he was the one who started singing, or maybe it was someone else.

At first the voices sounded like noise, but then Celia could make out a word here and there, and then more words as more voices joined in and repeated a chorus about being lost and wanting to go home. Littles shouted the words, jumped up and down, and threw themselves against each other as they danced.

The first song ended, and the next song had a harder beat that pulsed through the air. The writhing mass of Littles bumped into each other and sang louder. This song was about a ship filled with plague that was lost at sea. All of them yelled out the lyrics, and there was something beautiful and wild about it. The Littles moved together like one big monster made out of a hundred different parts.

They belonged together and took care of each other. A part of Celia longed to run forward and join them. The monster mark on her cheek throbbed. She stayed where she was and watched as each new song came faster and wilder than the last. Finally, after dozens of songs, the music slowed and a calm settled over the warehouse. Celia saw it on every Little's face. She felt it in the air and the way her own shoulders and arms hung loose. Even though it probably wasn't true, right now it felt like everything was going to turn out okay.

27

THE DIALECTICS OF MAGIC

The concert ended, and the Littles walked away in ones and twos. One of them walked by with a basket of green onions and stopped near Celia, avoiding eye contact. "Your tent is over there." He pointed. "I helped set it up."

"Thanks." Celia tried not to stare at the bony vertebrae that jutted out of the back of his neck.

Her tent stood apart from the others, sitting in the middle of some long grass. It was a small hoop-frame with duct tape wrapped around the crooked pole joints. One of the Littles had spray-painted onto the side of it: *Celia's Tent: KEEP OUT! Do Not Bother Her In Any Way Whatsoever. Do Not Do It!*

Celia walked to it, making sure to keep her distance from

every Little. She opened the tent, stepped inside, and zipped it back up. She ran her hand over the shadowed letters on the tent wall where the message had been spray-painted on the outside. She pressed her fingers against the thin material that separated her from the Littles.

Celia lay down on her back on top of the sleeping bag and felt the difference between here and her soft mattress at home. The lumpy surface of the grass pressed against her spine. Exhaustion washed through her, but she didn't close her eyes.

The air grew darker, and the light in the tent dimmed to a grayness she could almost touch. The Littles clanged pots, talked, argued, and laughed across the warehouse floor. Celia thought about all the other times in her life when she'd been scared at night, sure that a monster was out there, trying to get her.

Her body ached with exhaustion, and it felt good to be still, but her head kept going over the different parts of her day. She thought about her name being written all over the graffiti wall, and how the girls she thought were her friends had turned on her. She remembered being carried into the underground and how desperately cold the world had gotten. Her mind seemed to think that if she reimagined what had happened over and over again, she could make it all less terrifying.

It grew darker, and the noises outside died down until the only sounds were soft snores rising up from across the warehouse.

Celia stared at the roof of the tent. She imagined Littles

creeping toward her outside, with steps perfectly executed to make no noise. She imagined smoldering horns and red eyes, curled claws and jagged teeth. With just one lingering touch, she'd be ruined.

Demetri will protect me, she thought. But what if he crept toward her too? What if he led a horde of Littles to her? What if they were all about to tear her tent apart right now?

"I'm safe. I'm safe," she whispered, then stopped and listened to the silence. Every hair on her body stood on end, and she felt sure they were about to attack. Any second now. Any moment.

Celia sat up and unzipped the door of the tent. There was no way she was going to lie there and wait for something bad to happen.

A few yellow orbs hovered in the air, shining with spelled light. Pools of glowing orange smoke lay on the ground. Otherwise the sanctuary lay in darkness.

Celia searched for any monsters about to attack, but there was only stillness, along with the wonderful smell of a warehouse full of Littles. Celia squinted at an indistinct shape ten feet away. Was that one of them? No. It was just a small shrub. Her breath slowed as seconds ticked by and nothing happened.

Celia stepped out of the tent with bare feet. The air felt cool, so she reached back inside and slung the sleeping bag across her shoulders like a long shawl. Slowly, so as not to wake any sleeping monsters, she walked through the grass, and then along the soft, carpeted paths in between the mazes of garden plots and tents. With every step and inhalation of the sweet-scented air, Celia's night fears faded. They are Littles who don't attack kids, she thought. At least they try not to. Before long, without knowing where her feet were taking her, Celia found herself near the center of the warehouse, at the grassy hill with the tree at the top of it. Her bare feet sank into the loamy earth and soft grass as she walked toward the tree at its middle.

A few feet away from it, she heard a sigh.

"I knew you'd come here. It keeps happening, no matter what." Demetri spoke with a quiet voice. He leaned against the far side of the tree with his knees pulled up to his chest. He didn't look at her but held his yo-yo string stretched between his hands and rolled the plastic part back and forth.

She smelled his apple and sunlight scent and didn't know if she should turn around and go back to her tent.

"You might as well sit down."

"Did I do something wrong? I didn't mean to have to be rescued today." She sat on a patch of short grass near, but not too near, him. "I didn't want to need saving."

"You did nothing wrong."

"But you're mad at me?"

"I'm mad at the whole world, but not you." He leaned against the trunk of the tree and stared out at the warehouse. "I don't like how you and I keep meeting. It makes me think I have something to do with this doom prophecy, but I can't imagine what."

She nodded and looked out at the warehouse and all the little houses and gardens. "It's really neat here. You've built something amazing."

"We barely get by. We work all the time just to keep it going."

"I guess you don't like praise?"

He laughed, and it was the first time she'd ever heard him laugh in a happy way. She wanted to keep hearing it.

Celia ran her hands through the grass and plucked a blade out of the ground. She wound it around her finger like a ring. "Everyone here looks up to you. They love you."

"They like the idea of me. They like the hope I offer."

"You mean . . . it sort of sounds like you're saying you're lonely?"

Demetri looked away.

"It's okay," Celia said. "I know all about that. Ever since I came to this city, everyone has ignored me. Well, not since the earthquake, but before that . . . it felt like no one would ever see me again. Like whatever I was made of, it was all the worst things." It felt hard to say those words out loud. But also, as soon as she said them, she felt lighter.

Demetri nodded like her words made sense. "Can I tell you something, Celia? Something I never talk about?"

Celia nodded and scooted half a foot closer.

"This place, where I tell all my kind that they can be free? It's a lie to make them act better for as long as possible. Stories can do that, if we believe in them. I tell them they can be free of their fate, and that helps them wait longer before they steal the lives of more kids." His words hung heavy in the air. "But we are what we are. None of us will ever be free."

"If stories work, then maybe you should tell yourself a better one," Celia said. "You could be wrong. The world is always changing, isn't it?"

"It looks about the same as it ever was. When you're small and weak, others use you."

Celia sat with his words for a while. "Nothing stays the same forever," she countered. "Everything changes."

"Change is the one thing I can't do." He sighed. "Can I tell you another secret?"

She nodded. There was something about this grassy hill and the warehouse all around them that made Celia feel like either of them could say anything.

"Sometimes I want it to happen," he whispered. "Sometimes I just want to get it over with. Bigs don't feel bad about anything. The second I do something truly evil, it will change me. After that, I won't care anymore. Sometimes not caring sounds good. It would be a relief."

"But you won't. Not ever," Celia whispered.

"I will. Someday. But the longer I wait, the longer someone else gets to live a normal life. I'm not like Kristen. I'm nothing like Krawl."

"True. Even if I am extra awesome-smelling to you."

He groaned. "You shouldn't joke about that kind of thing."

"I think I need to joke about everything. I need for it all to be a little less serious or I'm going to be awake all night worrying about being the doom girl surrounded by monsters. Do you think it means I will bring doom, or that I'm doomed?"

Demetri shrugged. "Probably both?"

Celia tore up a clump of grass and threw it at him. "Thanks."

"It's just a word," he said softly. "Be yourself and you'll make the right decision."

He sounded so sure of that.

"There's one thing I've been wondering about. If we destroy Krawl, what happens?" Celia asked. "She's the first monster, after all."

Demetri chewed on his lip. "I have no idea. She's the mother of us all. If we destroy her heart, maybe . . ." He shook his head. "I keep having this feeling that everything is going to end soon." He shrugged and smiled.

Ending sounded like dying. Celia ran her hands through the grass. "Like, destroying Krawl will break the spell that made you all? What would that do to you?"

"I have no idea. I have been stuck like this"—he gestured toward his horned head—"for a very long time. Perhaps we will all disappear." He looked out at the rows of makeshift tents and houses littered across the warehouse floor.

Or one thing ending could mean new things starting, Celia thought but didn't say out loud. She yawned.

"If you really can't sleep," he added, "I can cast a spell to help."

"No thanks. The last thing I want to be is a sleeping princess in Little land."

"Oh. Yeah."

"But," Celia added, "if you did make a spell, how would you do it?"

"Humans can't make magic. You can *use* a spell, but never *make* one. Not since monsters were made."

"I know. But tell me anyway."

"Okay, to make a sleeping spell, or any kind of spell, I have to gather magic first. It's everywhere. It's in objects, or people, or even the air. You can collect it if you leave out bowls of tap water and sugar for a couple of days. You can store up magic in objects that have been prepared to hold it, or change yourself so you can hold more of it inside you. Animals lose magic as they age, but trees gain it, and rocks never change. I use magic from myself or inanimate objects only. I don't ever steal anyone's magic. Some monsters do, but I won't."

"Because . . ." Celia thought about that. "Because magic sort of sounds like life?"

"Yeah. Some people never see that, but it's true. Once I have magic, there's a hundred ways to make spells. They can be end-lessly complicated, but you only need three elements, really. It starts with wanting something and holding the image of it in your mind. Let's say I want this grass to grow." He ran his hands through the short blades. "In my head, I draw a picture of grass growing. I see it as clear as if it were there before me. Then I need an object." He took a round stone from his pocket and placed it on the grass. "Then I put the magic into the object—I do that by giving something of myself away. By making a sacrifice." He closed his eyes and smiled. The stone glowed with a soft blue sheen.

Celia watched the look of happiness on Demetri's face.

He opened his eyes and gestured at the grass. Without Celia noticing, it had grown a foot. Heavy stalks surrounded her and bent toward the ground.

"What'd you sacrifice?" she whispered.

"I gave it a memory I had of eating a hot dog. That's a small one. Bigger spells call for bigger sacrifices."

"So now you can't remember the hot dog?"

"No, I remember, but it's in black and white. It's lost all meaning."

"So, to make a spell, you imagine something happening, put it in an object, and sacrifice something," Celia said slowly, and then thought it through again, wanting to memorize the rules. "It sounds kind of easy."

"Not for you." He paused, gave her a funny half smile, and took a slim black book out of his back pocket. "You want to read this?"

"What is it?"

"My favorite magic book."

"You sure you don't need it?" The title, *The Dialectics of Magic*, was embossed on the cover in silver print.

"I memorized it long ago. It was the first book I ever stole from Krawl, and the one that eventually taught me how to banish her from the city."

"What did you sacrifice to get rid of her?" Celia asked. "It must have been a really big thing."

"The feel of sunlight on my skin. I miss warmth, but it was worth it."

Demetri held the book out, and Celia took it. He moved his hand away from her quickly, like she was fire.

"I wonder what big spell Krawl is making."

"It doesn't matter." He pointed to the looming man-statue in the corner. "Our golem will rise at noon tomorrow and lead me to her. With the golem's magic, I'll find her heart and destroy her." He added more quietly, "I'll try."

"Then why are you awake? Shouldn't you be sleeping before the big battle?"

"You're here." He sounded embarrassed. "It gnaws at me."

Celia thought that it must not be very fun to be Demetri. "Sorry."

"It helps to sit beneath this tree. You know what kind it is?"

Celia shook her head. She knew pine trees and palm trees, but that was about it.

"It's an olive tree, one of the ancients. When I first made this sanctuary, I planted it. It takes a hundred and twenty years to bear fruit."

Celia looked up at the tree's dark branches. She didn't see any olives on it.

"Give it sixty more years, and it will bear fruit. I plan to still be a Little and pick olives from it someday."

"A lot might be different by then," Celia said. "Robots, flying cars, and Littles who have learned how to never become Big."

"Maybe. I doubt it," Demetri said, but she heard the hint of hope in his voice.

"I'll come back here as an old lady and we can eat olives together. Deal?"

"No. All this ends tomorrow. Then you won't see me again," Demetri said, and turned away from her.

Celia sat there for a while trying not to feel hurt. She knew he said it because he liked her. Because he didn't want to destroy her. Even so, she wanted to keep being friends with him. Demetri might be strange and sad, but she liked him too. "If this ends tomorrow, mind if I stay up with you? Maybe we could talk about only good things. Maybe that could be its own kind of magic."

Demetri nodded. "I'd love that." He paused for a long moment. "We can't ever be friends, but know this, Celia. You are the first person in a century and a half who has treated me like I'm something other than a monster. All the Littles look up to me.

All the Bigs and hunters hate me. Thank you for seeing . . ." His voice trailed off.

"Who you really are?" Celia asked.

He nodded.

"Right back at you."

They sat near the olive tree and spoke in whispers as all around them the Littles slept. Demetri told Celia about a ginkgo tree on Charles Street that turned the brightest yellow every fall. Celia told him about the banana splits her grandpa used to make and how he'd always put extra whipped cream on hers. They talked for hours, and in the middle of a story Celia was telling about a time she'd gone kayaking down the Columbia River, she looked over at Demetri and saw that he'd fallen asleep sitting up.

She stood and started to head back to her tent. She walked through the grass and soft dirt to the edge of the garden, and then turned to look back at Demetri. Sadness covered his sleeping face.

Whatever I decide, Celia thought, whatever the doom girl does, I'm not going to do anything that could hurt him any more than he's already been hurt. That's what friends did for each other.

28

FASCINATING CREATURE

Back in her tent, Celia still couldn't sleep. She took a flashlight out of her backpack and began to read the yellowed pages of the magic book. The type was small and cramped, like whoever had written it had had too many ideas and not enough paper. She didn't know a lot of the words—alembic, quasimodic, alchymes— but the more she read, the more sense it made. It had a lot more details than Demetri had said, and described which different objects and sacrifices worked best for what kind of spells. Blood and memories of pain were good for hurting someone. A toy and the sacrifice of something precious were good for saving someone.

Celia grew sleepy but kept reading until her eyes refused to stay open. She slipped into sleep and dreamed of running fast while her fingers fused together and grew longer. Black feathers burst through her flesh, prickling her skin. She grew lighter, until she could bound forward and it would be a long second before she touched down again.

I'm becoming a bird, she thought, but when she jumped into the air, she fell to the ground in a painful jumble of feathers and breaking bones. She looked down at her body and saw not a bird, but a monster, wrong-angled and ugly.

She woke up panicked and confused, inside the blue world of her tent.

"Not real," Celia whispered, and breathed in the sweet-smelling air, so strong she could almost taste it. She ran her hands over her goose-pimpled arms and kicked her legs out of the sleeping bag. She felt sweaty and gross, and wished she could take a shower.

Outside the tent, sleepy voices called out to each other and the smell of fried potatoes wafted through the air. Someone argued with someone else, and others laughed.

Everyone stopped what they were doing and looked toward Celia as she emerged from her tent. Then they pretended not to be watching as Demetri walked toward her.

"Morning." His voice held none of the uncertainty from the night before.

How much does it hurt him to stand close to me? she wanted to ask. "Morning. How are you, Demetri?"

"Fine," he said calmly, but his breath came too fast and his eyes were dilated. Celia had read that when people were around their families, their pupils got big like that. She'd also read that cats, just before the kill, got dilated eyes too.

"I brought you clothes. You don't have to wear them, but I thought you might like to change."

He set the pile of clothing on the ground a couple of feet away, bending over stiffly and then stepping back.

"Thanks." Celia zipped back into her tent. Her old clothes smelled, and she was glad to get them off. She changed as fast as she could.

The pants were made of worn-down black corduroy with patches at the knees and hand stitches at the hem where the fabric had begun to wear away. The sweatshirt was thin but warm, and made out of a soft gold material with blue yarn sewn over the holes. Celia had never worn anything so used before, and she liked the softness of it. She liked how, when she came out of her tent, she looked like she belonged here.

But she didn't. Everyone watched her as she disappeared into the bathroom. When she came out, they stared at her as she took a path that wound through a garden with tethered pygmy goats. She came to the picnic table where Demetri and Daisy sat eating bowls of steaming porridge. Celia grabbed a chipped bowl and spoon and served herself some of the gray bubbling mixture from the iron pot hanging above a small campfire. Maple syrup and soy yogurt sat on the table, and Celia spooned some of each into her bowl.

As she ate, she thought about Demetri and his golem trying to stop Krawl today. She knew she would have something to do with it, and she was pretty sure that whatever it was would determine who won. It made her feel both excited and nauseated. Nothing bad will happen to any of us, she thought, like a prayer, like hope, before she began eating and wondering if siding with the Littles meant she'd already made some kind of decision. Demetri and Daisy watched her every move like she was a fascinating creature.

"So what's the plan today?" Celia asked.

"We wait until noon," Demetri said. "Then I wake the golem with some spells I've been preparing. He'll lead us to Krawl. With his help, I will find her heart and destroy it."

A Little ran toward them, clutching a sheet of paper to her chest with chicken-feet hands. She jumped over purple cabbages and pumpkins as she came close. She stopped before them, breathless and wide-eyed. "Soltminer whispered through the east tube that he needs to see you today," she said to Demetri. "Says he knows something about Krawl, and you have to hear it. He wants you to come and bring the doom girl. Says there's something he can only tell you in person." Her purple eyes flicked toward Celia as she spoke.

Demetri frowned. "How does he know we have Celia?"

The girl shrugged.

Demetri muttered in another language. "You should have asked him to give you the message instead."

"I tried! He said he'd meet you near Finney Port at the Crab Shack, and that you'd better come or you'll regret it. Then he was gone and I couldn't get him back."

The girl shifted from foot to foot as Demetri scowled.

"Thanks, Cathy. Good work," Daisy said.

The younger Little grinned and ran back to her surveillance station.

"A trap," Daisy said, and ate a lumpy spoonful of porridge.

"Perhaps." Demetri stared into his empty bowl. "Though it would be the death of him. We hold his heart. I'll do a quick meet-up and come back in time for the golem's awakening. Don't try to wake him without me: he'll be unstable until I put the last of the spells on him." He turned toward Celia. "You'll stay here with Daisy."

Dread pulsed through Celia. "Without you here, all the Littles, won't they . . ."

Daisy's checkerboard face went serious. "Celia's right. One of them will snap. They won't mean to, but they're already on edge with having to smell her lovely scent all night. I'm even feeling unsteady."

Demetri shook his head. "Every Big will still be hunting you out there, Celia."

"Bigs can't turn me into a monster. I want to come with you," Celia said, and then ate a big spoonful of porridge. It burned the roof of her mouth. "Besides, I have to decide something today."

She thought about the mural in the graffiti flats, and how it had both her name and Demetri's in it. "What if I miss out on my chance to do what I have to?"

Demetri sighed. "That's not how prophecies work."

Daisy shrugged. "Nobody really knows how they work. Also, I'm coming too."

Demetri glared at the world. "If you come, Celia, you promise to do everything I tell you, even if you don't want to? For safety."

Celia nodded.

Demetri closed his eyes and took a piece of smooth driftwood from his pocket. He placed it between them. The air turned electric, and Celia realized he was making a spell.

"I'll listen to you; you don't have to—"

Demetri opened his eyes. "Yes. You will listen. Sorry. I can't take any chances." Green light pulsed out from him.

The spell fell over her and crawled across her skin like a thousand wriggling ants. It lasted for a couple of seconds, then faded away.

"What'd you give up for that?" she asked.

"The smell of bananas," Demetri said. "I've always hated bananas. I can't remember why. Anyway, let's get gone."

29

OBSESSED WITH YOU

As they headed toward the hole that led out of the warehouse, Daisy ran over to a wooden filing cabinet and took out a box. She handed it to Demetri. He popped it open and took out a gray mushroom about the size of his fist. Soltminer's heart, Daisy told Celia. It pulsed and throbbed as Demetri put it into his bag. Daisy, then Celia, and finally Demetri slipped into the dark hole that led down to the underground tunnels.

Daisy turned on her flashlight. "Wonder what Solty knows. Wonder why he can only say it in person."

No one answered. Demetri led the way, taking them on a route through different tunnels than they'd come in on, as far as Celia could tell.

The darkness pressed in from all sides. Celia shivered, not because it was cold, but because of the memory of cold.

Daisy began singing about a bonny lass in a faraway field, and the people who lived underneath the hill. Her voice echoed back through the tunnels. At first it sounded like a song about fairies, but then the lyrics got stranger and stranger and it became about monsters who lured kids to their doom by disguising themselves as fairies.

They walked through a slimy tunnel for a long time before they came to a metal door blocking their way. It was covered with knuckles of rust and had a combination lock on it.

Daisy spun the dial.

"Freedom. That's the combination for all our locks, if you ever need it," Demetri whispered.

They walked through the door and up into an alley. Daisy held out her arms and spun around as she stared up at the blue-gray sky. Then she pulled the hood of her sweatshirt over her head and put gloves on, hiding her checkered skin and black-and-white hair. Demetri covered his horns with his hat. They looked like the homeless kids who hung out in packs and dressed like there were no new clothes left in the world and they had to patch and pin together everything that they wore.

"This way," Demetri said, and headed out of the alley. They walked by drifts of snakeskins and black garbage bags nailed to telephone poles with signs above them that read, *Skins*.

Celia checked her cell phone. She knew it wouldn't work, but she checked anyway. It was all the way dead now.

No one paid attention to Celia and the Littles as they turned down a street full of restaurants with writing on their cracked windows advertising the catch of the day next to drawings of happy-looking shellfish. The air smelled fishy and salty. Men and women stood out on the cracked sidewalks drinking coffee and talking to each other about how the port looked like it was going to be closed again today, because no boats could get in or out. A woman in an apron walked down the middle of the road carrying a wicker basket full of long loaves of bread.

When she passed Celia and her friends, the woman crossed herself and spit on the ground. The Littles hurried on.

"She can see you? She knows what you are?" Celia whispered.

"She senses us. She was probably attacked by a monster when she was young," Daisy said.

Demetri led them to a green door covered with a picture of a grinning crab sitting in a pot of boiling water. Inside, chairs lay thrown around the room and tables sat tipped on their sides. The walls were covered in pictures of cartoon crustaceans with forks sticking out of their heads as they sprayed lemon juice on themselves. It looked like the restaurant hadn't been opened since the earthquake.

"Soltminer?" Demetri called as they stepped inside. "You here?"

Something crashed and groaned from the back room.

They walked toward the sound, weaving in between the scattered chairs. A garlic-and-fish scent sat in the air.

"Solty?" Demetri repeated as they came to the windowless and dark back room.

A snarl erupted from a corner and something bared its teeth and hissed. Celia peered in, but all she could make out was something big and lumpy.

"You called us here," Demetri snapped. "Come out and tell me why." He pulled out the gray mushroom heart and squeezed it.

A groan came from the back of the dark room.

Demetri turned, righted a round table, and grabbed a chair. Celia found another and sat across from him. Daisy grabbed a stool, but instead of sitting on it, she started ripping off its legs.

"Daisy," Demetri warned.

The Little growled, "It helps. I can't stand being around *them*." She tore off the last of the legs, threw it on the ground, then sat down on a different stool.

The floor thudded as something lumbered out from the back room. A hunched-over beast, nine feet tall and covered in warts dripping green pus, emerged. He wore dusty jeans and a flannel shirt soaked through with his ooze.

"You brought the doom girl," he said in an oily voice as he licked his lips with a tongue covered in more warts. One of his eyes was swollen over, and he scratched at red welts around the collar of his shirt. He staggered to the table, sat down, and sneered.

His rotten-meat scent filled the air.

"Talk," Demetri ordered. He held the mushroom heart in both hands and his black claws tightened around it.

The beast flinched and coughed. He spit up a chunk of blue, claylike phlegm onto the table. The bad-meat smell grew stronger. Soltminer started poking and shaping the spittle with his warty fingers as he leaned toward Celia and grinned. "Good to finally see you, doom girl. Clever spell you wear. No wonder no one can find you." He laughed and his hot, foul breath hit her.

Celia leaned away from him.

Demetri squeezed the heart harder. "Speak now, Soltminer, or I end you."

"As you command, Little master." He snarled and coughed up more chunks of phlegm. His pocked hands kneaded and sculpted it as he scraped his own face to add pus to the mass. He worked on it until it resembled a snake coiled and ready to strike.

"Krawl's looking for the doom girl," the monster whispered. His hands let go of the phlegm snake, and it moved on its own as it slithered across the table toward Celia.

Celia jerked back from the table.

Soltminer laughed as his snake reared back and made a striking motion in Celia's direction.

"We know," Demetri growled. He squeezed the heart tighter. Blood bubbled up from the top of the mushroom and dripped down his knuckles.

The monster gasped and shivered.

"What does Krawl want with Celia?"

"She needs the doom girl to get *you*. The two of you are connected, but Krawl knows she can't find you. It's you your maker is obsessed with, Demetri. Always has been." Soltminer spoke in a grumble as he grabbed his phlegm snake and started kneading it in his hands again, spitting and rubbing more pus into it. "After all these years and decades gone, she's more powerful than most of us rolled together, and all she cares about is one stubborn Little? You worry her, Demetri. One of us shouldn't ever be so concerned about one of you." He coughed some more.

Demetri scowled and squeezed the heart mushroom. "You aren't telling us anything helpful. Why did you call me here? The truth this time."

The monster played with his phlegm ball as he talked. "Most of us don't care about a few Little ones getting free. We got our own hungers and desires to contend with." He licked his lips and fixed his gaze on Celia. "But Krawl? She thinks your pathetic resistance is changing the natural order of things." His hands let go of the phlegm. A hundred tiny gelatinous snakes slithered toward Demetri. "She's worried you're going to hurt all us Bigs."

Celia stared at the snakes, and the longer she looked, the more the snakes grew detailed and real.

"Parlor tricks. Look away," Daisy whispered, and kicked Celia's shin beneath the table.

"What's she planning with her big spell? Tell me something useful and specific, or I end you." Demetri poked the mushroom heart with a sharp black claw.

The monster yelped.

Soltminer rubbed his swollen eye. "Fine. Here's the truth of it." His hands grabbed the mass of phlegm and his fingers moved fast, kneading and sculpting the rubbery snakes. When he let go of it, he'd sculpted it into an image of himself in miniature—tied down, bleeding, and screaming. It was so realistic Celia leaned toward it to see the details. Soltminer whispered, "Krawl told me I had to lure you here and trap you, else she would kill me."

With a sudden motion, the beast's tail whipped up from behind him and snatched the heart from Demetri's hands.

Demetri and Daisy froze for half a second as Soltminer stumbled away from them, laughing and showing off rotten teeth.

Daisy's lips peeled back in a grin as she pulled a knife out of her pocket and jumped to her feet. She danced toward the monster.

Demetri reached into his pocket and threw something at the monster's face.

Soltminer roared as white light exploded and danced across his eyes. His eyelids snapped shut and he didn't seem to be able to open them again.

Celia got up too. She didn't have any weapons. She threw the nearest chair at him.

"Celia. You have to leave. *Now*," Demetri called out. He kept his eyes on the monster but pointed at her and then the door. Celia grabbed another chair and threw it, even as her feet started to back toward the door. She wanted to yell at Demetri that she would stay and fight, but her body responded without her will, helpless to do anything but obey Demetri's binding spell. Her muscles and bones made her walk away. She clenched her teeth and growled with frustration.

"Leave and don't come back," Demetri ordered. His words snapped through her spine and quickened her feet. She turned toward the door.

Something smashed to the ground behind her. Daisy yelped with pain.

Celia wanted to turn around and at least make sure she was okay, but Demetri's spell pulled her forward.

"This will be the end of you!" Demetri yelled at the monster.

Something else crashed.

The monster roared. "Don't count on it. Madame Krawl will be here soon enough!"

"Let her come," Demetri growled, and then yelled, "Run, Celia!"

The spell jerked her forward. Celia opened the door and ran.

30

LIKE FLYING

There's a way of running that's so fast it's like flying, with feet just accidentally hitting the ground. Celia flew down the road while her mind reached back toward the empty restaurant where Demetri and Daisy fought. She ran one block, and then two more, before she was able to slow down and look behind her. If she concentrated and clenched all her muscles, she could force herself to walk, not jog.

I need to go back to them, she thought. Demetri and Daisy were trapped. Krawl was coming for them. But no matter how she gritted her teeth and stomped her feet into the ground, she couldn't make her body turn around. The spell dragged her forward and away from them.

The streets were mostly empty around this part of Finney Port, but an old woman in dark glasses hobbled down the road. She paused and leaned on her white cane as Celia passed. "Are you troubled, child? Do you need help?" she asked with a watery voice.

Celia didn't know how to answer that as she hurried on. From somewhere many blocks behind her, a scream pierced the air. Was it Demetri? Daisy? Or, hopefully, the monster?

Another block gone, and she tried with all her will to turn around again. And for half a second she stopped walking, but then her body propelled her forward.

The frigid morning air seeped through her clothes, and Celia drew the soft hood of her Little sweatshirt over her head. Where should she go now? The safest place was probably back to the Littles' warehouse. She laughed. The safest place was the one full of Littles who could turn her into a monster with one touch? Great.

Or there was the cathedral. The hunters would show up there eventually. But would they help her or hurt her? Maybe, since she'd escaped the Bigs, they would be nice again. Or maybe they'd force her to eat their spelled sleeping coin.

So that left one place to go. Celia walked fast—she couldn't help it. She went out of the port neighborhood and through a fancy, hilly neighborhood called Green Slopes and then through downtown. Celia felt tiny as she walked between the giant office towers where scattered shards of mirrored glass littered the ground. The roads were buckled and curved. Celia passed blocks of ruined roads clotted with white snakeskins. She walked until she stood in front of her apartment building.

She looked up at the windows of her living room. Someone had pulled the curtains closed. She knew she'd left them open.

What if Celia's parents had found a way home? What if they were up there right now waiting for her, and when she opened the door she could get to be a kid again? She could tell them everything, and they would help her figure out the right things to do. They'd figure out a way to keep everyone safe.

Celia ran up the seven flights of stairs until she stood, breathless, in front of her door. It was open a crack, and that had to be good. Except . . . the dead bolt was busted and the door was tilted off its frame. Maybe her parents lost their keys and had to force their way in?

"Mom? Dad?" Hope fluttered in her chest as she pushed the door open. Unease gnawed at her belly. What if it wasn't them?

"Celia!" said a familiar voice. "You're back!"

31

SILENT WORDS

Ruby jumped up from the couch and faced Celia.

Amber walked out from the kitchen, holding a dish in her hands.

Celia's hands curled into fists as she stepped away from the hunters. She looked for something she could grab and fight them off with.

Both girls came closer.

Celia looked around for her parents. They weren't here. Of course not. She'd wanted to see them so bad.

"I thought I'd never see you again," Ruby whispered, and ran a hand through her purple hair. She bit her lip and shook her head.

"I thought you'd died. I thought the Bigs had taken you and

killed you in some awful way," Amber said, and burst into tears. "I feel so guilty, Celia. I'm sorry. We've been waiting for you all night and day and we were both sure you weren't coming back, but we couldn't leave because that would mean giving up hope." Amber put down the plate and took off her glasses. She mopped her wet face with the back of her sleeve.

"You should feel guilty forever," Celia said. She folded her hands over her chest. "Liars. Traitors."

"We deserve that," Ruby said. "That and way more. But we've changed. The Council of Elders didn't like hearing that if we found you again, we wouldn't hurt you, no matter what. But that's what we told them."

"That's so nice of you to not be willing to put me in a coma for a second time," Celia said. Whatever they said to her, how could she even trust they were telling the truth? "Leave. Both of you."

Neither girl moved.

"The Elders kicked us out of the hunters. They said real hunters do whatever is necessary. But we said no. We couldn't hurt you," Amber said.

"You would have, if the monsters hadn't broken down the door and attacked us."

Amber hung her head. "Maybe. I'm sorry."

Celia walked past them and sat down on the couch. She folded her arms over her chest and wished they would go away.

Both girls came to stand in front of her.

"You don't believe us, do you?" Amber asked. She pushed up her glasses and rubbed the scars on her arm. "I get it, since we lied about the other stuff."

"From here on out, I don't lie to you anymore. And I'm never hurting a kid for them, ever again," Ruby said.

Celia didn't have any magic spells or secret way of seeing if they were telling the truth. "If I told you to go away and never come back, would you?"

They nodded.

They'd cleaned her apartment while she'd been gone. Pictures were hung back on the wall, all the broken things were picked up, and they'd put every book back on the bookshelf. But everything was in the wrong place, and even if it had been the exact same, nothing would ever be normal again.

Celia closed her eyes and thought about Demetri and Daisy fighting Soltminer and Krawl. What was happening with the two Littles? Had the fight ended by now? Who had won? She wanted to run and retrace every step back to the restaurant, but just thinking that made the binding spell lock her joints and stiffen her muscles.

Amber sat down cross-legged on the carpet. Ruby perched on the love seat. Both of them watched her like they expected something from her.

"What?" Celia asked.

Ruby leaned forward. "We were so sure you were dead. How did you get back here? How'd you get away from them?"

Amber ran her hand over the coarse fibers of the carpet and added, "Good job, however you did it."

Celia bit at a hangnail on one of her fingers and wished she could trust them. "I just did."

Ruby studied Celia. "You're dressed different."

Amber sniffed the air. "And your clothes smell . . . sweet."

"No they don't," Celia said.

Ruby inhaled and frowned. "You were with a Little long enough to change into their clothes? How are you still human?"

Celia glared at both of them. She didn't want to give any of the Littles' secrets away. "After I was attacked by you two, Littles rescued me down in the subway tunnels."

"Littles kidnapped you, and then dressed you and set you free? That would have to mean they didn't have a Big who controlled them," Amber said. "How'd you keep them from changing you?"

"They *rescued* me."

"Tell us everything," Ruby commanded, and then added, "Please? I'm so curious."

Celia wondered what lies she should tell them. There was no way she was going to tell them about Demetri and the sanctuary. There was no way she was going to tell them about any of it, she decided. Celia wasn't going to say anything, but then she discovered there was something she wanted to say. "You know how much it hurts to have friends betray you? To find out they were just pretending to like you?"

"We lied about some things, but not everything. I always liked your stubborn self," Ruby said gruffly.

Amber added, "I liked you too. A lot. It made sense at the time that we should keep an eye on you, though. Sorry."

Celia looked at both girls and a strange thought occurred to her. Maybe they *should* keep an eye on me. Maybe I've been spending too much time around monsters and when the moment comes, I'll make the wrong decision, whatever that means. "So you two are really solo now?"

Amber nodded and wrapped the afghan Celia's grandmother had crocheted around herself. "For now. The hunters will probably let us back in when things cool down."

Ruby drummed her knuckles on the coffee table. "Whatever. What do we need them for? We can fight Bigs on our own. So what happened to you, really?"

Celia still didn't owe them a story, but she took a deep breath and started telling them as much as she could about getting rescued, without telling them it was Demetri and that he had a secret Little sanctuary. She had promised she wouldn't tell anyone about it. Celia told them she'd slept in an empty subway tunnel with two other Littles who were good at self-control. She told them that there was a rumor about Littles making a big golem spell to fight Krawl. Just as she was getting to the part about going to the restaurant and finding a Big, Ruby interrupted her.

"Who?"

"Soltminer."

"I mean, who were the Littles who nobly protected you and were so good at self-control that they could spend most of a day and a night with you and not attack you?" Ruby focused her gaze on Celia.

"Yeah," Amber said. "Most Littles would last about five minutes, tops."

"They were no one," Celia said quickly. "They were the most average Littles ever. I didn't even really catch their names or anything."

Ruby narrowed her eyes and stared at Celia for another long moment. Then she grinned. "You found Demetri, didn't you? He's real, isn't he? No other Little I've ever heard of has that kind of self-control."

"Promise you won't hurt him," Celia said, and then winced as she realized she'd just admitted the truth.

Amber shook her head. "Hurt him? No one has ever been able to find him. He's some kind of master magician, right?"

Celia shrugged. She didn't want to be talking about this. Hunters hunted Littles. They put them in locked cages and never let them out.

"He really didn't attack you? Not once?" Ruby said.

"Not just him, either. Demetri teaches other Littles how to stay in control."

She expected the hunter girls to argue with her. They both looked thoughtful.

"That's . . . amazing," Amber said. "If we could join up with them, we might actually have a chance to stop the Bigs in whatever they're planning."

"You'd really . . . work with a Little? Even though you hate them?" Celia asked.

Ruby frowned. "I just hate what they do. If they didn't attack kids . . . tactically, having someone on our side who could make spells whenever they wanted? That would change the game."

Something white caught Celia's eyes as it fluttered down outside the window. In the gap between the curtains, snow drifted down. But it was too warm for snow.

Celia walked to the window and pushed the curtains open.

The white stuff drifting through the air came down in flat strips and blew sideways in the wind, landing on the sill. On the strips there were black markings that looked like . . . writing?

Celia opened the window and grabbed a handful of the white stuff. It had the grainy but smooth texture of paper. She carried it to the coffee table.

Some of the strips were yellowed and brittle, while others were the fresh white of a new book.

"*The girl didn't know,*" Amber read out loud, grabbing one of the slips.

"*The boy was doomed,*" Celia read off a different piece.

"Books? It's raining shredded books? Beats snakes, I guess," Ruby said.

Outside, the falling whiteness grew thicker. The building across the street became invisible in the deluge.

"*The city will fill with silent words and the girl will decide,*" Amber read off another slip of paper.

"The last part of the prophecy," Ruby whispered. "We have to get to the cathedral and meet up with the hunters. I don't care if the council says we're out. We have to get them to help us destroy Krawl before she finishes this huge spell. It's going to take all of us: Littles, hunters, doom girl, whatever."

She said it like they could just go out and get it done, easy. But Celia didn't think whatever was coming would be so simple.

The end of the doom prophecy was here, and doomed things never ended well.

32

TROUBLE

They put on hats and buttoned their wool coats all the way up before leaving the apartment. Celia wasn't sure she wanted to go to the cathedral and be with hunters, but Ruby was right: they needed all the help they could get. And being surrounded by trained fighters sounded like a better idea than being alone right now.

"Strange weather," one of Celia's neighbors said. The middle-aged woman stood in the hallway wearing an old bathrobe as she stared out the window. "I've got extra canned food—you kids need any?"

"No."

"Stay indoors today," she whispered. "Wait until the strange things pass. That's what we always do in Youngstown." She pulled her robe tightly around her.

The three girls scurried past her and down the stairs. When they got to the foyer, the paper storm swirled and blew against the glass front door.

Ruby opened the door and a muffled silence entered the hall as bits of whiteness blew in and settled on the carpet. Ruby put her hand out into the storm. In a couple of seconds she held a handful of paper and threw it at Amber and Celia. It fell apart into a hundred pieces that fluttered to the ground.

Amber held her hand out to Celia. "Let's not get lost. Ever again."

Celia looked at her hand. "You trying to make sure I don't sneak off and decide things that you don't want me to decide?"

"Maybe. A little bit. Sorry. Is that awful?" Amber asked.

"Yeah."

"When all this is over, I'm going to prove I'm really your friend," Amber said. "I don't know how. But I'm going to be there for you, in a real way."

"Okay," Celia said, and grabbed her hand. The storm was a wall of white paper, and she didn't want to be alone in it.

They stepped outside with Ruby leading the way and Amber in the middle. The silence was so complete that it felt like deafness.

"Hello," Celia said, just to hear herself speak. Bits of paper clung to her lips. She pulled her coat collar up over her nose as black text swirled by in all directions. Most of it was too small to read, but Celia could make out a few words as they floated by.

Going.

Walk.

Stormy weather.

Amber's hand tugged her forward inside this blindingly white world. How was Ruby navigating through it? Celia couldn't see her own feet, let alone the road.

She squinted to keep the paper out of her eyes. With every breath, she inhaled the scent of a library. Her feet slid over the growing mounds of paper, and each step was uneven. She lurched forward.

Demetri.

The word floated by. Maybe she'd imagined it?

Demetri.

It flashed again on a slip of falling paper.

There are a million Russian books with that name, she told herself. Maybe these were the pages of classic novels. She'd heard of snow blindness. Maybe this was some sort of word blindness, playing tricks on her.

Demetri hurting.

The words flew by, written in bold black letters.

She tried to grab it, to hold the proof in her hand, but it swirled away, one piece among thousands.

Celia's eyes streamed tears as she tried to read other messages in the storm. Clots of paper stuck to her cheeks.

Demetri

Trouble

Trouble

Demetri

Her friend's name floated by, and Celia tried to catch it.

Amber's fingers jerked forward and slipped out of Celia's hand. Celia reached for her, but all she touched was more paper. Her arms groped into the downpour. She ran forward. Her foot caught on a bump in the road, and she fell.

"Amber! Ruby!" she yelled. Paper coated her lips and tongue.

Silence. Celia got up and walked, sweeping her arms in wide circles and yelling out for the two girls. The more she moved, the more she knew she wouldn't find them.

"I'm alone," she said, but could barely hear her own voice. The world, in every direction, was a downpour of silence.

Celia

A piece of paper drifted by, and this time she snatched it from the air and held on to the bit of proof. She stared at her name, written in bold letters. On the other side it read, *Demetri captured*.

Doom

Doom

Doom

The words drifted by, and she walked in the direction those

words came from. *I'll save him. If he's in trouble, I'll find him and save him.* She followed her name, and Demetri's, and when they came from the right, that's where she turned. There must have been cars, lampposts, and fire hydrants on the road, but Celia didn't run into any of them. She walked like the whole world only existed a couple of feet ahead of and behind her. The bits of paper led her forward, and on she went, one step at a time.

Her feet stumbled over some steps. She climbed their slippery, paper-covered slope and came to a red door.

Celia.

Doom.

Celia.

Bits of paper with her name on it blew against the door, held there for a moment by the wind before dropping to the ground.

Messages falling inside a magical storm had led her to this house. Someone wanted her here.

There were two great magicians in the city: Demetri and Krawl. Which one had called her here?

Demetri

Inside

Trouble

Celia spit out bits of paper that floated into her mouth and closed her eyes against the overwhelming whiteness. She searched for a plan, for any idea of what she could do to protect herself and her friends from anything bad that might happen.

She stood with her eyes closed for a long moment, then opened them and knocked on the door, because she couldn't think of anything better to do.

33

THE VICTIM

Wisps of paper blew against the door.

Enter

Enter

Enter

Celia found the doorknob and turned it. The door opened, and she stepped into a room full of the smell of apples and sunlight, carried on warm air. Demetri was here, somewhere. She had to find him.

The dimly lit room flickered with a dying fire in a fireplace that gave everything an orangey glow. The hardwood floors and the faded blue-flower walls reminded her of her grandma's house. Celia blinked and saw after-images of falling paper as she tried to figure out what to do next.

"Cookies?" a voice called out, and a door opened from a kitchen. The smell of cinnamon, sugar, and something like moldy potatoes and turned milk wafted into the room. An elderly woman with a round bun and dark sunglasses walked toward her. "Hello, dear. Cookie?"

"Uh, I'm sorry to barge into your house. I thought . . ." Celia squinted at her. She'd seen the old blind woman before: sitting in an apartment window after the earthquake, walking down the street after the night of snakes, and walking toward the restaurant when Demetri had been attacked.

"Don't be silly, Celia. We've been waiting for you. The storm brought you, just as planned." Her face crinkled up in a smile, and she pushed a gray strand of hair away from her face. She called out, "Your doom girl is here and she's lovely, Demetri."

Someone groaned. Celia turned toward the living room. Framed pictures of smiling kids hung on every wall. Polished sports trophies lined the shelves, and everything about this house was like a grandma's house, but there was something fake about it, like maybe it was too perfect. Celia stared at the blind woman and wondered who she really was.

A groan, louder this time, came from the living room. Demetri's horned head poked above the back of a big red couch.

"Demetri!" Celia ran to him.

He sat perfectly still with his fingers clutching the edges

of the seat cushions. His eyes tracked Celia, but nothing else moved.

"What did you do to him?" Celia turned to the beaming grandmother who'd come around and stood in front of the fire with her plate of sugar cookies held in one palsied hand.

"Sit, dear. I'll tell you a story."

Celia stepped toward her.

The woman tsk-tsked and flicked her wrist. Celia's body rose up from the ground and flew backward a couple of feet. She sat on the couch beside Demetri. Her body sank down into the soft cushions.

"Always respect your elders, dear. Kids these days."

A line of sweat ran down the side of Demetri's frozen face.

"Krawl? You're Krawl, aren't you?" Celia asked.

The old woman took a hobbled step forward. "Yes, dear. Those brave enough to speak my name call me that. How lovely to learn that you are brave. Or are you foolish? We shall see. Cookie?" She held out her plate full of white cookies dusted with sugar.

Celia glanced behind her at the door, then at Demetri's too-still form.

"You're thinking of escaping? After all I've done to bring the two of you together. I wonder, in that weak and fluttering human heart of yours, do you still hold hope? How sweet. Do you like stories, dear?"

I'll run, Celia thought. I'll grab Demetri and not touch any of his skin and run. She slid forward to the edge of the couch. I can move faster than her, she thought, sizing up the old lady.

Krawl tsk-tsked and flicked her wrist again. Celia's body slammed back into the couch, harder this time. "I asked if you like stories. But of course you do. All children love a good tale. Once upon a time there was a troubled Little monster named Demetri. He was different from all the other Littles, in that he wasn't very bright and liked to play pretend, even though he was far too old for it. He thought that Littles should run free and do as they pleased. He hid these thoughts from his maker, who trusted him to read aloud her books of magic." Krawl tapped her glasses and pushed them down her nose. Where her eyes should have been, her skin stretched flat from cheek to eyebrow.

Demetri whimpered.

"The old woman's other senses more than made up for her blindness, but for book reading, she needed her slave's help. The stupid boy was good at memorizing and practicing magic while she slept. One day, he rebelled." Krawl stepped forward and leaned over Demetri until her face was close to his. "I'd forgotten the lovely smell of your fear, child."

"He outsmarted you," Celia said. "He was a better magician than you could ever be."

Krawl snapped upright and smiled. "He stole some of the

best magical books in the world and, with knowledge in them, banished me from this city. Then he began to build an army of foolish Littles, tricking them into believing they could be free. His fairy tales spread across the world, and the name Demetri became a name of hope. Imagine, such a small, pathetic boy meaning anything. More and more slaves slipped away from their makers. They decided they would resist their nature. They came together and hid from us. You know what a creature who resists his nature is called?"

"A hero," Celia said. "A savior."

"An abomination," Krawl answered. "A cow who tries to hunt. A snake who tries to walk. A Little who believes he never has to grow up. The lies Demetri told spread throughout the world, as did his hiding spells."

"Good," Celia whispered. She launched herself off the couch and ran toward Krawl, but the old woman flung her back onto the couch with the flick of a crooked finger. Celia hit the couch hard. Her head snapped back. She gasped with pain.

All around them the photographs of smiling kids watched, looking like they enjoyed this.

"Soon there were fewer Big monsters being made, because Demetri convinced Littles it was wrong. Evil. Over time, with hunters hunting us down, our numbers dwindled across the world and there were fewer of us. In some places, we were even eradicated."

"Good," Celia said again.

Krawl swiped her hand through the air. Invisible nails scratched Celia's cheek. She gritted her teeth as blood trickled down her face.

"Bigs fought back. We made glorious examples of any Little rebels we found, but there was always Demetri out there. For every year that I was banished, the legend of Demetri grew."

"Monster," Demetri croaked. His jaw muscles bulged as he struggled to speak.

"Yes, dear, that is what we are. That is all that we are and we shouldn't pretend otherwise." She sneered at Demetri. "It took me a long time to figure out how to come back to this town—how to break your banishment. Did you know I destroyed two bird species just to examine your spells clearly? Other monsters helped me. We couldn't have you in the world. Even though I care little about any of them, I united them to pool our powers together. To end you, Demetri, dear. Or else we might someday face extinction."

Celia glanced toward Demetri. His eyes, trapped in his frozen face, looked furious.

Krawl touched Demetri's chest with a bony finger. "And here you are."

Demetri rocked backward, howling in pain.

"Stop it!" Celia yelped.

Krawl watched him for a long moment and then touched him

again. He went suddenly still and silent.

"He's stronger than you are. Better than you will ever be," Celia said.

"He was merely more clever for a short time. But I've bested him, ever since the night of the earthquake and the beginning of the largest inevitability spell ever cast. He met you that night, didn't he, Celia? He touched you soon thereafter, yes?"

Celia felt the blood drain from her face. Her hands and feet went cold. An inevitability spell? What was that?

"I fell. He touched my cheek. By accident." She tried to get up from the couch again.

Strong, invisible arms wrapped around Celia and held her down.

"You had to fall, doom girl, and he had to touch you. That's what the spell did. I didn't need to break any of his wards to set it in motion. I didn't even need to find him. The very air of the city enveloped everyone, but only worked on him. On the night of the quake, he would inevitably meet someone he would change, and you were in the wrong place at the wrong time." Krawl's shrunken form swayed with pleasure.

Celia flinched and stared at Krawl as her words sank in.

"Did you think you were special, Celia, dear? Did you think that was why we searched for you? Why psychics saw you and Littles dreamed of you in their nightmares? No. Not special. You are the victim, the unfortunate one. You were merely the closest child to Demetri when the spell hit him. That's all you are, doomed girl."

So that was what it meant. Celia wasn't supposed to save the city, or anyone or anything, from doom. Celia was *doomed*. Celia sat next to Demetri, just as frozen as he was.

She hadn't even wanted to be the doom girl at first: hadn't even believed it for a while, but then, part of her had thought she *was* special and that she could do something good.

I'm nothing. Just the girl who was in the wrong place at the wrong time. Just doomed, that's all.

What would Demetri think of her now? His still form was impossible to read.

"And the next part of the spell, the snakes? They brought you together again, for a longer period of time, yes? He should have changed you then, but Demetri was too strong and resisted. Anyone else would have fallen, but we had to make the paper storm—the end of the spell that would drive you both inevitably to me. It took the largest spell ever cast, but we caught you both. Demetri, your reign ends today, one way or another. No one will ever say again that there is a Little named Demetri who lives free."

Krawl took one of the sugar cookies off her plate and held it out for Demetri. Slowly, mechanically, his hand rose up and grabbed it. He began to move it toward his mouth. His muscles clenched. His eyes watered.

Krawl laughed as he tried to resist her control over his body.

Celia tried to lunge toward him and knock it out of his hand. But the invisible arms tightened around her, and all she could do was sit there and watch it happen.

Demetri put the cookie into his mouth and chewed it mechanically. He swallowed. Tears rolled down his face.

"Good boy," Krawl said. She took something out of her pocket: a plain silver necklace. She slipped it over Demetri's neck and then turned and walked toward the front door, trailing one hand along the edge of the faded wallpaper. She stopped at the coat rack and wrapped a white shawl around her shoulders. "Goodbye, children," she said. Then she left.

Celia looked at the door and then at Demetri. Krawl was gone? That was it? She couldn't believe it. She turned toward Demetri. "Come on! Let's get out of here. Now!"

"You should leave," Demetri whispered. "I'm not going anywhere."

34

THE WORST MONSTER

"I'll carry you if you can't move. We'll have to be careful not to touch, but I can do it." Celia scooted to the edge of the couch. "Come on. I'm sure she'll be back soon."

Demetri shook his head and kicked his legs out. "I can move fine now, but I'm staying." He laid his head back on the couch. "Krawl is clever." He wiped cookie crumbs from his mouth. "Sorry I didn't see this coming."

Celia looked behind her at the door. It seemed like they should be running, but if Demetri said he couldn't . . . "She couldn't come here for so many years because you banished her. You're the clever one. What should we do now?"

"They always win." Demetri's voice sounded soft and far away.

"No matter what, they always own us, but at least for a little while they didn't." He spoke slowly, like each word took effort.

"What do you mean?" She looked around, trying to understand what was going on. The house felt empty. "What did she do to you?"

"The cookie was poisoned, and there's only one antidote to keep it from killing me."

Celia jerked upright. "Then why are you sitting here? We have to find it."

"The poison flows through me." Demetri sighed. "I've always wondered what being a Big would be like, but I've never thought about death. I think it'll be peaceful." When he blinked, it looked like it took effort to open his eyes again. His skin grew gray. His sunlight and apple-pie smell turned to rotten apples.

"We have to get you cured. Tell me where to get the antidote."

A tear rolled down his face and his hand slowly rose to brush it away. "There's nothing to be done. Get as far away from me as possible."

And then Celia understood how this trap worked and what it really meant to be the doom girl. Krawl would make it so that no matter what, Demetri would no longer be the hero to the Littles after today.

She knew what the inevitability spell was for.

"I'm the antidote," she whispered. "Right? The poison won't kill you if you become Big. So either you'll become a Big monster today or you'll die. Either way she wins." Celia stared at the silver necklace she'd put around him. "And that's not just any necklace, is it?"

With effort, he whispered, "This necklace would control me if I turned Big. I would be Krawl's forevermore. The perfect trap. I will die or be hers again."

Celia's breath caught in her throat as she realized this was it. This was the moment when she made a decision. The girl will decide, just like the prophecy predicted. Celia would be the one who turned Demetri into a monster or not. And Demetri as a Big? He was decades older than any other Little, and already a powerful magician. If she changed him, he'd become the worst monster ever. Under Krawl's power, he might destroy the whole world.

But if she didn't touch him?

Her friend would die. Demetri had been suffering his whole life. He didn't deserve that.

His horned head fell forward. He raised it slowly back up. "It's not hard being around you anymore. It feels nice. When I'm gone, Celia, remember to be a little bit happy every day, okay? And if you're lonely, like we've both been, think of me and know how much I liked being your friend, even if it was just for a little while. Thank you so much for seeing that I was more than just a Little." His skin took on a granite-gray hue. His breathing came slow and labored.

Celia blinked hard as tears slid down her face. "I'll think of you all the time. Every day. Every hour. You're the best friend I've ever had." It was true, even though she hadn't had nearly enough time with him. Everything was happening too quickly, and there had to be a way out of this. Celia thought about what she'd learned since the earthquake, but there was no solution, was there? There was no choice, here at the bottom of everything. Demetri was a Little, she was doomed, and the Bigs always won.

"Despite it all, I'm glad we met, Celia. It's meant so much to me," he whispered. His body went still. He slumped forward. All his muscles relaxed and he sank into the couch. Demetri let out one last sigh and stopped breathing.

Celia closed her eyes and said a silent prayer for him. Then she said a prayer for herself, and grabbed onto Demetri's bare hand with both of hers.

35

THE BEST ADVENTURE

For an awful moment, nothing happened. Then Demetri inhaled and jerked back to life with an electric shock that ran through both of them.

"No!" Demetri said. "You can't! You don't know what you're doing!"

Celia swallowed hard over the lump in her throat. "One of your rules is that Littles always help each other. Which I think is also what friends should do for each other. You needed help." Celia squeezed his hand and didn't want to think about what came next.

"I become evil as soon as you let go. I become owned and you turn into a monster," Demetri said. The grayness faded and his skin glowed with a strange inner light. "Krawl wins everything." His voice broke.

Celia bit the inside of her cheek. "Maybe. That's one story."

"You don't know what you've done. You can't know, not really." He clutched her hand. "Oh, Celia. I'm so sorry."

"You think I could just sit here and watch you die?"

"It would have been better."

"I had to save you." Celia breathed hard. She felt too warm.

"There's nothing to save. I'm already gone," he said.

"Maybe we can hold hands forever and neither of us will change," Celia said. "We can live in this old house and be like conjoined twins."

Demetri smiled and touched Celia's cheek, right on the monster mark, with his pointer finger. "We'll both change soon enough, Celia. There's no other way this ends."

She took a deep breath. "Then I need you to tell me a story about how things should have been: what our life should have been like."

His hand squeezed hers, and his voice came out hoarse as they both shifted closer together. All she could see, her whole world, was Demetri. "We should have met in school," he said softly. "We should have both been miserable and lonely, and not even noticed each other for a while, but then one day we would have met in the library."

"Because we both like books. And then we'd start talking,"

Celia said. "And it would feel like we already knew each other, and like everything about the other person was interesting. We'd be instant friends."

Demetri's sweet breath was tinged with a new scent, something smoky that filled the air as he spoke. "Best friends. And we'd go on long walks through the city, and never have a moment when we didn't have something to talk about. We'd tell each other everything, even the boring parts of our day. We'd have so much time together."

Celia ached for that reality. She bit her cheek to keep from crying. "We're only thirteen, so we wouldn't even know about the bad things in the world yet. The worst thing would be flunking a final, or getting in a fight with our parents."

Demetri nodded. "And then years would pass and we'd get to grow older, and we'd always have each other, Celia. For our whole lives. We'd get to grow up and do a hundred different things. I'd be a carpenter, or a mailman, and you could be . . . I don't even know what you want to be."

"A biologist. Or a writer." Heat rose up in Celia, like a furnace blasting within her. She started shaking harder. So did Demetri. She spoke faster. "We'd never be lonely. Promise me that, Demetri. In the way things should have been, we'd always be friends." Celia panted as the heat burned through her.

"I promise."

Everything was starting to go bright, and a ringing filled her ears. The heat intensified. Celia held Demetri's hand tighter and imagined that perfect story of what her life could have been like, should have been like, because she knew she was about to lose it all forever.

"I want you to stay Demetri, no matter what. Whatever you change into, I want you to still be Demetri," Celia whispered. She closed her eyes and imagined that as vividly as she knew how to. She imagined it from all sides until she could see it in bright detail.

A new burst of heat ripped through her, and she jerked away from Demetri, but still clutched his hand as pain flared high and bright. From deep inside she felt a pulsing change begin to rip through her and remake her into a different creature.

A creature who was good at doing magic.

"Give me your yo-yo," she whispered.

"What?"

"Yo-yo. Now." More pain twisted through her as Demetri pressed his yo-yo into her free hand.

She knew what she wanted—for Demetri to stay Demetri—and she had an object—his yo-yo. She had all the magic and more that she needed to make a spell. It pounded and pulsed through her. Now the only thing left to do was make her sacrifice.

Celia couldn't hold anything back—she had to give the spell something huge: the thing she least wanted to give up. So she gave it the story of what they could have been together. The happily ever after that would never be. Celia closed her eyes and sacrificed all of it for the spell, and with it she felt her memories of every time she'd been with Demetri fade to gray. What it had felt like to be his friend, and how it had been a tiny universe opening up between them. Even though she couldn't let it go, even though she wanted to hold on to her friend, she had to feed it to the spell to try to save him. Everything about him faded from her mind as Celia felt it flow out from her and arrow toward the yo-yo that pulsed and throbbed in her hand.

I'll never be able to remember why Demetri was worth it, she thought as she ached and shook all over with the magic that filled her and twisted her in strange new ways. With a cry, Celia put the last of her sacrifice into the yo-yo and closed her eyes to envision the one thing, the one impossible thing that she wanted to happen. Demetri wouldn't turn evil like every other Big. However he was remade, he wouldn't be changed, not deep down.

Demetri gets to stay Demetri.

The boy's hand slipped out of hers as he howled. Celia heard a matching scream and realized it was coming from her own mouth.

They fell off the couch, both of them lost and writhing in such overwhelming pain that there was nothing else.

Celia and Demetri changed.

36

A THOUSAND SHADES OF BLACK

Celia went somewhere else, up and out of her body into a white-hot place made of pain so total and brutal that when she returned a moment later, her mind couldn't remember it.

She lay on the floor curled up in a tight ball in front of the fireplace. Was it done? Was it over?

A crash sounded nearby.

Celia opened her eyes. The world looked sharp and hard-edged. She looked down and saw bone-white fingers clenched around Demetri's yo-yo. The plastic toy had turned black with the spell, and it pulsed with a steady rhythm. Celia stretched out her other hand and studied the chalky paleness of it. Thick black nails, like claws, jutted out from each finger.

Something flew by her, wicked fast. The dark blur hit the wall, bounced off, and changed directions. It zoomed across the room and hit the living room wall. The whole house shook with the impact. For a moment, the dark creature stood still and Celia was able to see what Demetri looked like now. He still looked like a boy, mostly, but shiny onyx scales covered his arms and neck. Obsidian claws jutted out of his fingers and stabbed through the ends of his tattered tennis shoes. Wings had burst through the back of his hoodie and lay folded across his back. He stood watching her with a midnight-black face.

He scowled and sparks fell from his mouth. They bounced and hissed across the floor before going out.

Celia got to her feet and faced him. She felt a hundred tiny differences in her body: her balance was shifted to the front of her feet, her heart beat faster, and her muscles felt twitchy and fast. More than that, she felt the invisible tether that stretched between her and Demetri. I would do anything for him, she thought. Not because he was her friend: he wasn't anymore. All of those memories were dead and gray within her. No, this bond was because he was her maker. Her owner. The magic that had made them connected them, and even if she knew the desire to obey him was a new kind of poison, she wanted to rush to him, fall to her knees, and vow to serve him forever.

If my spell didn't work, he's evil, she thought. He'll hurt me and keep on hurting me. I should run now while I have the chance.

But all she could do was watch as he burst into motion again and hurtled his onyx body across the room again and again. He bashed himself against the walls. His wings flapped wildly behind him. Sometimes they lifted him up a couple of feet before he crashed back down.

Celia shifted her weight from side to side, feeling the lightness and hollowness in her bones. She felt agile and coordinated, and like she could sprint for five miles and not get tired. She looked at her hands some more, and at the whiteness that was pale as snow and so different from what she used to look like. White like I'm invisible. Like I'm someone no one notices, she thought.

Demetri stumbled and flew toward her, impossibly fast. He managed to come to a skidding halt a foot away from her. His glassy, black eyes bored into her. His hot breath blasted her face. Up close she could see how his scales covered him like an armor and his wings had fine blue-black feathers that looked like a crow's.

"What did you do, Celia?" His voice sounded the same but held an underlying hiss. "It wars within me." He put a black-scaled hand over his chest.

Celia inhaled deeply and said in a rush of words, "You said when someone becomes a Big, it burns away who they are. I made a spell so that it wouldn't. So that you'd still be . . . you."

Demetri snarled. More sparks fell from his mouth onto the wood floor.

Celia stared at him and tried to see in him the boy who'd been her best friend, but she couldn't remember why she had felt that way. She knew that should make her sad, but she felt only a landscape of gray indifference. "My spell worked?" she asked. "You're still . . . Demetri, aren't you? You're still good?"

His mouth opened and sparks fell from his lips as he laughed and shook his head. "Somehow, you have done what no one thought was possible." He smiled and let out an angry hiss at the same time. "Still me, but changed."

Up close, Celia could see how the silver necklace that Krawl had put on him crackled and hissed where it touched his skin.

Celia reached for the necklace. Before her hand came close, lightning crackled out from it and struck her fingers. She yelped as the electricity stung her.

"It won't come off until she's dead," Demetri hissed. "Show me what's in your hand."

Celia held up the burned and blackened yo-yo, and they both stared at the pulsing object that had become his heart. She knew she should hold on to it, that she might need it if the Big parts of him were more powerful than the Demetri parts. She held it out to him. "It's yours."

He focused on it for a long moment. "You should keep it safe for me."

Celia was fairly sure, in the history of all Bigs, that none of them had ever let their Little keep their heart. Which meant that he really was still good. Celia slipped it into her coat pocket. "It's not the only heart I want. Krawl won't have gone far."

A smile slid across Demetri's face, and for a second Celia almost remembered why she loved that smile. The points of his wicked-sharp teeth showed and sparks fell from his mouth again.

"Are you going to be able to fight her?" Celia eyed his necklace.

"I have to try." He turned from Celia. His long feathered wings stretched and extended out across the length of the room. They beat once, twice, and Demetri jumped into the air. This time he moved with grace as he pumped his wings and flew toward the front door. His wings beat faster as he neared it. He lowered his head and burst through it with a spray of broken wood.

Celia walked after him, feeling both hollow and heavy in her new body. Demetri's heart beat in her back pocket. She stepped through the dragon-shaped hole in the door and went out into the bright, white world. The paper storm had stopped, and everything lay covered in bits of meaningless text. She could read any and all of it if she focused on it with her keen Little eyesight. Krawl's house was only a couple of blocks away from her apartment, on a street she walked down all the time, but the paper turned everything strange. The dragon boy flew overhead in wild, erratic circles. Demetri disappeared over apartment buildings and then swooped back. A steady stream of sparks fell from his mouth down to the road. They ignited wisps of paper that burst into yellow and orange flames, like tiny firecrackers.

"Krawl?" he howled. "Show yourself."

"Yes, dear?" The old woman appeared at the end of the block, coming out from the shadows of a doorway and standing on a papered stoop. She tapped her white cane against the ground and walked slowly into the middle of the street. "You are mine again," she said with a smile as she tilted her face up toward the sky and Demetri. "I have missed you. You see now how together we will rule the world?"

He spit fire down on her. It went out a dozen feet above her head.

A look of confusion crossed Krawl's face. "You are mine?" she repeated, but sounded less certain.

"Never!" He spit more fire. This time it arced and fell toward her small form.

"We shall see," Krawl said as she held up her palm. The fire disappeared. She pointed toward Demetri and then lowered her finger until it was aimed at Celia. "Destroy your Little." She spoke with a voice that had commanded monsters for over a century.

The necklace around the dragon's neck flashed with a blinding white light. Demetri howled and thrashed through the air. Flames burst from his mouth. His wings beat out of sync with each other, and he started to fall out of the sky.

I should run, Celia thought. But even though he was

commanded to destroy her, she couldn't leave him.

"End her!" Krawl commanded with a voice that echoed everywhere. She whipped one hand through the air in a complicated set of gestures and held her cane up in the other. A thick white stream of magic flew out of the tip of her cane and hit Demetri.

"You. Do. Not. Own. Me!" he screamed back as he crashed into the ground.

Paper went flying in all directions. Some of it caught fire, bursting into orange and red flames that died out quickly. Demetri thrashed on the ground as Krawl's magic writhed around him, covering him like a blanket. He screamed and tried to pull the magic off, but it clung to him.

"I will never hurt her," he growled. His fisted hands began gathering their own smoky magic as he started muttering to himself.

"If you won't obey me," Krawl said, "then stay, dog." Demetri's necklace flashed bright again. The white magic convulsed and tightened around his small and rageful form.

He growled and lay still on the papered ground.

Celia swallowed. Fight it, Demetri, she thought. Fight her with everything you've got.

Demetri made a mournful keening sound. He didn't move a muscle. Celia watched him, willing him to get up. He didn't.

Krawl had taken him down in less than a minute. What chance do I have? Celia wondered.

Demetri lay on the street halfway between Krawl and Celia. Krawl walked a couple of steps toward him, tapping her cane in front of her. "What did you do to him, Celia, girl? All the tender parts of him should have burned away. What monstrosity have you made?"

Demetri tried to speak. All that came from him was an angry cry.

"He's still Demetri," Celia answered. "He's not yours. He never will be."

Krawl touched the white bun at the top of her head. She swayed from side to side and her tongue flicked out, tasting the air. "I see," she said. "Your magic flows into him and creates a strange bond. It holds him back. A clever use of your transformation, I will admit." She made a tutting sound and shook her head. "There's only one remedy to break that spell, my dear. When you die, so does that disgusting tangle of magic you have trapped my poor Demetri in."

Demetri growled. Flames shot out of his mouth and burned the paper in front of him. More of it caught fire around him.

Krawl tsk-tsked and pointed at the fire. It went out. "No more of that," she ordered.

Demetri whimpered in pain. His mouth snapped shut.

"Now where were we, Celia? Oh yes, your imminent death."

Celia pawed the ground with one foot. Her new body felt so fast. Strength buzzed through her. It wouldn't be hard to race down the road and knock the old lady down. Anger, just as bright as Demetri's fire, burned through her.

But ... one of Demetri's rules was that Littles didn't fight Bigs, because they always wanted to, and they almost always lost. And Krawl was the first monster, and more powerful than any other. Be smart, Celia told herself. You have to find Krawl's heart.

A boom filled the air and something large lurched into view, two blocks behind Krawl.

The old lady turned and sniffed the air as the thing, huge and misshapen, stumbled closer. The Littles' golem had been awakened, and he moved unsteadily down the road. He was as tall as the three-story buildings he passed. He walked with lurching strides on his long chicken-wire-and-mud legs. The Littles from the sanctuary surrounded him and pushed on his ankles and feet, urging him forward.

"A golem?" Krawl smiled. "I once made one when Demetri and I were both young. It destroyed two city blocks. How droll. I haven't fought a golem in ages."

The giant dragged his feet on the ground, sending up clouds of paper with every step. He let out a strange cry that sounded like a hawk's. His hand hit a streetlamp and knocked it over. His foot kicked a motorcycle that smashed into a storefront.

As Krawl watched the golem, Celia began to move closer to the first monster. Her feet moved silently over the papered ground. She stared at Krawl's back and at the pocketed skirt the old monster wore. One of those pockets has to have her heart, Celia thought.

"So lovely to see you rebel Littles," Krawl cried out. "Have you heard the good news? Demetri is a Big now. He failed, just like all of you will fail."

The Littles froze and stared at Krawl. They looked down the road and took in Celia's pale form and the dark unmoving lump that was Demetri.

"Lies!" Daisy yelled back. She jumped up and grabbed the golem's pinky. She held on to it and pulled the giant man forward. "Demetri would never—"

Krawl laughed. She moved her pointer finger around in a circle.

Demetri's shimmering, scaly body rose up into the air behind the old woman for everyone to see.

Krawl snapped her fingers. Demetri fell like a stone.

"No!" the Littles called out in one collective voice. Even from a block and a half away, Celia could see the shock and pain on their faces.

The golem swayed from side to side. Celia wasn't sure what kind of magic he could do, only that Demetri and all the Littles had made him to help destroy Krawl. She also knew the golem hadn't been finished when they'd left the sanctuary this morning, and that Demetri had needed to add more spells to him. Though the Littles had figured out how to get him moving, the giant looked like he might crash to the ground with every step he took.

Krawl raised her cane and pointed it at the sky. A burst of white magic flew toward the golem. The giant watched it arc toward him with a confused look on his crinkled face. The golem raised one stiff-fingered hand as if to catch the magic. The Littles pushed at his feet and tried to get him to move away from it.

Too late, the magic flowed into his palm and wound up his arm in pulsing white rivulets. It moved over his torso and up toward his head.

The golem raised his head and cried out with a piercing bird shriek. He lowered his head and started running forward, arms akimbo. He kicked a car and a fire hydrant. His hand smashed into windows. Glass rained down on the street. He pitched forward.

Littles on all sides of him pushed and pulled at his ankles and shins to keep him upright.

Celia moved toward Krawl. She passed Demetri's tense and still form. He watched her with his midnight eyes.

Run, he mouthed.

Celia felt the twinge of her maker's order wind through her muscles. It tried to control her. She gritted her teeth and walked faster toward Krawl. She wasn't far from the old lady now. Her hands flexed into fists. A rage, deep and animal, roared within her. She lowered her head and pawed the ground with one foot.

Krawl spun around to face Celia just as the golem crashed to his knees.

"A funny thing about me being blind," Krawl said. "Did you know, dear, that I can sense what's going on behind me just as well as in front?"

Down the block, the Littles frantically tried to get the golem to stand up.

Celia took another step toward the old lady. What chance do I have against Krawl? Celia wondered. The answer was none, but she had to try.

"I will give you this," Krawl continued. "You are more interesting than most children." She touched her bun. "The clever ones are always the most trouble." She walked down the road toward Celia, leaning on her white cane and closing the gap between them.

Celia's rage billowed. This was the monster who had hurt her maker. Who had attacked a dozen orphans and stolen their lives. She ground her teeth together, even as a part of her whispered that Krawl only had to raise a pinkie to kill her in an instant. Something moved on the edge of Celia's vision. She looked left but saw nothing.

Krawl walked closer on silent footsteps buffered by layers of prose.

More motion fluttered at the edge of Celia's sight, this time on the right side of the road.

"How shall I destroy you, child?" The dark circles of her glasses seemed to stare at Celia. "I will make it useful, of course. Death magic is wonderful stuff. But in what way should I shape it? Dismemberment? Drowning? Or being engulfed by flames, always a classic. . . ." She came closer.

Celia lowered her center of gravity. She didn't know how far her Little body could jump, but if Krawl took a couple of steps closer . . .

Down the block, the golem got to his feet and started walking again.

Motion scurried along the edges of Celia's sight. She caught sight of Amber's long black braid disappearing behind a school bus. She spied other hunters, moving between the papered cars and mailboxes. Krawl still hadn't noticed anything.

Celia took another step closer to Krawl and spoke loudly, trying to cover over any sounds the hunters might make. "Even if you kill me and use Demetri, you'll still just be an evil monster. You can make the world worse, but that's all you'll ever do."

Krawl stopped hobbling forward. She threw back her head and laughed. "Oh, Celia, my dearest. Please carry on. The last words of the hopeless are always such poetry."

"I'm better than you," Celia said. "I will never be like you, for as long as I live. I'll never destroy other people's lives. For a day or a lifetime, I'll never turn evil like you."

"Never, says the girl of thirteen? Says the freshly made Little?"

Krawl laughed some more and raised her deadly cane into the air. She moved it in slow circles, and white magic built around the tip of the cane. It pulsed and grew brighter with every rotation.

Celia crouched and jumped toward Krawl. She sailed higher and faster than she had expected.

Krawl snarled and snapped, "Fall."

Magic flared off her cane.

It hit Celia's body. She slammed into the ground, knees first.

Before she could get up and hurl herself at Krawl again, the monster added, "Stay."

Magic pushed Celia down, like hundred-pound weights placed on her shoulders.

"Hey Krawl, why don't you pick on someone your own size?" a voice cried out. Ruby jumped up onto the hood of a paper-covered SUV. The purple-haired hunter held a glowing green soda bottle in one hand. To her left and right, and on the far side of the street, other hunters popped up from their hiding places. They each held glass bottles filled with a glowing green liquid.

Amber jumped up onto the car beside Ruby. She held two of the glowing bottles. Amber looked at Celia, squinting behind her glasses. The hunter hesitated and then threw one to Celia. "Catch."

When Celia caught it, the glass sent shocks through her hand. She tried to get up from where she knelt, but couldn't.

Krawl's tongue flicked out to taste the air. She touched her bun as she turned around in a slow circle.

The hunters spread out across the road and made a ring around her.

"Hello, hunter children," she said. "So nice of you all to come to the day's slaughter. I'm getting so many items crossed off my to-do list today. And you brought parlor tricks with you. Lovely!"

The glowing bottle burned cold and then hot in Celia's hand, pulsing painfully between the two extremes.

"Not tricks. This spell will destroy any monster," Ruby replied.

"Then it's a good thing I'm not just any monster," Krawl responded. She raised her cane and turned around in a wide circle. White magic fell from it and made a protective halo around her. The hanging magic pulsed and then drew tight around Krawl. The old woman glowed from head to toe.

Ruby threw her glass bottle at Krawl. It sailed through the air, aimed right at her. Krawl smiled as the bottle hit her shimmering form. It shattered on her left arm. Green magic splattered onto her hand and forearm. Krawl's white magic fizzed up against the glowing green spell.

Krawl's smile fell off her face. Her eyes went wide as she made a hissing sound. The green magic burned through the white. Where it touched her, Krawl's skin turned a smooth green marble, hard like a statue.

Krawl tried to move her arm. It didn't budge.

The hunters launched a dozen more bottles at Krawl from all directions. She raised her cane with her free hand and battered some of the bottles out of the air with streams of white lightning. Other bottles crashed into her.

Wherever the green magic touched her, she turned to stone. She couldn't move her right leg, then her left foot, and then her thighs.

Celia, still on her knees, threw her own bottle. It flew end over end through the air and smashed into Krawl's torso.

The green magic splashed across her, and the Big stood immobilized and snarling. Over half of her body was frozen. Krawl struggled against her bound form and breathed with an audible rasp. "This won't hold me for long," she hissed.

"Good thing it won't take long to find your heart," Ruby yelled. "Hunters, attack!"

The hunters ran toward her.

Krawl raised her head toward the sky. "To me," she whispered in a frail old woman's voice. Something flashed off her body, so fast that Celia couldn't track it.

"Careful," Celia warned. She tried to get up. Krawl's magic kept her down. Celia gritted her teeth. She strained all her muscles. She stayed put.

Amber was the first hunter to get to Krawl. She reached into one of Krawl's skirt pockets. "Nothing," she called out.

The hunters searched every pocket. They patted her down

and looked under her shawl. Krawl kept her face lifted toward the sky, ignoring everyone as she muttered under her breath. A couple of cracks grew in the green marble that encased her arm.

Faster, Celia thought, wishing she could join them.

A screeching filled the air. A shadow passed over the street. A keening sound joined the first cry, followed by a deafening roar.

Celia looked up in time to see three winged monsters fall out of the sky. "Did you think I wouldn't bring backup?" Krawl laughed.

The hunters fell back from her as a snarling blue-skinned man with swirling black tattoos and long, leathery wings landed beside Krawl. His lower half was furry and thick, like a grizzly bear. The hunters pulled together into a wary clump. The next monster to land was a strange jumble of body parts that was hard to look at. It had legs, eyeballs, hands, and arms, all pushed together into a lumpy mass held aloft with dozens of mismatched wings. It stood on seven different legs and stared at everyone with its many unblinking eyes. The third was a winged horse with a pearly white unicorn horn jutting out from its silvery white head. It nickered and moved its horn through the air as it sauntered to stand with the other monsters. Celia recognized all three—their images had been painted on one of the walls at the graffiti flats she had visited with Ruby and Amber.

The blue man folded his thick arms over his bare chest. "Orders, Madame Krawl?" he asked with a thunder-laced voice.

Krawl, still frozen in marble, nodded toward the hunters. "Keep them occupied and away from me, in whatever way you wish."

The three new monsters flowed past Krawl and ran at the hunters.

The hunters fell back, retreating down the block. They scrambled to pull out spells and weapons from their bags. More cracks grew in Krawl's marble as she watched the hunters.

Celia clenched every muscle and fought to get up. If I could just get to Krawl and find her heart before Krawl is able to move again, Celia thought. She wasn't far away, but it might as well have been a thousand miles. Celia tried to move her knee. She failed.

Weights pushed her to the ground. It was all she could do to keep sitting up.

Small chunks of green marble fell off Krawl.

Celia looked around, desperate for any help. In one direction, the golem had stopped walking. He studied the sky with an empty look stretched across his gaunt features. In the other, the hunters threw handfuls of spells at the three advancing monsters. The air filled with fizzing explosions that smelled like rain and peppercorns. Ruby raised her twin swords against the blue man. She struck him in the arm with one of them.

The Big laughed and whipped his cut arm toward her.

His blood splattered across her torso. It caught fire wherever it hit her. Ruby screamed and fell backward. She dropped to the ground and rolled around until the fire went out. Bits of paper caught fire but then went out, too.

Another hunter took her place, using a slingshot to hit the blue man with paintballs that exploded with yellow magic that danced across his tattooed skin. He howled and cut his own hand open with a knife. He used it to set two more hunters on fire as he advanced toward them on powerful furry legs.

Celia kept trying to get up. The weight of the world pushed back on her. More chunks of marble fell off Krawl.

Amber ran with her long braid flying out behind her. She twisted through the air and threw a handful of exploding marbles at the floating misshapen Big. Mouths opened up all over its lumpy form. Tongues reached out and grabbed the round spells. It ate all the marbles, then ran toward Amber on its many legs. A dozen arms reached for her. Amber and four other hunters ran away from it, throwing more spells at it as they did. The thing gobbled them all up.

Other hunters surrounded the winged unicorn. It hummed a song, and, as if in a trance, the hunters swayed to the sound of it. None of them seemed to notice the battle happening all around them. The Big kept humming as it lowered its gleaming horn and ran at the nearest hunter. The boy snapped out of his daze and jumped aside just in time.

The other hunters moved into action. They threw spells and

rocks at the horse's pearly-white hide. The horse fought back, biting the air and charging them with its lowered horn. All three of the Bigs pushed the hunters down the road and away from Krawl.

Krawl muttered under her breath as the marble that held her grew thinner and paler. Cracks spiderwebbed across it as its hold on her weakened.

The golem took a couple of long steps closer. The Littles did everything they could to keep it moving and avoid crashing into the nearby buildings.

The thin green marble exploded off Krawl in hundreds of flying pieces. Krawl raised her white cane up. Great strands of magic flowed off it and flew down the street. The magic streaked across the papered ground and whipped around some of the hunters' legs. It yanked them to the ground. As soon as they fell, more of Krawl's magic covered them and bound them. Five hunters fell, then four more, and another three.

The remaining hunters turned and fled from Krawl's magic. They ducked and zigzagged. They threw spells and jumped into the air. A few of them made it to the end of the block and disappeared around the corner. The three winged monsters chased after them.

The golem shuffled his feet slowly along the ground, kicking up tufts of paper.

We aren't going to win this, Celia thought. We're just a bunch of kids. Bigs always win. Her rage grew hot at the thought. It coursed through her with every beat of her heart.

"Now where were we, Celia, dear?" Krawl turned to face her. She looked older and shrunken. "Oh yes, we were discussing your death! And how it will be just the thing to enslave Demetri to me forever. Oh, Celia, I shall love eating your fear and seeing you die." Krawl gave her a grandmotherly smile.

Celia groaned and found a way to force one leg up. Somehow, pushing against all the weight that held her down, she ground her teeth together and got herself up to standing. She faced Krawl.

Krawl walked forward until she stood in front of Celia. She reached out with one hand and touched Celia on her cheek.

Celia slammed back to the ground again.

Behind them, the golem loomed closer. He ran into a wall. He kicked a car. He scratched his nose and stared blankly up at the sky.

37

THE DESIRE TO DESTROY

Krawl followed Celia's gaze and stared at the golem. She made a tutting sound. "So many distractions. A moment, Celia dear. I will get to you soon enough." Krawl walked by Celia's fallen form and faced the towering golem.

The giant stumbled over some garbage cans. Around him, the Littles pushed his feet and struggled to keep him moving. If they could just get him to Krawl, the golem was full of spells that would hurt her.

Daisy glared at Krawl. Her black-and-white face was flushed with anger. "Think you can take us all, Krawl? You think you're big and bad enough, old lady?"

"Come closer, Little rebels, and find out," Krawl called back and cackled. She began to sway from side to side, muttering and tapping her cane along the papered ground. Magic grew on it like a cloud of cotton candy.

Celia focused on Krawl's back and somehow, some way, forced one leg up again, and then the other. She sagged under a thousand pounds that pushed down on her shoulders. She dragged one foot a couple of inches forward, then the other. Krawl had to be stopped. Out of the corner of her eye, she saw Demetri, trussed on the ground and watching her. The bond between them pulsed and strengthened her. She took another step forward.

The Littles got their golem to take three steps forward, but then some crows flew by his head, and he stopped to watch them. Daisy screamed at him to keep moving and kicked his foot. The golem smiled at the birds.

Celia took another impossible step closer to Krawl.

Krawl muttered and moved her cane through the air in precise gestures. More magic clung and grew on the tip of her cane.

The golem needs to attack now, before she's done with that spell, Celia thought. If he just ran at her right now . . .

The giant reached toward the crows that squawked and circled his head.

Celia gritted her teeth and slowly forced herself closer to Krawl. All her muscles screamed. Her bones bent with the effort. I'll never get to Krawl, she thought. Celia took another step forward.

Daisy kicked the golem's shin. All the Littles yelled at him to keep walking. The golem looked around. He spotted Krawl and started lumbering toward her.

Krawl's muttering grew louder. Her magic grew brighter. She'll destroy him, just like the rest of us. She's going to get everything she wants, Celia thought.

Krawl raised her cane at the golem.

Celia, with everything she had, ran forward and shoved Krawl in the back.

Krawl fell. Her magic flew upward.

For a brief moment, Celia thought it might miss the golem, but then the magic hit him in his knees and burned through them, leaving gaping, wide-open holes. The golem opened his mouth in a surprised O shape. He began to fall.

Right toward Krawl and Celia.

Krawl raised her head up from the ground and lifted one deadly hand toward it.

Celia fell on top of her and knocked her down again.

A heartbeat later, the golem landed on top of both of them. His open mouth covered their entire bodies.

Krawl screamed from inside the golem. The sound echoed off the walls.

The pressure on Celia's body disappeared. She was suddenly able to move again. She sprang up into a crouch inside the small dark cave of the golem's mouth and backed away from Krawl until she was pressed against the thin wall. Light shone in through the nostrils and mouth. Celia blinked, and her new Little eyes adjusted instantly to the darkness.

Krawl sat up just as a flock of origami cranes flew out from the dark tunnel of the golem's throat.

They flapped their bright-colored wings and swirled around Krawl's head and shoulders, pecking at her and leaving tiny spots of blood where their paper beaks bit her.

Krawl muttered under her breath. Her fingers glowed bright. She batted away the cranes. They burst into flames the second she touched them. More flew out from the throat and moved in undulating circles around the monster's head. The air filled with bright bursts of fire.

Krawl's heart, Celia thought. I have to get it. She stood pressed against the wall of the golem's head, unable to move, this time because of fear. If I don't get it . . . if I fail . . . Panic fizzed through her.

She swallowed and looked through the blur of cranes at Krawl's many pockets. One chance, she thought. Krawl is the mother of all monsters, and maybe, right this second, I might have one chance. Dizziness washed over her. She looked Krawl up and down.

Krawl's bun had fallen to one side, and some of the white hair had been pushed aside. Something red peeked out beneath it. It seemed to be moving. Not just moving, but beating.

Celia's breath caught in her throat. Could that be . . . ?

Celia pushed off the wall and lunged for it.

A new flock of cranes burst from the golem's throat. The wild paper birds were everywhere. They blinded Celia. She reached, unseeing, for the bun. Her hands closed around something round and alive. She yanked on it, hard, and fell backward.

Krawl screamed. All the origami cranes exploded into flames. The paper fell smoldering to the ground and the cave of the golem's mouth lit up with hundreds of soft flickering embers.

Celia looked down at her hands and saw that she held a small red rubber ball. It pulsed in and out with the steady rhythm of a monster's heart.

"No," Krawl whispered. "No!" she screamed, and raised her deadly hands.

"Don't," Celia whispered.

Krawl's arms fell to her side.

Celia stepped back, pressing her body against the wire-and-paper wall of the golem's skull. She looked down at the red rubber ball and remembered Demetri saying Kristen had brought a red ball to play with the orphans at the park. She remembered Demetri telling her how much he had liked that girl named Kristen.

"Whatever you wish me to do," Krawl whispered. "I am yours to command, evermore. Together—Celia, I can do things for you. We can rule the—"

"Quiet," Celia whispered.

Krawl's mouth snapped shut.

Celia stared at the throbbing red ball as she heard banging come from the far side of the golem's head. "Once upon a time," Celia said, looking at Krawl, "there was a girl who thought she was important, but she wasn't. Not at all. She was the most normal girl in the world. There was nothing even a little bit special about her. All she was was the victim of a nasty spell."

"Are you talking about you or me?" Krawl whispered. She was an old lady, but her voice sounded young and sad.

Celia shrugged. "The beginning of this story could be about either of us. But then you changed twelve kids and became more powerful than anyone else. Me? All I wanted was to make some friends. Our stories have different endings." Celia squeezed her fingers around the warm pulsing rubber heart and watched the mother of all the monsters.

Krawl flinched. She whispered, "I wanted friends too. I didn't mean to hurt any of them. I didn't know, not really, what would happen when I touched them. All I knew was that I was so hungry and so, so tired of being all alone," she whispered. A tear ran down her cheek.

Every monster started with a kid being hurt. "What if we could be different than the stories they tell about us?" Celia whispered.

Krawl blinked slowly and stared at the heart that beat in Celia's hand. "I don't understand."

"I made Demetri different than every other Big." Celia took a deep breath and couldn't believe she was saying this, except that a long time ago, Krawl really had been just like her. "Do you want me to try to help make you become different too"—Celia swallowed—"Kristen?"

Krawl's eyes went wide. "That name," she whispered. More tears fell down her face. Krawl covered her face with both hands.

Then, before Celia could squeeze the heart and command her not to, the old lady attacked her.

38

A DELUGE OF FIRE

Krawl bashed into Celia's side. Both of them tumbled to the ground. The wind got knocked out of Celia's lungs. She couldn't breathe. She couldn't order Krawl to stop.

The monster's gnarled hands wrapped around Celia's fingers and started prying them off the heart. The rubber ball throbbed in Celia's hand as she fought Krawl. The old lady kicked her in the shins and yanked on the heart, hard.

Celia felt the red ball slipping out of her grasp. She grabbed onto it with her claws.

A squelching sound filled the small dark space.

Krawl fell away from Celia.

Celia stared down at her hands. They held half of a rubber

ball that dripped blood onto the ground. The old woman held the other half. Already, Krawl was starting to change. She grew thinner and older with every passing second.

A great roaring filled the air. A wind rose up and battered them from all directions. The air itself caught fire with a hundred different colors and someone was screaming and there was laughter and rage and sorrow sparking and breaking all around her and—

39

THE UNLUCKY ONE

Celia blinked. An empty blue sky filled her gaze. The world smelled like ash. She sat up and saw burned paper wafting through the air and shifting across the ground. She rubbed her eyes and noticed the whiteness of her strange hands. "What happened?" she whispered.

Something moved to her left.

Celia tensed but then saw it was just a kid. For a second, Celia thought it was Daisy, but this girl had smooth brown skin instead of a checkerboard face. The girl stared at her for a long second. "What happened? A lot," she said slowly. And the girl's voice? It was Daisy's.

Dizziness washed over Celia. "You're . . . human? Normal again?"

Daisy chewed on her lower lip and nodded. Other Littles from the sanctuary crowded around them. Only . . . none of them were Littles anymore. Celia recognized each of them, but they looked totally different without their horns, strange-colored skin, and other Little traits.

"Krawl died and you all became . . ." Celia shook her head.

"Normal. You freed us," whispered a boy. He reached up to touch the tip of a horn that was no longer there. "You broke the great spell."

Daisy nodded. "We're all just a bunch of normal kids again. Those Bigs who were chasing the hunters? They changed back into kids too." She grinned and bounced up and down on the toes of her worn shoes. "No more monsters."

Celia got up and took a step toward them. All of the kids moved away from her. "But . . . me. I'm still . . . ?" She studied her black clawed hands.

"You and Demetri are the only ones. He's still a Big. You're still a Little. He said the spell broke with Krawl's heart, but not all the way. The magic still needed to go somewhere. It's in you two now: the one who broke the spell, and her maker. It's in you two, and nowhere else."

Celia blinked and tried to take in all the new facts of the world. The wind shifted and Celia caught scent of the former Littles. They smelled like fresh-baked cinnamon rolls on a Saturday morning. Or the first nibble of a good chocolate bar. She inhaled the scent. A hunger roared through her.

I'll get used to that, she thought unsteadily as she bit her cheek and forced herself not to run at them. I'll learn to deal with it. All she wanted was to hold their hands. Was that so wrong?

"Where is he? Demetri?" Celia asked.

A girl who used to be covered in boils pointed at the sky.

The midnight-black body of Demetri was just visible as he flew in between two skyscrapers. Celia watched until she couldn't see him anymore.

"You can live at our old sanctuary," Daisy said. "That's where some of us will be staying, those of us who were monsters for a long time and don't have families anymore. We can make a section of it just for you, and it could be okay, even if you're a Little."

Hunger flashed through Celia again. She shook her head. "That's not where I belong."

She started walking, and the normal kids trailed behind her. They passed a mirrored plate-glass window, and Celia stopped to stare at herself. Her skin was a pale white porcelain, and her irises were bloodred. Her hair had changed from brown to jet black, and she reached up to the top of her skull to feel two small red horns that jutted out of her head. They were smooth and needle sharp at their ends. Celia pulled the hood of her sweatshirt up and over her head to hide them.

A half block later, the burned paper ended and the world was covered in bright soft paper again. Some kids came out of their apartment building and started playing in it like snow. They threw handfuls of it all around. The former Littles moved away from them by habit, but then, one by one, they remembered they were kids again. They ran forward and started throwing paper everywhere. Daisy cast a grin toward Celia and then ran into the mess of kids playing and laughing.

Celia chewed on one of her thick claws and pretended not to notice how the kids smelled. She left them behind and kept trudging forward.

Streetlamps began to flicker on, one by one, and a soft hum filled the air. Maybe a normal girl wouldn't have been able to hear the electricity flowing back into the city, but Celia heard the rushing hiss of it move across the wires and into buildings. She heard people cry out as they realized that things were getting back to normal.

This will be something everyone talks about, Celia thought. They'll rebuild the city and their lives, and tell stories about earthquakes, snakes, and strange paper storms, until that's all it becomes: a story.

For them.

Footsteps ran up behind her. Celia turned to see Ruby's and Amber's grinning faces. The smiles fell off them as they stared at her and saw what she still was. They took a step back from her, and another.

"We thought . . . we saw Bigs turn back into kids. And then Littles. But you're . . ."

"The last Little." Celia smelled the sweetness of their scent and turned away from them. "I broke the spell, and Demetri and I are the last ones left." She started walking.

With her sharp hearing, Celia could tell they were keeping pace behind her as they all moved through the drifts of paper.

"You did it, Celia," Ruby said. "You did the impossible and made it all go away. I can't believe it."

"Where are you headed?" Amber asked.

"Home. I just want to go home."

"Um . . . have you looked in the mirror lately? You can't live with your parents," Ruby said. She hurried forward and walked beside Celia. So did Amber. "You don't fit into their world anymore. They won't even be able to see you."

"We'll help you find a place," Amber added. "We're still your friends. Even though you're a Little. We can help you keep from touching any kid. But you can't go home."

Celia closed her eyes and wished her friends didn't smell delicious. Her apartment building came into sight, half a block away. She stared at the window to her living room. "I think I'm done with being told what I can and can't do."

Ruby stopped and stared at her for a long moment. She nodded slowly. "If anyone can pull this off, you can. We'll hang out soon. We'll figure out how this is going to work, and we'll be there for you, Celia. I promise."

Amber nodded.

"You'll watch me and keep me from doing anything bad?" Celia said. She had no bitterness behind those words. Not anymore. She had a feeling she was going to need all the help she could get.

"Always," Amber said.

Celia left them standing in the paper-covered world and went home.

AFTER THE END

All the lights were on in Celia's house when she opened the door. Her parents sat on the couch, holding each other and crying.

Celia ran toward them. "Mom! Dad! I'm back!" She threw herself into their laps and hugged them as hard as she could.

They didn't hug her back.

"I have a bad feeling about this," her mom said. "Celia should be home. Why isn't she home?"

"She'll come through the door any minute," her dad replied. "She will, she will, she will."

Celia pressed her face right up to both of theirs.

They looked straight through her.

"I'm right here!" she screamed, inches from their faces.

She jumped up and down on the orange couch and then shook her mom. Celia tried tickling her dad.

Her parents sat there and worried some more about her.

Celia threw blankets into the air and turned the TV off and

on, but whatever magic hid her from them hid her actions too.

Her parents walked to the kitchen. Her mom picked up the phone and made a call. "Hello, I'd like to report a missing girl. Yes, I know there was an earthquake and a lot of people are missing. My daughter is thirteen. Yes, I'll hold."

Celia's dad looked up the numbers to all the local hospitals and paced as he spoke tensely into the phone, describing what Celia used to look like.

Celia broke dishes at their feet. She yelled at them even louder, and sometimes, for half a second, they would look at her, but then their gaze would shift away. Celia slammed every door in the house. She grabbed a pile of paper and wrote in huge letters that she was right here. She put it on the kitchen table.

Her parents went to the couch again. They held each other and cried some more.

Celia ran into her bedroom and grabbed sunglasses and a big hat. She went to the bathroom and covered her face and hands with her mom's concealer so that her skin was a beige color. She did everything she could to make herself look like she used to. Then she went and stood in front of her parents.

Her mom flinched. Her dad's jaw dropped open. They stared at her.

"Celia?" her dad whispered.

"Honey, what . . . ?" her mom started, and then they all fell into each other, hugging so hard that it hurt, but in a good way.

"What happened? Where were you?" they asked.

Celia took a deep breath and pulled back from them. "Some bad things happened, but I'm still Celia. And I'm okay, but this is going to be a lot to get used to."

Her dad frowned. Her mom started crying.

She sat holding their hands and told them the story of everything that had happened. Celia stopped now and then to make sure that they were still listening to her. Now that she had their attention, they seemed to be able to focus on her. She told the story again and again, until it made sense to them. She answered every single one of their whispered questions.

They talked and talked, until they understood.

Then Celia took off her hat and wiped off some of the makeup with her sleeve while they stared at her. She kept at it, until she looked like her new self and they could see what she had become. Everybody cried some more.

Every day, Celia had to remind them what she was. It took a full month before they stopped closing doors in Celia's face, speaking over her when she talked, and taking plates of food away when she was still eating. Slowly, they became more and more able to see her red eyes, chalk-white skin, and horns. It felt like they would never stop crying.

Then another month passed, and Celia's mom started calling

her "my little monster" and rolling her eyes every time Celia forgot to do the dishes or left the lid off the pickle jar. Her dad started asking her questions about her day and acting like Celia was his daughter again.

Celia never left the house unless she was with one of them, and when she did, she tried to stay far away from all other kids. Amber, Ruby, and Daisy would come by to try to hang out, but that didn't feel safe. Whatever happened, she couldn't touch anyone and hurt them. She wouldn't make more monsters and start the whole cycle all over again. No matter what it took, she just wouldn't.

Winter turned slowly into spring, and one morning Celia's mom came into her room with her arms full of books. "I ordered homeschooling stuff. You can study six hours a day."

"Super fun," Celia replied.

"You have a lot of catching up to do."

"Because monsters need to know algebra?" Celia asked.

Her mom looked straight into her red eyes and didn't flinch. "Because my whip-smart daughter is going to get an education, regardless of what she looks like." She leaned forward and kissed Celia on her forehead, careful to avoid the sharp points of her horns.

"Yes sir."

They grinned at each other.

Celia spread out the books on her bed's quilt and opened up every window in her room. A warm breeze blew in. It smelled like a dozen different blossoms. There was a fat biology book with a picture of a duck-billed platypus on the cover, an American history book, a geology book, and even some novels that had questions at the back of them for reading comprehension. Celia stared at all of them and an idea surged through her.

It was time.

She went to her closet and pulled out a small cardboard box from underneath a pile of stuffed animals. Inside was a blackened and pulsing yo-yo. Celia tapped her claw against it a couple of times and then put the heart carefully back in the box and hid it again.

Outside, the sun was starting to set and everything glowed with a soft light. Celia sat on her bed and started reading one of the novels about a girl who gets stranded on an island. The scent of apple-cider vinegar and smoke hit the air a moment before a boy-sized dragon flew into her room. He landed on her carpet and stared at her with his coal eyes.

"Hey, Demetri," Celia whispered. She tried not to stare at his scales and feathers.

"Do you need help? Are you in danger?"

Celia shrugged and chewed on her lower lip. "I kept waiting for you to show up, but you never did," she said, and felt the strange connection between them. "So I decided to call you here instead."

"I thought it would be better to keep my distance." He looked toward her window, like he might jump out of it and fly away.

"Even if we're the last two monsters in the whole world?" she asked.

He frowned. "Even so. There is a darkness that runs through me, Celia. I fear I might try to steal my heart back and own you."

"You're the Little who figured out how to not attack any kid ever for decades. I'm pretty sure you can handle not destroying one more."

A smile flickered across Demetri's lips. "Also, I wasn't sure you'd want to see me."

Celia wanted to reassure him that nothing that had happened was his fault, and of course she wanted to see her friend. But he wasn't her friend anymore. Every memory of that was covered in gray. But maybe she could make friends with him all over again. "You know you're the only kid it's safe for me to hang out with, right?"

"Safe," Demetri whispered. He looked around the room. "How is it that you are home with your parents?"

"It's complicated, but we're making it work."

"Of course you are."

"I did call you here for a reason," Celia said. "I need help."

"Anything."

"I've always hated history, and that book isn't going to read itself." Celia gestured at her books and scooted over. She patted the empty space on the bed.

Demetri stood frozen for a moment. Then he moved and perched on the edge of her bed. Sparks fell out of his mouth and made burn marks on her patchwork quilt. He watched her for a long moment before grabbing her hand, careful to not let his talons cut her skin. "You're really okay?"

She nodded.

"I've been so worried."

"Me too. Is it the worst being Big?"

"Sometimes I'm filled with rage and must burn things. But also, the other night there was a storm and I flew up into it and danced with lightning. And I sleep on a roof full of crows who seem to like me."

"Crows like me, too," she said, "and rats and roaches and everything gross. And I love doing magic—I've been reading your book and practicing. Just small things. I turned an apple into a potato."

"How useful."

Celia rolled her eyes. "I don't really know what we're supposed to do, now that we're the only ones left."

Demetri didn't say anything for a while. "Maybe there's

nothing we have to do anymore. Maybe we can just be . . ."

"Free?"

"I was going to say friends." He grabbed the history book. He opened it to the first page and started reading. So did Celia. They stopped every once in a while to talk about everything interesting that they read.

They stayed sitting next to each other, reading and talking, until Celia's mom called her for dinner.

ACKNOWLEDGMENTS

Thanks to my mom, who taught me the magic of books by reading pirate adventures at bedtime and always ending them on a cliffhanger. Thanks to my dad for teaching me about creativity in its many forms. Thanks to my whole family for always taking in stride my quixotic quests and oddball self.

Thanks to my writer friends who read this book in all of its messy manifestations: Rachel Swirsky, Philips Patton, Erin Cashier, Micaiah Huw Evans, Randy Henderson, Kris Millering, Neile Graham, and Lauren Dixon.

Thanks to the HarperCollins team, who gave this book such focused care, with special thanks to Stephanie Stein, Jocelyn Davies, Renée Cafiero, and Megan Gendell.

Thanks to the dreamiest dream of a literary agent, Linda Epstein, and the inimitable Emerald City Literary Agency.

Thanks to my little Sparrows for giving me no time to write but so many stories.

Thanks to Elijah for having the fiercest faith in my story-telling.

Thanks to libraries, which hold vast universes, and thanks to the librarians who are my favorite cosmonauts.

Thanks to teachers, who gave you, me, and everyone we know the gift of reading.

And thanks to every person who gets hurt by monsters and refuses to become one, even when that is hard. I love you.